OSHUN
RISING

Trinity Forest Book 2

JENNIFER ALSEVER

GET FREE DIGITAL CONTENT

Curious to hear Oshun sing? Want to see the crazy Woman Notebook first hand? I'll send you digital extras. Just tell me where to send it.

www.trinityforestseries.com/sign-up-now-venus

For my Pop, who taught me the word resiliency.

1

EMBER

The world comes to me in snapshots.

The sound of laughter at a party. A hailstorm of camera flashes.

Reality is like a dream that turns to vapor the moment you try to remember. Here one minute, gone the next. I fight for consciousness as though drowning and gulping for air. When it finally comes, it's too brief and I can't control my body, my speech, my actions. I'm like a passenger on a ship that was once mine, but now someone else is steering and all I can do is watch. Scream silently in my head.

Awake for an instant, I glimpse lines of paparazzi. I climb out of a limo, wearing silver platform boots up to my thighs, a skirt made of strands of silver chains, and a mesh top that barely covers my breasts. They're taking my photo—*why?*—and the flashes come in successive bursts.

Rose-scented perfume.

Large headphones, pressing against my ears.

My mouth touches something metal and I sing breathy

words to a pop song. The beat thumps in my chest, fills my vision with black leather and bright blood-red splotches. They pulse and spin like a wheel on a truck.

I stop singing and hear myself talk, but it doesn't sound like me. "Really? I should so fire you right now."

The yellow sound of a tinkling coin dropping onto the pavement. Clicking heels. The smell of hamburgers cooking. I cast a quick glance back over my shoulder; a young girl picks up the coin. She looks up at me, curious, with large round eyes, sorrow coloring her downturned lips and chipmunk cheeks.

The theme song for a reality TV show. I catch something the host is reciting, about people living in a forest. A stark hotel room with sleek, modern furniture. I brush the soft, silky texture of my pajama top with my fingertips. In my other hand, I'm clenching a toothbrush, swiping it fiercely across my teeth and gums until the metallic taste of blood fills my mouth.

Plumes of cigar smoke. A toilet flushing. My hand, squeezing clear liquid into a drink. A man with a bulbous nose unknowingly drinks it, and then he freezes. His eyes grow wide. He grabs his throat. Begins to cough.

I stand stock-still, watching as he struggles to breathe. He's dying. I stare at him for a long time... smiling.

The cotton-candy pink sound of an ocean wave, and the smooth texture of chocolate pudding in my mouth. I'm on a deck, and the sun heats my skin. A glass of white wine sits on a nearby table. Dots of condensation slide down the glass.

Black-colored humming voices, chanting. Flickering candles. The smell of campfire. The shuffling of feet. Lines of people wearing dark hooded robes moving past gray stone walls, past a girl with short brown hair lying still on a stone table. A fire burning beneath her. The room feels electric, and an energy pulses through my veins. Hypnotic and powerful, the sound crescendos into a chorus.

I feel sick. I want the nightmares to stop.

2

MADDIE

"*Morphology* comes from the Greek word for 'shape or structure.'" The monotone voice of my professor and the hot, dark auditorium make the perfect recipe for a nap. I doze. My head nods and I jerk it back up, glancing around the auditorium to see if anyone noticed.

My phone beeps—a text from Jared.

Check this out. Doesn't this chick look like my sister?

I click on the link. It's a news story about a pop star named Oshun. Apparently, she sold two million copies of her *Seasons* album and now she's all the rage—and she's only seventeen. I scroll down to the video of her song and, without thinking, hit "Play." The electronic beat screams from my phone, and I jump. The whole lecture hall turns to stare at me—including my professor. He stops midsentence, his nostrils flaring.

I jab at the volume on my phone until it's turned all the way down and, as the professor drones on once again, I watch the video without hearing the song. The blonde singer—Oshun—wears black leather boy shorts and no top; only long, shiny strands of pearls cover her breasts. As she sings, she's climbing over a pile of dead bodies. *Well, that's pretty effed up.*

I pause the video on a close-up of her face. I guess it *does* kind of look like Ember. But Oshun's lips are different. They're pouty, and her teeth are crisp white caps—lined evenly, like miniature piano keys. The nose is slightly different, too, tighter and narrower, slightly upturned at the tip. And holy crap, her boobs are huge, and she's super skinny, too. And of course there's the bleached blonde hair. No curls. *Come on, Jared.*

Just the thought of Ember is like a spark to a tinderbox of longing, buried deep in my chest. I miss her so much. People say by now she's probably dead. But I can't believe that. Sometimes I think if I could, it would be easier. If she were dead, at least I would *know*. Not knowing anything is what hurts the worst. The mystery of it all still makes me nauseous every time I remember the way she disappeared. From my life. From this world we were supposed to navigate together.

Yet this crazy pop star is in no way Ember.

I tap my gentlest reply to Jared.

Kinda.

The girl in the seat next to mine glares at me before shoving a handful of caramel popcorn into her mouth. Her low, steady crunching is way more annoying than me and my phone.

My professor continues to pace back and forth in front of a smart screen, wearing a headset, absorbed in his own voice. He says something about sternal angle, the second pair of ribs, and whatever else. If I'm ever going to get my nursing degree, I need to pay attention. But my mind wanders.

I think about Jared, remembering all those days we spent together after graduation, looking for Ember. One night, we sat on the floor of his grandma's living room, surrounded by stacks of *Missing Person* posters featuring Emby's smiling face, and piles of orange search vests and flashlights for volunteers. By the time the clock hit 1 a.m., I was feeling pretty buzzed from the beer we'd drunk to calm the jitters and the nonstop ache of her disappearance. Then I hit a wall—both emotionally and physically.

"You need sleep," I told Jared. He wore dark circles under his eyes and looked like a shadow of himself. When Ember went missing, it buried him and his perennially upbeat, laughing personality in his own private grave.

I squeezed his hand, and a small smile inched up his face.

"I gotta get this stuff ready for the reporter. He said he'd cover the search." He took a swig of beer and shuffled a pile of papers containing lists of what Ember liked, places she frequented, links to the fundraising page—a donation collection for the cash reward.

"Yeah, but seriously, you need to take care of yourself," I said. "How about we go for a walk. Take a break? I don't know... sleep?"

He leaned his head in close to mine, rested his forehead on my shoulder for a minute. "You're the only person who gets this, Mads," he whispered. "The only person who really understands."

Her disappearance bound us together. It still does.

My phone vibrates. It's another message from him, and seeing it sends a little dopamine rush to my brain.

The girl with caramel corn breath shifts her gaze to me like a spotlight. I pretend not to notice her and read Jared's message.

I know it sounds crazy. But I think this girl IS Ember.

I sigh. Part of the reason I've never been able to move on is because somehow, I feel like she's still alive. And yeah, maybe I'm experiencing a healthy dose of denial. But this? Deciding that Ember is some slutty pop star who climbs over dead bodies?

My heart just breaks for Jared. He wants his family back so badly, and there has been no closure for him. He needs to hope.

I debate about how to respond. Too harsh and I hurt him; too supportive and I encourage this loony line of thought.

Finally, I type a reply. *Maybe...*

A second later, another message pops up. This time from Mom.

Get vaccinated!!

Attached to the message is a link to a story with a headline that reads: *CDC Warns Citizens to Protect Against Virus.* There's a quote from a guy named Jeff Culver, head of the Centers for Disease Control, and a photo of him: droopy eyes, leather skin, a mole on his left cheek. He looks... *.off* somehow, but I can't put my finger on why.

Mom bugs me practically every week to get vaccinated. She says the virus is spreading fast and I should worry. I know it is. It's raging in California, New York, and parts of the Midwest. Took out half the population of Leadville after graduation, which is one of many reasons why our family moved. But I still haven't gotten the vaccine. I feel like a lot of people who do get it only get sick anyway.

I type out my message to Mom. *Remember, I hate needles.*

She responds instantaneously. *Do you hate breathing too?*

My phone vibrates again. Another message, another distraction. I am so failing this class.

It's her. I know it.

I sigh at Jared's message and put my phone away.

Early the next morning, I stare at my phone with blurry eyes, reviewing a string of random, obsessive messages that came in overnight from Jared.

2 a.m. *Look at this pic I found.*

2:15 a.m. *And this one too.*

2:16 a.m. *Call me?*

4 a.m. *I sent Oshun a message on Instagram. Told her that I'm looking for her. Sent her a picture of Ember. Think she'll respond?*

4:05 a.m. *Hiring a PI. Going 2 bank 2mrw 2 get loan. Found 15 private investigators in LA*

4:15 a.m. *Can't sleep. But this guy looks good. Dewey Slaughter: "Find the truth about anyone. I don't search public records and the Internet. I follow up on leads and interview others. You'll find so much more from me than you would on your own. Call now! 310-555-7898."*

Clearly, he's not letting this go.

I sigh and flop back on my pillow. The dying horse snores of my roommate, Emily, fill the room. I turn my head to look at her in bed, and she's a mess of wild black hair covering her face, her body spread-eagle on top of the covers. I shouldn't always be so annoyed by her; it's not her fault the residential housing people screwed up and overbooked the dorm rooms, thereby forcing me, a junior and an R-freaking-A, to live with a roommate. Yet here she is, lying in a bed where my futon couch used to be.

She's kept me awake so many times with that deep nasal snore, not to mention her late-night make-out sessions with whatever randoms she brings home, and her long-winded yapping on the phone to her BFF from high school. I truly believe she's responsible for the C in my Concepts of Pharmacology class, because even the foam pillow over my head didn't block out her noise the night before my last quiz.

Quiz. Tests... I have a midterm today. Crap. My least favorite course: Pathophysiology. I so don't want to be thinking about alterations in the musculoskeletal system. Not when Ember is still missing, and Jared is clearly going off the deep end.

I climb out of bed, toss some clothes and bathroom

supplies into a duffel bag. I shower, brush my teeth, and pull on a pair of faded jeans and my favorite loose-fitting tank top —cream colored with embroidered T-straps. I size myself up in the mirror, wishing my arms were thinner and my skin tanner, but ultimately deciding I don't look too bad. Not that Jared will care what tank top I'm wearing. He sees me like a sister, always has.

I pull it together and remind myself he needs a friend right now, one who can talk him off the ledge. Which is what I plan to do. And doing it by text isn't an option.

3

XINTRA

When Father gave me the whistle so many years ago, he told me I had a knack for calling on the dead. I still admire the Egyptian design of the hard-carved wooden duat—a stick-figure star with a circle around it. I stroke my fingertips over it, the sign of the dead, before tipping my head down and blowing the whistle just the way he taught me. The airy, high-pitched sound coils around my ears and rises in the dark room. The candles in the sconces flicker.

Arms outstretched, I watch as they slither like snakes from the corners of this basement room in Trinity, writhing across the floor, slinking across the ceiling. Some hover along the edges of the stone tunnel; others wait above the heavy wooden door, looking more and more like black cobwebs floating in and out of the dark hole from the universe. Their faces are imprinted on the air—stretched in horror, impassive, seething, pained—their eyes like pieces of burnt coal, recessed and hollow, feeding on the negative energy of the world.

My black vortex.

The faces of the dead. The spirits from beyond. They

come to me at my command and their fury lifts me up—me, their queen—and I hover just inches off the ground, floating, as they fill my body, empowering me. It's delicious. The energy pulses in my veins, running along my arms and throat.

I focus on Molly, the girl standing before me, so broken and ruined. She will be saved through rebirth, and in the end, she will save the earth.

"Look upon this broken girl, ye gods," I say, pacing and inserting her blood onto the hot stones, inviting the demons to mask themselves in her DNA. I raise my hands. "Transfigured souls and spirits of the dead. Thine spirits of the dead will say, 'Here I am!' and you will take her place. She will be mine. She a slave, and I the master."

Molly transforms before my eyes, mouth dropping, face cringing. And then the fog emerges, rising and pulsing in puffs like smoke, turning to black ash before evolving into another indistinguishable funnel-like shape. I see her memories float away, and like scenes from a movie projector, they run along the air before dissolving. The black spirits flow into her fingertips, into her eyes, into her mouth. Her skin transforms into a beautiful, unearthly glow—I call it the rebirther dazzle.

A chill spikes the air and my fog slowly dissipates. I sink back down to the ground. My bare feet kick up plumes of dust above the dirt floor. I don't even have to turn around to know someone is here in my den with me. The black spirits, they whisper her name.

"Zoe," they say, howling like the wind in the trees.

I throw my arms down. Molly crumples to the floor, and I spin around, the sound of my silky robe exhaling on the air. "Why are you here?" I snap.

"He's not breaking yet, Xintra," Zoe says, clasping her

hands in front of her stomach. "I'm not sure he will ever give in to rebirthing."

"He must. He's been in there for a week now."

"Twelve days, actually," she says. "Since Ember—"

"You know, Ember is the only one you screwed up," I say, irritation flowing through me. "It's your fault that her rebirthing was rushed, and that Tre saw it. Did you know that there are holes in her chakra now? Holes that Ember could potentially find. Tell me I don't need to explain to you how bad that would be."

"But she's still under your control," says Zoe. "Right?"

"For now," I say. "If you want to be useful, help me carry Allura to be trained."

Zoe lifts the feet of what used to be the lost girl Molly, and I take her arms, and we carry her across the room and heave her onto the stone table. Next to her are the gems of other rebirthers, now named Konrad and Roark. They lie, clad in plain clothes, on stone slab tables. I found one in the vortex in Egypt. The other in Peru. Above them, energy swirls with my dark spells, sucking down from the universe the information and skills they need to complete their missions, to use their gifts and embody the rich and powerful. They will slip into their assigned positions, and through this rebirther spell, the world will never know they hadn't been there all along.

I watch them and my heart swells with pride, feeling the tingle of energetic power rush through my scalp. The more lost people I rebirth into the world, the more powerful I become.

I point to these recent conquests lying on the tables and then turn to Zoe. "We need more rebirther candidates entering the vortexes. Quickly."

"But your father claimed—" Zoe stops when she sees my scowl.

"That's in the past." I slice her words off with my own. I don't need to be reminded of Father's call for patience. He believed that if we drew suspicion about the vortexes, it would ruin it. That if we rebirthed people too quickly and they looked too much like their former selves, it would draw suspicion. Father is not here. For good reason. And I have a plan, one that needs to be implemented quickly. Otherwise, all my work will be for naught.

I brush past Zoe and march down the dark hallways, a labyrinth which few know as well as I. Zoe trails behind me and we come to a heavy wooden door.

I hold up my right hand in front of it, watching the faint sparks fly from my fingertips, the tiny veins of electricity hovering in the air. Drawn from the power of Trinity's dark vortex, they unlock the ancient Annunaki door. One among many of my gifts as the Chosen One.

Once inside, I breeze over to the table with the coins, each imprinted with the name of a vortex—a collection that always fills me with pride. I pick up fifteen of them and drop them in Zoe's cupped hands. They land with a tinkling sound.

"Get these out. Get me my people. I need more; the big day is coming soon."

I envision the whole world at my fingertips. The dead filling the souls of my human puppets.

I push past her, and she trots behind me down the dark hall, the door slamming behind us. A few doors down, I open a peephole to look inside the room where Tre sits, huddled in the corner. Meager stubble dots his chin, and his cheekbones protrude from his gaunt skin. He folds and unfolds his hands, rocking back and forth. Shattered. Just how I want him.

"He won't give in," Zoe says, wringing her own hands. "And he now refuses to eat."

"Well, let the next round of torture begin," I say musically, pulling away from the peephole.

Zoe nods and disappears into the back hallway. I wait, checking the weather on my iPhone until Zoe begins the next round of punishment. Then, I peek through the hole and see the snake rising in the dim light of Tre's cell, sweeping back and forth like it's painting the air. The pit viper.

Tre shakes his head and squints, bewilderment scrambling his face. I smile with bared teeth. He can't comprehend how a South American pit viper could get into the locked basement cell in Trinity, a forest in Colorado. *Because it's a dark vortex, Tre, and I control it. I control everything—including your destiny. This is what you get. What you deserve.*

The green and yellow snake rises in the dim light, sweeping out and back, flicking its tongue past inch-long fangs—fangs that, once plunged into the skin of its victim, would cause a person's blood pressure to plummet. It's beautiful, and perfect for the physical necessities of rebirthing. I suppose it *could* kill him. It would be a bit of a drag, but still interesting to watch.

Tre shakes his head and then does something unexpected: he talks to the snake.

"Hey there, buddy, hey there."

I begin to giggle and have to pull away from the door, covering my mouth to stifle the noise. Once the laughter has passed, I lean back in and watch him squirm backwards, pushing the heels of his boots into the dirt, pressing his back against the stone wall.

I grin. "It's pointless," I whisper. These snakes can locate their prey by detecting differences in temperature. His stress-induced sweat will only make it easier for the snake to attack.

The snake hisses and inches its head out, searching for Tre, sensing him in the dark. I press the palms of my hands together as the snake slithers closer. Now you can see the real length of this green guy—maybe five or six feet long. I inhale and bite my lips in anticipation.

For kicks, I toy with him. I press my fingertips against the heavy wooden door, the sparks igniting and unlocking the hidden mechanism. The door swings open wide, and I hide behind it, peering through the crack by the hinge. The flame from the wall sconce dances in the hallway.

Tre pushes off the wall, climbs to his feet, and leaps up into the air to escape the snake, moving swiftly towards the doorway.

I see something move, fly through the air—and then Tre collapses onto the ground. I grin.

4

OSHUN

The woman looks hideous. Red streaks atop her black and silver wiry hair. She even smells old, like a musty closet and cheap perfume.

I shake my foot, signaling to her that she needs to move faster. She laces up my shoe, kneeling on the ground. She looks up at me with eager eyes. "You like them, Miss Oshun?" Her voice has a hint of an accent to it. Russian perhaps.

I examine the shoe: a black high heel that laces up from my toe to my mid-calf with shiny black string. It's like a corset for my foot, and it's perfect.

"I like them, but you tied them too tight," I say. "I guess putting shoes on my feet is the only job left for people as inept as you."

The woman's smiling expression melts off her face like wax. She licks her lips and inhales. "Oh, I am so very sorry."

"Get out," I snap. "But leave the shoes."

The woman gathers her purse, puts the boxes of shoes in a bag, and hustles out of the dressing room without a word. She takes with her that awful old woman smell, too.

As soon as she leaves, my assistant, Kaat, peeks in the

door. She pushes her round glasses up at the bridge of her nose. "Oshun, you're on in an hour," she says.

"Fine. But I still want to see what the stylist has in mind for the Grammys."

"It's not a great time now. You need to be ready to go onstage," she says, clearing her throat and glancing around the room. She's too afraid to let her eyes land on me. She knows I can crush her.

"I want the stylist. Now." I run my fingers over my silky red robe and glare at Kaat.

She opens and closes her mouth like a fish before nodding and tapping on her phone. "Right, right, we'll just multitask."

A few seconds later, my makeup artist and stylist swirl into the dressing room behind her like a tornado, jostling Kaat in the narrow doorway.

"Oshun, baby, Oshun, you look like heaven," the stylist says. "You don't even need clothes to look that good."

The stylist carries a black garment bag and hangs it on the back of the door. "Let me show you the goods. Promise you will love. L-O-V-E." He's a dark-skinned giant, and he juts his hips and swats the air with his hand.

He holds up a number of dresses. One looks like an upside-down hot-pink teacup. Another is a silver dress that sparkles like a thousand diamonds. "Hot. Right? It's an Hervé Léger," he says.

"Well..." I say slowly, and he leans in, waiting, with wide eyes.

They hang on my words. They shrink in my presence. An electric power flows through me and I gnaw it, sucking his power dry to feed myself.

"I'm sure you will make me a goddess," I say finally. He exhales and grins and moves swiftly around me.

I shrug. "I like the silver one, but I need diamonds to go

with it. Kaat. Order me a necklace. Makes sure no one else has anything like it." Kaat nods and urgently taps on her phone. "Oh, and make reservations for the jet. I want to go to Monaco this weekend to shop."

She nods and begins to type on her phone but then stops, looking up abruptly. "But you have a concert on Friday."

"Well, book the plane right after. Is your head full of rocks or what?" I point a ringed finger at her and then jab it at my foot. "If you want me to hurry for this show, put on my other shoe."

She kneels and begins strapping the black shoe on my foot. I gaze down at her short-cropped hair, watching the fog emerge around her head. It moves in brief bursts that seem to echo her nervous energy. In the hazy aura, I see visions. Kaat's father's square jaw and his faltering disapproval the day she told him she was going into the music business. He wanted her to go to law school. She has other secrets, too. The binge eating and purging at night. The hatred for her small breasts and large hips. She thinks about being thin most hours of the day.

I see it all.

"You always had such a small waist—so tiny," I play.

"Oh, why thank you." The sound of her voice is pink, the color of new spring flowers, and the flattery fills her chest in a single breath.

"Have you stopped working out?"

Her face withers with the words. I adore seeing the effects of the master manipulation. That is what we do—rebirthers. How we keep those beneath us groveling.

"Um, no..." she says, an awkward smile attempting to climb up her cheeks.

"You can go now," I tell the male stylist.

"I didn't show you all of them," he says.

"*Out.*"

He nods and hurries to pack up a half a dozen garments into his bag.

The makeup artist applies foundation to my face, then thick winged eyeliner and fake eyelashes to my eyes. While she works, her breath tickles my face and her hair drags along my shoulder.

Another girl enters the room and brushes my blonde hair, twisting it into a dramatic ponytail with a knot high on top of my head. "We should really bring back your natural color," the girl says, tugging on my hair. "I bet it's a pretty brown underneath. And the curls—girls would die for curls like yours."

"I want it blonde," I say. "And straight."

I watch the news on a big-screen TV on the wall as a cool breeze from a fan blows on my face and my bare thighs. The man on-screen leans into a microphone at a press conference. He looks familiar. Jeff Culver, head of the Centers for Disease Control. He has droopy eyes, leathery skin, a mole on his left cheek, and a slight twang to his voice. I enjoy this game of spotting other rebirthers, Annunaki members. I see them, I know them. It's as if we have radar for each other.

"No one would think that we'd have these kinds of outbreaks, but we do," he says, speaking slowly, reading from a teleprompter. "And it's important for all citizens to be inoculated against this new threat. We've set up free clinics across the country for people to receive the vaccines."

A grin spreads across my face. The vaccines aren't the cure. They're the poison. And when the chords for "Lie Down" play tonight, the pink fog will be sprayed, emitting the virus to more people. The weak will inhale it and die within six months. It's kind of a drag that some of my fan base will die off, but it's important for the cause. I know this because I saw it. I had a vision this morning when I heard the tomato red colored song play on my stereo.

"Miss Oshun, it's almost time," Kaat says, biting her bottom lip. Her voice sounds milky yellow; even the color looks like it skitters and cowers on the floor. I think someone once told me I have synesthesia, which means I can see colors when I hear things. I also see visions when I hear things, and I simply *know* things. Another sign of the superiority of rebirthers.

She opens the door, and a young girl with a headset and an iPad rushes down the hallway outside the open door to my dressing room, flashing a tense smile. The hairdresser tugs on my hair, sprays it. The scent of alcohol and peaches wafts into my nostrils.

"Almost finished," the makeup artist says, dabbing glittery makeup on my cheekbones with a brush. "You look beautiful." She stands back, brush in hand, a painter proud of her art. When her moss green eyes meet mine, I watch her aura and story rise in puffs around her brown face, flickering in waves like hot steam from a shower. I see her story in the fog: she's going to die next week, coughing and heaving from the virus. The small droplets of her aura rise and fall, billow up and out, shrink and dissolve at the edges.

"Good," I say. "Now get out." I stand, slipping off my robe to reveal my stage outfit. I gaze at myself in the mirror, adjusting my double-Ds in this tight, shiny silver bikini top. The breast cups point out like two pyramids. I tug down on the miniskirt, which starts high on my waist like a 1930s swimsuit and then hugs my body, stopping high on my thighs. I admire my thigh gap in my reflection. My lips are glossed and my eyes are heavy with makeup. A goddess. I smile.

From my dressing room, I can hear the crowd chanting, "O-shun! O-shun!" and the sound appears in my mind as inky black and blood red swirls. The sound and dark colors make my heart beat faster. A few minutes later, I stand onstage, in the dark, waiting for my entrance. A steady, strong drumbeat pounds magenta and gold, and I *feel* the crowd's energy. I *smell* their sweat. The adoration. The euphoria of seeing me, Oshun, standing here before them.

The microphone is smooth and heavy in my hand, and my voice is breathy and raspy. A powerful pied piper. *"Whoa, whoa-ooo-a-whoa. Yeah, show me what you got."*

5

MADDIE

The town looks weird. I drive with one hand on the wheel, truly distracted by the dark mood of downtown Leadville. No one is here. No one walks around the street like normal. No cars. Nothing. It makes me feel nauseous, and I crane my neck to get a better look at the line of sad, empty storefronts.

My phone rings. Mom.

"Yeah."

"Hey, sweetie, are you there yet?"

"Just got here."

"Tell me how to track your location on the phone again? I tried but I just keep getting the screen where I see your phone number. Then what do I do next?"

"Mom, I'm fine." I feel my shoulders tense. "Shouldn't you be pouring all this worry on Hunter already? He's the kid still living with you."

"Well, excuse me for being a mother."

I roll my eyes. "Ma..."

"I want to know how to find you. Seriously, honey, what if you get sick? Are you wearing that mask I sent in the care package?"

"Yeah," I lie. Though I did eat the chocolate chip cookies in the box she sent.

"Where exactly are you in Leadville?"

"What?"

"What street?" she asks.

"I'm driving down Harrison now." My voice trails off as I look around. All those new restaurants that opened just before graduation are closed. The consignment store. The cookie place. That outdoor store. They're all empty. It makes me feel like I'm in an episode of some zombie apocalypse TV show. "Whoa, it's like a freaking ghost town."

"Why do you think we left? You should have just called Jared instead. You didn't have to drive all that way."

I don't answer. I watch a single person shuffle along the street. He wears sunglasses and a T-shirt that says *Pizza to the People*, and he moves his mouth as if he's muttering to himself.

"It's been three years," Mom says. "You need to leave it alone now."

I grip the steering wheel tight, and my whole body clenches with irritation. I don't get how she can say this. Ember goes missing and I'm just supposed to forget? Supposed to just leave Jared on his own when he's completely falling apart?

"Ma, Jared is, like, totally freaking out."

Mom sighs. "He's a big boy. You need to focus on school."

"Listen, I gotta go. I'll call you later." I click off the phone. I know it's rude, but I can't deal with her negativity right now.

I pull up to the crooked house that Ember hated so much. Even that little trailer where she and her family lived in middle school felt homier than this place. This feels like a mausoleum for dead people.

I ring the doorbell, and Jared answers with an incredulous expression on his face. "Mads, what in the world are you doing back in this hell hole?"

"I came to rescue your ass," I say. "Living in this house is making you a total nutjob."

I want to say, *I came here because you need me, because you're falling apart and I need to fix you like I couldn't fix Ember. And a text won't do it.*

He smiles and shakes his head. "Well, you might be too late." He hugs me tight, and I catch a whiff of body odor. That can't be a good sign.

Inside the living room, the air smells stuffy and faintly like mothballs. The floor creaks beneath the nappy green carpet. "Where's Gram?" I ask, looking around. Everything is the same. The olive-green couch. The crystal chandelier. The oil painting of the old mining structure that hangs over the potbelly stove.

He shrugs. "I think she's working on something in the garage again."

He offers me a soda and we sit in his kitchen for a while, catching up on what I'm doing at Colorado State. I tell him about the toga party I went to last weekend, and how I had to wear my only clean sheets—which had Hello Kitty cartoons on them. I tell him about my meager dating life and the recent spontaneous road trip that my friend Lia and I took to Dallas to ride all the roller coasters at Six Flags.

"Okay, so the Texas SkyScreamer was the best." I wave my hands above my head. "A 124-foot circle at thirty-five freaking miles per hour. I couldn't open my eyes for the longest time, but then I finally did and I was, like, four hundred feet above the ground, and I could see everything. The AT&T Stadium, downtown Dallas—"

It's then when I realize that despite the fact that I am clearly reliving my roller coaster euphoria, Jared is still stuck in that place. That place he's hovered in for three years. His lips turn up in a grin and he shakes his head, but his mind is somewhere else.

"So anyway," I say, taking a self-conscious drink of my soda. "You texted me saying you had some friend who was some hot-shot reporter or something?"

"Yeah, yeah." He nods. "Come on, I'll show you what I'm talking about."

I follow him upstairs to Ember's room. Or what was supposed to be her room, but she didn't unpack any of the boxes after her parents died. It smells like cardboard and dust.

I am a little surprised that after all this time, Jared hasn't opened them, cleaned this place out and gotten rid of some stuff.

He stops and turns to look at me, a haze of sunshine descending on his heart-shaped face from the dirt-streaked window. "You look good," he says, throwing his chin towards me.

Something blooms inside me. I shrug nervously, shake my head, and laugh through my nose. "Whatever... I just threw on what I had. I had to hurry, you know, just to make sure you didn't start clipping letters from magazines to make creepster letters to Oshun."

"Riiight."

Girls in my class used to go nuts over this boy. He had that crooked smile and the square shoulders and the eyes that crinkled, telling you he was really present, really seeing you. He had this way of making you feel like the most impor-tant person in the world. Sydney always liked the way he kind of sways when he walks, too. Me too, I guess, but he was always Ember's big brother. I saw those nasty blackened socks he had strewn across their shared bedroom floor, and I heard him burp, and I even saw him scratch his balls once while he watched football. That killed any bubbling crush I had freshman year. Maybe not killed it, exactly. Just tempered it.

After she disappeared, Jared got pretty skinny and kind of looked like he'd been hit in the face with a sack of flour. Pale. Tired. Gaunt. Just totally worn out. He might have a little more color back in his face today. He still looks like Jared, but just a flattened version of him, like someone stuffed him in a closet for a long time. I want to shake out the wrinkles and let him soak in a cool mountain breeze and some sunshine.

I take in the sight of him in red athletic shorts and a dirty T-shirt that says *Lettuce. The taste of sadness.* He looks like he hasn't combed his hair in months.

"Looks like you eat a lot of lettuce," I say.

"What?" he asks, tossing his head back in confusion.

I point to his stained T-shirt. "The taste of sadness?"

"Ha. Ha. Ha," he says. "What's that supposed to mean?"

It means I want him to smile. I want him to be Jared again. I loved the sunshine he brought to everything way back when. I just shrug and slap his arm. "Kidding. What did you want to show me?"

"So check this out," he says, squeezing between a pile of boxes and picking up Ember's laptop. "Remember how the cops hacked into her computer to see if there were any clues about where she went?"

I nod.

He sits down on the bed with the laptop and starts typing. "Well, I went in there again and found this video she did freshman year. She's singing and playing guitar in it."

I nod, sit down next to him and pick up Ember's old stuffed black teddy bear from the bed and then scan the piles of boxes covering half the room.

"Wow, look at all this stuff," I say.

"Yeah, I haven't had time to get rid of it."

No time in three years? I nod and shake the bear. "She

loved this guy." She called the bear Yoda and claimed he held all the secrets to the world.

"Yeah, she did," he says.

I want to give him permission to let her go, but I can't. Our shared hope that she's alive is what binds us.

He becomes animated, his eyes brighter. "So I called this dude, Dax, who was in my frat at CU. He was a senior when I was a freshman, and he's become, like, this *star whisperer* with that breakout story about Booker Lee. You remember that?"

"Nope," I say.

"No?" Jared is incredulous. "You been under a rock or what? That story was huge. Dax was this newbie reporter who happened to pull enough strings through a neighbor's cousin or whatever and got an interview with Booker."

I gaze at him, waiting to understand how this connects to Ember.

Jared leans forward and talks slowly like I'm an idiot. "He sings that song 'Rain Check' and just about every other pop song—"

"I *know* who he is, Jared."

"Oh. Anyway, Dax got him to pour his heart out, share all this stuff about his divorce from Ambrosia, and how his past girlfriend left him after he broke his neck skiing, and then his mom committed suicide and how he killed some girl in a car accident when he was drunk and only fifteen... Heavy, personal stuff—it all pours out of him in the interview and he starts crying and bawling about it."

"Sad."

"Yeah, well, Dax just gets underneath people's skin, you know? And now, apparently, all these stars just call him, literally begging to be interviewed."

"Okay." Inside, I'm rolling my eyes. What does any of this matter? What rabbit hole are we tunneling down now?

He taps on the computer and talks without looking at me. "So I asked him to interview Oshun."

I bite my lip, inhale deeply, and stifle a sigh. He may seriously be dipping into madman territory. Where is my Jared?

He turns the computer to show me an email from Mrs. Nusca to Ember senior year. The first line reads, "Blast from the past."

"When I found this video of her singing, I sent it to Dax to ask if he thought they sounded the same and if he thought she looked similar."

"Oshun has those big boobs," I say. "And straight, bleached blonde hair. And bigger lips. Uh... and the nose isn't even the same."

"Plastic surgery," Jared says. "Hair dye."

I don't respond.

"Well, Dax thought it was interesting, and he's getting an interview."

"Huh." It takes everything inside me not to wince at this. Maybe Jared has really lost it. But I can't turn away from him. I want to take care of him, help him put himself back together.

I need to get him out of this house, to heal and to figure out how to live again. And I can't watch that video of Ember because hearing her voice will be another sledgehammer to my chest. We need a distraction.

"Road trip," I say suddenly, standing up.

He looks at me and frowns. "What?" He stays seated on the bed, looking up. Confusion muddles his face.

I don't know where we'll go or why I even said that. But I am the Road Trip Queen—some nerdy kids at school even called me Mad Kerouac after *On the Road*. I still haven't read the book, but I kind of liked the nickname.

But camping in the desert or driving to another roller coaster won't be enough for Jared. He needs to put these thoughts of Oshun to bed. To see for himself. Because then he will. See, I mean. And maybe then... maybe then he'll be *him* again.

"Yup, you and me. We're going on a road trip to see this Oshun in concert."

6

TRE

My foot feels like it's been stabbed by a knife. A torrent of hysterical words flies through my head. *Snake. Bite. No way. Pain. Dying. Blood. No! Why?*

I crawl on my hands and knees in the dim hallway, my path lit up in fragments by flickering wall sconces. My pulse races, and a painful burning closes in around my foot.

Someone is nearby. There's the muted sound of shuffling feet and the whisper of something else moving—maybe the hem of a long dress—which kicks up a little breeze over my sweaty face. The pain is unbearable, distorting the stone wall into a blur of gray. "Help!" I gasp before screaming out in agony and squinting up to see the person standing above me. I get a glimpse of long hair, a pale face with delicate features.

She says something indecipherable.

"What?" I whisper, writhing on the cold stone floor.

"That must hurt," she says in a British accent. I recognize that damn voice.

"Hell yeah!" I yell, reaching out and clutching her leg with my hand. "Help me! Do something, *please!*" I hold out irrational hope that this woman, who undoubtedly put the snake in the room with me, who held me hostage for days, will help me.

"You have to stay calm," she says. "Otherwise, the venom will spread quickly."

"Calm. Right, yeah, of course," I say, gritting my teeth. "Why didn't I think of that?" Waves of searing heat pulse through my foot, and I'm panting like a horse. Fear and panic and nonsensical words run circles in my head.

Who is she? A snake. Bite. Die. Help. I'm dying.

I can't see her, but the young woman's presence looms like a mountain lion stalking its prey. "I need a doctor. Seriously." Knives stab and twist my flesh.

My fingers tremble as I take off my boot, and I breathe out slowly through tight lips. My sock is soaked in blood and I gasp at the sight, pressing my shoe back on to keep from bleeding out. I tie the laces snug, panting, irritated that this chick just stands over me, looming, watching, doing nothing at all. Her face is still hidden by the shadows.

"You can't just let me die!" Rage overcomes the pain. "Help me, dammit!"

She stands there, unmoving, with her head tilted, watching. She's curious, maybe even enjoying herself, and anger roils inside me. I kick at her shin with my good leg, smacking it hard with my boot. She backs up a couple steps before finally squatting down next to me.

"Don't kick me," she says. Her tone is harsh. "You won't die."

She removes a syringe from her pocket before leaning over, roughly yanking down my sock, and plunging the needle into the wound. The pain makes me howl, and it hurts so bad I think she might have just poisoned me further. My head fills up with what feels like burning hot water, and I sink back down to the ground.

"Don't forget what I'm doing for you," she says.

Later—I don't even know how long—I sit up, groggy, peeling my sock back to look at my wound, sure an infection is taking hold. It's caked with dried blood but doesn't look infected yet. In fact, the bite looks light pink, like perhaps it's healing— faster than I could ever have imagined. I don't even know how long I've been here. I remember writhing in misery, remember her dabbing something onto my wound, chanting some strange words. She came and went; I stayed splayed on the cold stone floor.

The pain has lessened some, and now the bite just aches dully, like a torn ligament.

"You heal faster here in the Trinity vortex than in the outside world, Tre." Her voice comes from somewhere in the hallway, followed by the butterfly flutter of her dress. She's near me again, though it's too dark to see her clearly. "Of course it helps that I treated you with some antibiotics, ancient spells, and healing herbs—you're welcome."

I stare up at her in the darkness, confused.

"Get up," she says sharply. "You can walk now."

Slowly, I climb to my feet, and she's right. I put my weight on my other foot and hop. My knees feel like jelly. I take a small, slow step, putting delicate pressure on my bad foot. I do feel markedly better, and I can walk, though I still shuffle and slouch.

She leads me up the stairs, back to the Trinity living area. The sunlight from the windows is so bright I have to squint and shield the sun with my hand.

When we get to the living room, she turns around and points to the sofa. "Sit."

I collapse onto the white couch, not because this chick told me to do so, but because I need to rest. My foot still aches and I don't feel strong. In the light, I can see the girl clearly now. She's dressed in a weird robe and looks familiar. Maybe it's the way she stands with a hand on her hip and the way she holds her mouth. Her red hair is so shiny it's like it's been shellacked, and her face is heart shaped with incredibly pale skin. Her eyes are pretty striking, too. You don't see that color green every day, the color of a shallow sea. This must be the girl that Ember saw downstairs when she explored Trinity on her own—before she went through rebirth. The mere idea of that, of Ember just losing herself, everything that I loved about her, makes my chest tighten again.

"What'd you do to Ember?" I say. "And Lilly. She disappeared, too. Where are they?"

She ignores my questions. "I feel pretty bad for you, Tre," she says, pouting. "Life pretty much sucks, huh?"

"Because of you."

"Let's see, twelve days inside a little dark room, dealing with rats, eating maggot-filled bread. Oh and then the snake bite?"

I clench my jaw. I hate this girl, more than I have ever hated anything before in my life.

"And on top of it, your little girlfriend, Ember, abandoned you." She perches on the edge of the couch and clicks her tongue. "I assume you've had enough."

"You can't get to me like you did the others," I say, looking out the window at the aspen trees, their green leaves twisting in the breeze. I'm not giving in to this place, no matter what. But I can't help but wonder how long I'll be trapped here, in this time vortex.

"Ember decided she would rather get out alone than stay here with you," she says.

That right there hits me hard. My heart squeezes.

I've heard people talk about falling in love, but with Ember, I didn't just fall—I catapulted headfirst, eyes shut, arms thrown out wide. That last night with her, I was so freaking excited. I hadn't felt that much hope in forever. But when I went to look for Ember that night, she was gone. I remember feeling that crazy sense of panic where my fingers tingle, how I started mumbling to myself in raspy breaths. I looked for her everywhere.

When I found her downstairs, where she had seen that creepy séance earlier, it was like the life was draining out of me. I took it all in. Her dark curly hair tumbling over her shoulders, eyes wide; candles flickering against the walls; people in robes moving around her, humming. My whole body seized up as hot rage and desperation coursed through me. I pounded on the door relentlessly, pleading, sobbing for hours.

But I failed. I couldn't stop it. My eyes fill at the memory.

"Oh, poor Tre." The redheaded lady brings me back to this time and place and my miserable existence.

I sneer at her. *She did that to Ember.*

Then with sudden grit, I run at her, the pain in my foot momentarily gone. I am ready to bowl her over, wrap my bare hands around her throat, squeeze the life out of her. But in a flash, I'm thrown onto the polished floor and an electric shock shoots through me. The pain is incredible, and my whole body spasms like I'm having a seizure.

When the current diminishes and my body stills, I lie gasping on the stone floor. Every now and then, my muscles twitch uncontrollably, burning and aching at the same time. My head buzzes, ears ring. She must have hit me with some kind of electric shock. It's the most bizarre and frightening thing ever, like waking up one day and discovering the sky is actually beneath you instead of above.

She walks over slowly and gazes down at me with a small smile. "Ouchie," she says. "Tre. You shouldn't blame *me* for Ember. She *chose* rebirth. She chose me over you."

I shut my eyes and grunt, from both the pain of the electric jolt and the reality that Ember went through rebirth. She wanted desperately to get out of Trinity Forest. What happened? It's like all of a sudden, she totally gave in to it. She just veered off the road so suddenly. That's why it was all so freaking devastating. That, and the fact that I love her so much it feels like I can't breathe when she's not with me.

Xintra watches me for a moment before standing and moving to the floor-to-ceiling window. She gazes out at the shimmering trees with her hands folded in front of her. "Soon, the next group of people will come to Trinity, ready to change." She spins around to look at me. "But you... you still haven't submitted to your destiny, to rebirth. Why is that?"

"I don't want your rebirth. I want to be *me*. I want *my* life back."

"Oh, Tre, when will you figure it out? Even if you *did* get out of Trinity, you would have no one. It's been decades. You have no identity. No family. No friends. No future."

"I have my dad, my mom—"

"Your mum will have forgotten about you," she snaps. "She always does."

I feel so small, lying on the ground, the stinging still coursing through my muscles, and the aching from the snake bite in my foot extending up to the top of my calf. "What the hell is that supposed to mean?" I muster.

"It *means* your mum is not as perfect as you think. It *means* she will forget about you. In fact, she already has." She turns away and gazes outside again.

What the hell was that? How would she know what my mother does or doesn't remember?

I stand up gingerly. I'm not sure where I'll go, but I'm definitely getting away from this girl. I weave through the white leather furniture toward the large front door, and she calls to me from behind. "Trinity is the queen bee of black vortexes. It holds a phenomenal power that's beyond you." I stop, turn around and look at her. She walks toward me, waiving her hands. "But you know all that, right? Because you read Ember's mum's notebook about Trinity."

"Yeah, I know you have some bullshit plan. But I have no clue why that plan would include me and Ember."

"Do you know who I am?"

I stop at the edge of the couch. "Yeah, you're a *Xintra*. Some eighth-generation Annook-something-or-other that supposedly wants to rule the world. I got news for you, lady: torturing me isn't going to help with that. It's not going to do anything but piss me off." I begin to limp away. I don't care about her power or Trinity's power. *My* only power is not listening to her.

I need to get out of this house. I'd rather die in the woods than here.

"It's Annunaki." She repeats it slowly. "A-noo-na-key. We have psychic abilities and we share DNA with ancient beings. We're powerful, Tre. I'm powerful."

I glare at her. Under normal circumstances, I wouldn't buy it. But Trinity is not normal circumstances, and nearly three decades have passed in the outside world while I've been stuck here. "Whatever. Great. Keep your effing DNA."

"And I am not *a* Xintra," she says. "My *name* is Xintra. And my DNA might be of more concern to you than you think. Tre, I'm your sister."

7

EMBER

I stand in high heels in front of a white background. Large photography lights surround me. It feels like real life, but not quite. As if I'm watching a movie of my life—or not really my life, but me, trapped in someone else's life—through smudged binoculars.

"Ahhh perfect, yeah, pout a little more, lips open, tongue sensual." The photographer's voice is light tan, and he wears a white button-down shirt and jeans. Shaggy sandy hair pokes out of the bottom of his navy knit cap. "Let's get some pics with you on your knees."

I always wondered what lucid dreams would be like. As far as I can tell, I'm dreaming right now.

Without my consent, my body moves. I climb onto my knees, place a hand on my hip, elbow out behind me, and drape the other arm over my head. I arch my back and lift my chin and gaze directly into the camera with smoldering eyes. This *feels* so real, so unlike a dream. The metal looping rings of my belt pinch my fingers.

If I am actually lucid dreaming, I should be able to

control my movements, right? I want to stand up and go get a glass of water, or maybe I can go fly around the room instead. But I don't. I can't.

"A natural, baby, oh yeah," the photographer says. "Chin down, eyes up. Tell the camera you want it. You want to be devoured. Yeah, honey."

I do as he says, and my heart thunders in my chest. I have never felt my heart beat in a dream before.

Then, I dip down into darkness.

Again, I'm moving. This time in a choreographed dance. A kick, a swivel of the hips, one foot stepping in front of the other like a catwalk model. But I don't know how to dance... do I?

I'm in a dance studio, and sweat drips down my forehead, stinging my eyes. It feels so real. My pulse races. I'm breathless. The pop song is shiny black and purple and it's my voice singing the tune. A familiar power flows through me.

"One-two-three. One-two-three!" a woman shouts at me, as a series of sinewy men and women slink and crawl on the floor to the beat of the music behind me.

I open and shut my legs in a low crouch. The moves come easy to me, as if I was born for this, premade and preprogrammed for it.

When the music ends, one of the dancers slithers up to me, stroking my hair and talking like a close girlfriend. "You look amazing. Absolute natural," she says.

I nod and smile. "Yeah," I say. "I know." This isn't me, none of this, and I'm confused why I would act like someone else in this dream.

It hits me then, for the first time. Like gasping for air after drowning for so long. A gasp, and then a breath. This isn't a dream. This is real. These moments are glimpses of clarity. I'm swimming in some strange, dark place. I paddle hard to the surface to stay alert, to take control. But it doesn't work. I sink down again beneath the surface. I'm held captive in my own body.

8

MADDIE

It totally looks like we're on Mars. Twisting, bulbous spires made of windblown sandstone sprout from the barren, sandy desert floor. On either side of us, towering mesas and planes of flat red rock climb and flatten, curve and dip. It goes on like this forever.

"Doesn't it look like another planet?" I ask Jared. "The red rock looks like ripples of frosting on a cake."

He drives my blue Honda Accord, holding just two fingers on the bottom of the steering wheel. With his free hand, he shoves popcorn in his mouth. "I don't know." He shrugs. "Looks like Utah."

Road trips are better than boys, chocolate, or rainbows. They're better than lying in bed until noon, reading trashy magazines and eating ice cream out of the tub. They're better than mountain biking down a rocky ravine. It's like I need to get one in every couple months or I'll stop breathing. I just want to see things—new things—and feel synapses explode in my head.

"I've been to Utah a bunch of times, and I'm still amazed," I say.

"Weren't you nominated 'Most Likely To Go To the Moon' or something like that senior year?"

"I think it was 'Most Likely to Get a Nobel Prize.'"

"Riiiight," Jared says. "It wasn't 'Most Likely To Be On Reality TV'?"

"That was Sydney," I say, referring to our polished vale-dictorian, who swept me under her wing when Ember ditched me senior year.

My phone buzzes. It's Mom. I swear she has radar when I'm outside of Fort Collins. She's been calling incessantly, which is like a form of road trip torture. I enact standard road trip protocol: put my phone on mute. "Do you think we have time to stop and go climb into some of those slot canyons? Maybe rock climb or something? *That* would be killer."

"You're some sort of rock climber now?" Jared asks.

I'm trying to move on. Can't you come with me, just for a little bit?

"No," I say out loud, "but we could hire a guide. It would be fun." I desperately need to see a bit of spontaneous, fun Jared again.

"With what? We don't have much cash."

"You used to be so optimistic, Jared. Remember that one time when we went on that hike over to Turquoise Lake, and I said, *we should just take off all our clothes and jump in*. And you did! I just *mentioned* the idea, and *bam* you did it. I remember your butt was so stinking white."

"People change."

"Your butt is no longer white?"

"Ha. Ha." He chugs his Mountain Dew and steps on the gas. I thought maybe this trip would be fun and could lighten him up, but he is hell bent on getting to Los Angeles as soon as possible. "Besides, everywhere we go, the virus is shutting down the world. I wonder if anyone will even go to this concert."

"Don't be such a downer." I put my feet up on the dash. "It was only, like, two gas stations that were closed so far. It doesn't mean people are dying everywhere because of the virus. *We* are still living, right?"

"For now," he says. "Are you gonna get the vaccine?"

"And live in fear and let the government experiment on me?"

"Don't be so paranoid."

"Something rubs me the wrong way about it." I crane my head to look up at a weird orange spire shaped like a trippy mushroom. "Call it a gut feel." I find enough bars on my phone to stream Oshun's album. "We need to start prepping for this concert. Get to know her music."

Jared shrugs.

I play the first song on the album, which has an electronic dance beat and sounds a lot like other pop music played on the radio. It's catchy. Then Oshun's voice comes in. It's a strange combination of salty and sweet, cooing and riffing, rising and falling with repetitive phrases. I can't make out all the words, but her voice is familiar. I understand why Jared thinks it sounds like Ember. It *does*. I always thought her voice was unique, but she would never sing this kind of crap.

Just the thought of Ember and how her dreams unraveled senior year crushes my heart and lungs together. At one point, Ember and I knew each other's passwords, and we spent every day together, binge-watching *Ghost Whisperer* and having all those Pinterest dessert parties, where we made all the recipes of pictures we saw online. We'd eat until we felt sick and then a couple hours later we'd go run three miles, believing that the sugar might just slide off our butts if we ran fast enough.

The memory is sweet and sour at once, and I wonder when the sourness of thinking of Emby will go away. I glance at Jared, listening to the song and chewing popcorn intensely.

His brow creases together, and I take his hand and give it two squeezes. It's just something we do. We spent so many long hours together after Ember's disappearance that now I know that the two-lined wrinkle between his brows is a pained look, not a focused look. It's like we communicate through a private Bluetooth frequency, without words. Whenever I'd start tapping my fingers, he did the same thing for me— clasping my hand, squeezing it twice, and flattening my jitters.

School helped me get away from it all, find a purpose. But Jared remained in that black hole, too far away for me to squeeze his hand regularly.

"So are you ever going to go back to school?" I ask, turning down the volume.

He shrugs, throwing the empty popcorn bag on the car floor and then digging his hand into my licorice stash. He bites into a red piece, letting the end dangle from his mouth like a cigarette. "I think about it sometimes, but Gram needs help."

"Uh *whatever*," I say, taking a piece of licorice, too. "That old lady does *not* need anyone. It'd take her a few months to even notice if you were lying dead on the couch."

"Harsh," he says, glancing over at me with a grin. "You just don't know her like I do." His eyes look earnest. Maybe he has figured out how to thaw her. "She just has issues, you know, with expressing how she really feels. But she cares. And I have that job down at Safeway, unloading produce at night."

"Really? You didn't tell me you had a job."

"You didn't ask."

Sometimes I feel so incredibly close to this guy, but it's like other times there's that wall that I just can't see through.

"So did you hear from Dax about that Oshun interview?"

"He says it looks promising," Jared says, nodding. "And he's got us free tickets."

"Cool!" I say, though I never thought I'd be excited about getting free tickets to an artist I hardly knew. "But is he *really* going to ask her if she's Ember?" I couldn't help but wonder if Dax thought Jared sounded as crazy as I thought he did. Besides, asking that question could ruin all of his professional credibility.

"Yeah, he says he's going to do it," he says. "Or at least bring *me* up as the freak who has that theory."

I purse my lips and nod. "Cool. Well, if anything it'll be fun to go to a concert again. I haven't been to one in forever." Jared once drove Ember and me to see this indie band in Denver sophomore year. We had to tell my mom that I was sleeping at Emby's so she wouldn't freak, and we drank and danced until we were so sweaty we looked like we'd been caught in the rain.

"Remember that one concert in Denver?" As soon as I say it, I cringe because Emby is in that memory.

"Yup," he says. Then he flashes a grin, which puts me at ease. "*That* was fun. Remember that dude tried to hit on you?"

"Oh yeah! He was, like, forty, and you totally chased him off. What a creeper. I still think the pink Hawaiian shirt he wore would have looked great on you."

"Looked everywhere but couldn't find one like it," he says, shaking his head, playing along. "But I needed the leer to complete the look. The leer went with the shirt." He turns and squints out of one eye, raising his cheek in a deformed smile.

"Yes!" I sing, throwing my head back on the headrest, laughing. "I can't believe I didn't land that guy! Tomorrow at the Oshun concert, you better not fall for any middle-aged female creepers with bad Hawaiian shirts."

"It will be tempting." He smiles. Pauses. Then he points to the back seat. "Hey, grab my duffel bag, will you? There are some *missing* posters in there. We'll stop up here at the gas station and hang one up."

And just like that, the darkness dawns and we are back in our post-Emby, post-happy world. Alone, together.

That night, we camp by the side of the road somewhere in Utah. We laugh and curse as we struggle—and nearly fail—to set up a tiny tent in the dark, lamenting the fact that we didn't bring any headlamps or real camping equipment. Then we eat hamburgers from McDonald's over a microscopic campfire.

My hamburger bun is crunchy on the outside, and I chew as Jared finishes off a story, complete with waving arms and obvious exaggerations. The moment fills me with a sense of comfort and familiarity. Warmth. Like old times, even if I know the moment is fleeting.

After their parents died, Emby went underground and Jared became the great entertainer, burying himself in distractions. At parties, he was usually drunk. I remember at Breezy Deckers's house the end of junior year, he slung an arm around my shoulder and announced that I was the best "extra" little sister ever. I remember the weight of his sweaty arm, and the way he ordered all the graduating seniors to deliver me drinks, even though I barely sipped them. He leaned in close and I felt his warm breath in my hair. "I always have a blast with you, Mads," he said. That mere touch gave me a syrupy feeling inside, and those sweet words —even if they were drunk ones—made me feel ten feet tall.

I lean back against the tire of the car as Jared continues his story about how he saw a lady and a five-year-old girl walking on the side of the highway on Vail Pass in the freezing cold last winter. He stopped to help her, but the lady was acting so weird, telling him that she knew his cousin Kelly—only he didn't have a cousin named Kelly. He'd gotten out of the car to call the police, talk in private, when the lady hopped over to the driver's seat of his van and drove off, leaving him in a snowstorm in the dark with no coat. By the time a tow truck driver picked him up, he had stopped shivering, which was a bad thing: hypothermia.

"I huddled down by the heaters and couldn't get enough warm air," he says, shaking his head.

"So did you find the lady? What happened? You never told me this."

"Police found her sitting in my van, reading a newspaper at a bus stop in town."

"No way!" I laugh and take a bite of my burger.

"And when I saw her sitting in the back of the police car, she starts waving like we're good friends."

"Last time you try to be a good Samaritan." I suck up the last of my soda through the straw and it makes that annoying slurping sound that Mom says "ladies don't do."

"Naw, I'd do it again. I think she just needed some mental help." He points to his head.

"Seriously, you'd still pick up another random person in a snowstorm?"

"Of course, if someone needed help."

I gaze at him longer than I should. I can't help but drink up the shape of that crooked mouth and the way his hazel eyes perfectly match his golden hair. *Ack.* I shake my head and look at my feet.

He pulls out his phone, frowning again.

"Checking for a message from Dax?"

He nods. "I've never felt so close to finding her," he says. "Part of me wants to just jump in the car and head over to her house."

"Yeah, that would *not* work," I say.

"I know she lives in Malibu."

"Can you say 'stalker'?"

"Well, if that's the case, then you're my official accomplice." He holds up his McDonald's cup of soda so we can clink our drinks together, and after a momentary hesitation, I do. "We're in this together," he says.

9

TRE

When I was just a kid, maybe in third or fourth grade, Mom drove me to a soccer game from our house in Mill Valley, winding through the twisting roads of Muir Woods and into Stinson Beach. Dad always wanted to buy a huge mansion in Oakland Hills, but Mom felt like it was too showy. Which is funny because Dad thought nothing of landing his helicopter on my school playground to take me to a baseball game in San Diego.

I remember how Mom was lost in thought that day on our drive, and I went searching for a piece of gum in her purse. Her wallet was open slightly, and I saw a photo of a little redheaded girl with freckles. She couldn't have been older than two.

"Who's this?" I asked.

Mom glanced over and immediately grabbed her wallet, snapping it shut.

"Who is it?" I asked again.

She wouldn't answer me for a while. But I kept asking, even popping my gum with my tongue because I knew it irritated her.

Finally, she answered: "Your sister."

I thought she was joking at the time, and I tossed her leather purse onto the floor of our minivan. "Yeah, right," I said, and kicked my feet up on the dashboard.

Mom got so flustered she had to pull over and put the car in park. "She's your half sister."

I stared at her, wincing while I listened to her explain. "Her father, my ex-boyfriend, ran off with her one afternoon. Took her."

"Kidnapped her?"

"Yeah." Mom's voice cracked, and it was so sudden, so unexpected. With that one word, a stream of tears raced down her cheeks, like they had been waiting there all this time. "It happened after we broke up, and I was with your dad by then and had you. I've looked for her for years now, and I'll never stop looking."

I remembered vague recollections of Mom talking to people on the phone, demanding "someone find *her*." She also used to be so moody and so sad every December. Before that drive, it all went over my head, conversations overheard when I got a glass of orange juice in the kitchen or as I passed through the hallway to find a screwdriver in the garage. But all of it made sense after that Muir Woods drive with Mom.

Standing here now in the Trinity living room, I gaze at this redheaded witch in front of me. No way is she my sister. Another lie. Another manipulation.

"My *sister*? What the hell are you talking about?"

She crosses her legs on the sofa and points to a chair opposite her. "Sit down."

I stand and lean against the wall, my body still feeling weak and tingly after that weird electric shock. She sits daintily, waiting for me to submit to her.

"Where have you been, if you're really her?" is all I can think to ask.

"I disappeared for a while," she says, "and eventually came here. Just like you did."

"Why?" My brain has so many questions, but that's the only word that seems to come out of my tangled thoughts. *How? What have you done? Why are you doing this? I don't get it.*

She scratches her nose and bites her lips together—just like Mom. That's why she looks so familiar. She has these minute mannerisms that just remind me so much of Mom. And the eyes... Mom's are that watery blue, like clear swimming pools. Xintra's eyes have the same quality, but they're that translucent green.

"Go ahead and stare," she says. "I did the same when you came. I always was curious to know what my baby brother looked like."

The idea of this girl being my blood relative and calling me her baby brother hits a nerve like a hot iron. "You're not really my sister. You have a different dad," I say sharply.

"Yes, I do have a different father." Her accent makes it sound like *fatha*. She sighs. "But your father was a total loser, from what I understand. I guess that's because he had no Annunaki blood. He was inferior."

My dad was messed up, for sure. He had an addiction, something that told his body that drugs were more important than food, water, shelter—and me. But I don't blame him anymore. In fact, hearing her cut him down makes me feel defensive.

"Who even cares if you have Annunaki blood?" I spit. "Clearly you've got problems of your own, what with being a massive bitch and taking to torture the way you do."

"Ah, well you *would* care if you knew what was going to happen to the world. The Annunaki will inherit the world."

"Whatever."

She raises her eyebrows, a smug expression clouding her face.

The questions tumble out of me. "How did you even get here? Why?"

"That's not important."

"Get me out of here," I say.

"You can't tell me that you, too, don't have traits—psychic traits, that is." She tilts her head, studying me. "You've probably had visions, but you chalk them up to happenstance, right? Like when you think of an old friend and then the next moment they call you?"

She's right. When Ember showed up in Trinity, I was taken aback, because it was like a giant case of déjà vu. The night before she arrived, I imagined this short girl with long, curly dark hair walking down the hill with Lilly to the swimming lake. I remember thinking she was beautiful and feeling so drawn to her, knowing that she was different from the other people I'd met in Trinity.

The next day, that same girl, Ember, comes walking down the hill.

"And you probably see visions of people elsewhere in the world, connecting to them somehow through the energy of the universe, if only for a brief moment in time," she says. "That's the power of Trinity's vortex. It heightens everything. But you also have some latent psychic abilities."

I guess I do see things every now and then, but I always figured it was my imagination or coincidence. Last night, I saw Pete, another guy I met in Trinity—before he was rebirthed—dressed in all black, setting off a bomb at a subway.

"Pete," she says, as if reading my mind. "Poor guy. He's what we call a sab, put out in the world as a sacrificial lamb for the cause. Setting off bombs, committing mass shootings, evoking fear and uncertainty."

My heart sinks to my stomach, so heavy, it's as if it was tied to an anchor. Pete wanted so badly to have a better life out there, and he was just a piece of toilet paper, used by Xintra, flushed away. My stomach rolls, and I clench my teeth. I want to punch her.

"And the others? I'm sure you've thought of them all," she says. "How could you not? Lying there in the dark alone all those days?"

It's true. Another time, in the dark cell downstairs, I saw Chris, dressed in a suit and tie, as some government official, talking to a reporter, telling people to go get vaccinated for a virus. I even saw a vision of Lilly on the set of a movie, running from some zombie.

Worst of all, just the other night, I imagined Ember singing onstage. She was dressed in some Catholic school skirt, tall socks, and a black bra, marching around in the spotlight. She didn't look like herself. Her breasts were enormous. Her nose narrow. Her hair was so blonde and straight she hardly looked like herself. But it *felt* like her. Felt kind of shitty for having that dream, to be honest. But I refused to believe it was more than what it was. A dream. Kind of a smarmy dream, but a dream nonetheless.

"Sure, everyone lets their imagination go wild," I say. "When they're locked in a freaking *cell* alone, for weeks."

Xintra clicks on the TV and pats the couch next to her. "Come. Sit."

I shake my head and stay where I am. She flips the channel. "There was a big interview set to air on TV today," she says. "Well, not *today* today. But in the outside world."

The TV flashes scenes of TV news and infomercials about workout equipment and police dramas. Then, Ember appears on-screen, looking exactly like I dreamed.

"That stuff you saw in your mind about everyone was real," Xintra says.

There's a clip of Ember holding a microphone with her middle finger and thumb. Smoke billows up around her onstage. She's wearing the Catholic school skirt. The tall socks. The black bra.

My heart squeezes. She's out there, rebirthed, singing like she loved. But she would never do it this way. Not like this. This isn't her, and it wasn't what she wanted. I ball my hands into fists and my body trembles. I can't swallow.

"You really loved her," Xintra says, sighing. "But Ember chose a life as a star, singing onstage out in the real world instead of moping around here with you."

I glare at her and my jaw clenches tighter. She's getting to me now. Is it possible? Would Ember *really* pick that lifestyle? Not many people would pass up being famous, rich... for someone like me. But she seemed so strong, so different, so ready to fight. That's what I always loved about her. During the time we were together, I watched her change. I noticed how she started to stand taller. Her eyes shone. She genuinely smiled and even snorted when she laughed. She discovered the strength inside her that I always saw. She had forgotten it was there, but she found it again. With me.

"She left you. She never loved you."

I can't say that her words don't chip away at me—that her little chisel doesn't hurt. I remind myself that it's not true. It can't be.

"She's the reason you were put in that dark room. She's the reason you were punished. You slept with rats. You got bread with maggots for dinner. She's the one who told you how the food was all a facade here, drawn from the power of spells and Trinity's energy. She took the joy of food away from you. She took the beauty and luxury of this place away. And now, you still refuse to free yourself?"

"You mean lose myself?"

"I suppose you can stay inside that cell downstairs until you die. Suffering, sad, wallowing in a meager, worthless existence."

No way am I going back down there. I realize how far I've fallen, and the situation I'm in now. No way out. No way forward except for the crazy, evil magic my bitchy half sister is promising. Holding over me. How long can I sustain my objections? And what will they get me, in the end?

Xintra clearly picks up on my moment of weakness. She pounces like a jungle cat.

"If you were smart," she says, "you'd choose to be my partner. Brother and sister, like we were meant to be. And you can live in luxury. Like me. Honey to the queen bee."

10

OSHUN

We climb into the back seat of my limo, pull down the long driveway, and after a few minutes, we're in thick traffic, inching past tall palm trees and silver skyscrapers. Kaat sits next to me, wearing glasses and reading headlines from her phone.

"Here's one: 'Oshun Bought a Nineteen-Million-Dollar Mega Mansion in Malibu,'" she says. "Um, here's another: 'Oshun Reveals How She Goes Unnoticed Riding the Subway in New York.'"

I wave my hand to quiet her. "I own the media. I've heard enough."

After a couple minutes, the car pulls up to our destination. A red carpet awaits me, and lines of paparazzi with their enormous cameras stand, waiting like vultures. A rush of power throbs in my chest.

I climb out of the car, lower my sunglasses, and gaze at the cameras before holding up my fingers into the shape of a triangle, my thumbs touching at the bottom, forefingers at the top. I hold the triangle up to my eye. The sign of the pyramid eye—a signal to other rebirthers, of our solidarity and the coming Dark Day. I raise my voice above the shouts from photographers. "Oshun Beach Party, June twenty-ninth!" I say.

I wear silver platform boots up to my thighs, a black checkered miniskirt, and a silver slinky top that wraps tight to my torso. My hair is straight and parted severely in the middle. I pout my lips and gaze at the cameras. It's silent for a moment, outside of a few shouts of my name and the *click, click, click* of the camera shutters, like a thousand turning locks.

"Come to the beach to win a two-week trip with me later this year," I say, flashing my ivory smile and then posing with a smirk, my head tilted down, one leg out to look slimmer.

When I decide it's enough, I sway my hips and stride to the nightclub, the click of cameras capturing my backside.

Two bouncers wearing black T-shirts stand at the entrance to the Hollywood Club. They dispose of their standard fierce scowls and offer me, Oshun the Pop Star, beaming smiles. They move aside quickly, as if they themselves are two large wooden doors swinging up open just for me.

Inside the dark club, the walls vibrate with the thump of rap music. The sound is black and red streaks. A strobe light distorts the faces and bodies, sweaty and hot, pushing together like a wave, crowding against the bar. Most of the faces are unfamiliar, but I know they are the important people in the world. The rich. The famous. The powerful. The beautiful. All but a few are also rebirthers—dressed in every kind of attire. Sparkling long formal gowns. Revealing dresses. Baseball caps, baggy jeans, and T-shirts. Suits with no ties. The air is electric and transcendent. Add to that thrill, I know there are thousands of us out there.

"Want something?" Kaat shouts over the music into my ear.

She doesn't belong here. She is not a rebirther, nor is she powerful. She is my gnat, and I have no clue how she got this job. I should fire her.

I nod. "Vodka. Straight."

I move to a railing that overlooks a crowd of people below, laughing, talking, and gyrating on the dance floor. I can easily spot all of us rebirthers, who have the dark, heavy energy that hangs in clouds above our heads. The clouds move like clumps of ashes that ebb and flow, crumbling and reforming into various muddled shapes.

Then, I see her. My target.

I stride up to the middle-aged woman with coifed blonde hair, dressed in a red designer business suit. She stands out like a weed in a rose garden, glancing around the club and sipping a glass of wine.

I hold out my hand and smile. "I'm Oshun. I'm so glad you could make it tonight. As my special guest," I say, raising my voice above the noise.

She nods and flashes a nervous smile. She leans forward and shouts over the music, which thumps in my chest. "It's nice to meet you. Quite a scene."

"Yeah, it's great." I point to a booth in the corner. "Why don't you join me at a table over there?"

She pauses and touches my arm. Few people can get this close to her. "Oshun, can you tell me exactly what you wanted to discuss? Something about a nonprofit?"

"Yeah," I say. "I want to solve world hunger, and thought you could help. Plus, I wanted to make a donation to your presidential campaign."

"Oh." She nods with large, eager eyes and flashes a smile that reveals crooked teeth. She won't become president with *that* face, but she could steal important votes from a better candidate. *Our* candidate. We walk toward a booth, and in the commotion of the club, I subtly slip the tiny bottle of carby-lamine-choline-chloride from my purse.

Poor Jane Baxter. She doesn't even look like a woman who will suffer a deadly heart attack tonight. I grin and place my hand on her back.

11

MADDIE

I push the tack into the Missing Poster on the cork bulletin board in the coffee shop, bustling with clattering dishes and buzzing conversation. A hand squeezes my neck, trying to scare me, but I know it's Jared, so I spin around and put my hand over his face.

He laughs and leans away from me. "I was able to put up a poster in the record store and the juice bar around the corner," Jared says.

My job was to talk the owner of this coffee shop into letting me hang up the posters with Ember's face on them. I had to fight him for it.

"It's kinda depressing—ruins the vibe," the owner told me, rubbing his goatee.

"Yeah, but wouldn't it be great if someone in your coffee shop changed someone's life by recognizing and finding a missing girl?" I responded, reciting a conversation I've had with hundreds of business owners across Colorado in the past three years.

"But she's been gone for years, and she's not even from LA," he said.

"Have you ever heard of cars and planes? It doesn't matter where she's from. She could be anywhere." I gazed at him wide-eyed. Still, he was unconvinced. "Do you want me to create a scene and put it on YouTube? You'll look like a jerk."

I swear I saw his top lip quiver. I won. My poster is up, though I don't know if it will do much good.

"Dax should be here any minute," Jared says. "Can't believe he got free tickets for us. Then we'll go check into the hotel and get ready for the show, alright?"

"Sounds like a plan," I say.

Jared gets in line to order a cup of coffee while I take a seat at a table by the window and pull out my phone. Jessica Rengel posted another picture of her cat. Molly Fenton put up a video of herself eating a whipped-cream pie. I lean my head against the wall, bored, when a hand touches my arm. I look up.

A middle-aged woman stands at our table, smiling, with long gray braids and a round, smooth face. "I know your friend," she says, pointing to Ember's poster on the bulletin board.

"What?" I ask.

"I know Ember," she says. "I had a dream about her."

Jared returns to the table, takes a seat across from me, overhearing this woman. I give him the Look. We've had this scenario before. People calling the police, claiming to know exactly where Ember is. One guy said she was abducted by aliens and tossed out on the streets of Mexico. Another lady told us her vision of a terrible, gruesome story that only gave me nightmares. I inhale, ready for this lady's wild prophecy.

"Tell us more," Jared says, sipping his coffee.

"May I sit?" the woman asks, motioning to the seat next to him.

I look at my phone, because I'd rather look at cat pictures than talk to a lady who probably has a thousand cats. But

Jared doesn't seem to mind her plopping down right next to him. "Yeah, sure, sure," he says.

She sits across from me and I glance up at her hands, folded on the table, dotted with brown henna lines that climb up her wrists. She smells like patchouli oil. "I dreamt about Ember, over and over. She was banging on the walls of something, screaming to get out."

I glance at Jared, and he's rapt. I roll my eyes.

"Go on," Jared says. Great. Another total whackjob to yank his chain one more time.

"I saw her. The brown eyes, the curls," the woman says, touching her eyes and hair. Her voice is light and gravelly. "She was trapped inside another body. I could see her banging on the translucent skin of a body."

Creepy. Totally creepy. Is she saying someone *ate* Ember?

"Wow," I say. "Thanks. That's great information. We'll pass it along to the investigators." I begin to stand up, but Jared reaches across the table and puts a hand on my arm, keeping me from leaving.

The woman keeps talking. "And then I dreamt of the ocean. Waves crashing down at night, hitting rocks. The waves, rising, rising. And I believe she is Oshun, the singer."

Oh, what the hell. This is *not* what he needs. How did she even get wind of his crazypants idea? She had to have overheard him on the phone earlier or something.

Jared leans toward her, bracing himself on the table. "Really?" His voice is rushed.

Great, now he's encouraged. I can picture it now, the total BS from this woman's lips turning him into a real celebrity creeper. We need Dax to bring him back to reality, stat. Maybe the concert was a terrible idea.

"Yes," she says, leaning back in her chair and nodding her head slowly. A shadow of sadness crosses her face. "I can't reach her, though. I won't be able to come within five feet of her."

Of course not. She's a total weirdo. Oshun probably has a restraining order out on her.

"But *you* can," she adds. "You have access I do not. And you must give her something to find her way home."

I glance at Jared, hoping to exchange the *here's another crazy one* look. But his eyes are locked on hers.

He runs his hand through his hair and waves the other in the air. "What are the odds? We're actually going to her concert in just a couple hours."

"I know," she says. "I dreamt that, too." She reaches out long fingers draped in silver and turquoise rings and touches his cheek. Her eyes soften with a hint of emotion and familiarity.

He doesn't pull away, letting her keep her hand on his cheek. It kills me the way he's so hopeful, and I want to slap at her for pumping his head full of ideas. She's probably going to figure out how to get money for this. She'll pull out a crystal ball and charge us to look inside.

"You look just like your father," she says softly. She sighs. "Ahh, I know Ember is the only hope."

She gently pulls away and digs into a large woven purse, removing a necklace made of a dozen or so crystal rocks. In the center of the strand is a large stone that looks like it's made out of a chunk of gold. It has a handmade, bohemian look to it, and it's kind of funky and cool. "This," she says. "Give her this."

Jared takes the necklace and studies it. "Okay, yeah, I'll try. My friend is a reporter who's interviewing her, so maybe he can give it to her."

"Perfect," the woman says, perking up.

"But what's so special about the necklace?" Jared asks.

"She will feel it." She touches the big, chunky rock at the

center. "This contains a thin piece of iron, which has a high magnetic permeability. That ferromagnetism should be able to block out Xintra's magnetic force, and allow me to reroute lines of magnetic flux around Ember, shielding her from Xintra's pull."

I frown. Her gobbledygook words are incomprehensible. This necklace is from a complete whackjob and is probably coated in anthrax. We are *not* delivering it to that pop star. "You should probably just give it to her yourself," I say.

Jared waves me off. "No, no," he says. "I'll give it to her."

She nods. "Very good. And I've something for *you*, too, sweetie." She nods at me and removes a bracelet with a looping cross from her bag. "It's an ankh cross. No matter where your life may take you, your true path will be shown to you. You'll know what to do with it when it's time." She pushes it across the table. It's silver and has what looks like clear quartz in the middle of the looping cross.

"I couldn't," I say, pushing it back to her.

"No, you must," she says, shaking her head and putting up her hands. "I insist. It's got quartz in it. Very powerful energy. It can counter black magic."

Great, just in case I happen to come across black magic. It's what I've always needed. Whatever. I squirm under her gaze. It *is* actually a cool bracelet. I take it, nod, and avoid eye contact. "Well, thanks. Nice meeting you."

"And you as well." She rises and turns to walk out the door.

"Thank you..." Jared calls. "Oh, I didn't catch your name."

"I am Lodima."

12

DAX

"J-Man!" I yell, swinging open the glass door to the coffee shop. I take off my black sunglasses and walk toward Jared, who's sitting at a table with a cute round-faced girl with dark brown hair and a sullen expression.

I move my arm to cover the coffee stain on my beach shirt. After a crap morning, this is the last place I want to be, but Jared drove across the country, so I needed to show up. He stands and walks toward me with open arms. "Hey, buddy!" We clap each other on the back and then Jared points to the girl. "You remember Maddie, right?"

I have no idea who she is, and she's quick to pick up on this.

She raises her eyebrows. "You met me during the search for Ember?" she says. Her low, raspy voice sounds kind of sexy. "We walked about two miles together?"

"Right, right," I say. I still don't remember.

"So, you're some kind of big writer, huh?" she asks.

"Well, I don't know about *big*, but yeah, I like to write." I offer my practiced humble wince. Sure, my writing career took off last year. But I always try to remember where I came from.

Two years ago, I was handing Uncle Phil wrenches while he fixed up his 1965 Dodge Coronet, and we got to talking about my cousin Antonio, who went off to work at some Hollywood agency. I went on a rant about how everyone famous is glossy and fake—a brand or a package. "They're not authentic," I said.

"Hand me that cold chisel," he said without looking at me. I didn't know which one was a cold chisel, so I handed him a long gold wand off the counter. He frowned and reached for another one.

"Look at Marilyn Monroe," I continued, pointing to the poster in his garage. "She was this gorgeous girl named Norma Jean, but they made her change her name, change everything about her. She was a marketing machine. A brand. She couldn't be her real self—and she died inside."

"Well, whatcha gonna do about it?" my uncle said through a gritty sigh.

"What?" I tried to see his face, but his body was twisted around a rusty car door.

"You're the reporter. You've got the Alvaro good looks. Make people talk to you."

I grimaced and studied a rusted can of motor oil. "Naw."

Uncle Phil stopped working and squinted at me with those dark eyes and bushy brows. Mom always said I was a mini-me of her brother. He leaned over the car door, his white T-shirt smudged with black oil. "Get a credit card, buy some decent clothes, and call up your cousin in Hollywood. Maybe he can get you access." He laughs and picks up a compressor. "Cause it's clear mechanics ain't your thing."

Jimmy did hook me up. And eventually, I learned how to pull the humanity out of those polished celebrities. The irony? I'm now officially an A-list Hollywood reporter who's making more waves than I did covering real news.

I pull my wallet from my back pocket and remove two paper concert tickets. I hand them to Jared. "I don't have a lot of time, but here are those tickets."

"Thanks, that is so cool," Jared says. "How'd you get them? Did Oshun give them to you?"

"Her people did offer me free seats, but that puts me in ethical hot water if I take them. You know, it'd be like she was buying good coverage. So I just bought these for you." I may be in Hollywood, but I have to have some journalistic standards.

Jared tries to hand them back. "I can't let you pay—"

But I back up with my palms held up in the air. "No, I insist. My treat."

Jared needs a pick-me-up. Besides, I owe him. I remember senior year, kicking back on the front porch with him, whining about Keya, my ex-girlfriend who tortured me for two years, reeling me in with those legs and lips and then tossing me to the curb.

"You gotta get back out there and live, man," Jared told me. That day, he got me out on a mountain bike, and I was addicted. Eventually, I moved on past Keya and Jared became a good buddy. He was like that with everyone. He hooked BJ Sops up with a job at The Kitchen. He tutored that handicapped chick in physics. Organized all the music for our annual luau and our big funk party. Unlimited energy. Then he threw that energy into finding Ember.

He dropped everything for Ember's search and posted constantly to social media with updates on any tips and clues. It consumed him from the inside out. When I saw him at the frat house last summer, he wasn't even the same guy. Usually he was the one organizing the party, chatting everyone up like a social butterfly. Girls were glued to his side. I mean, hot girls. But last summer, he just sat in a lawn chair with sunglasses on all day, not talking, just drinking so much beer he puked all over the grass.

I look at my watch. I've got to give myself enough time to prepare for this interview, and so far it's been a crap day. Spilled my coffee on my way out the door only to find my car has been booted from unpaid parking tickets. Add to that a wicked hangover from that Peppermint Club after-hours party. If this bubblegum Oshun doesn't give me an authentic interview, I'm screwed. Good-bye, parties. Good-bye, girls. Good-bye, career. You're only as good as your next story. I can feel a stress headache creeping up the back of my neck.

"Listen, I need to run because I'm actually set to meet her before the concert, and I've only got a little window of time."

Jared's face lights up and he shakes his head. "Oh, will you give her something for me?"

Maddie's nostrils flare and she crosses her arms across her chest. She definitely has attitude. They look like a little married couple.

Jared pulls a necklace out of his jeans pocket. "This lady literally just came up to us and said she had a dream about Ember and that I needed to give this to Oshun. Can you do it for me?"

I wince. Jared is grasping, big time. Still, I take the necklace and pretend this is a totally normal request. "Wow. It looks handmade."

"Yeah, it's cool, huh?"

"Why exactly am I giving this to her?"

"She just said she had dreams that Ember was Oshun and thought she needed these crystals to find her way home. Then something about a magnetic force." The words fall flat on the concrete floor. I gaze at Jared, and his Adam's apple bounces when he swallows. The guy must realize how ridiculous this is. He *has* to hear himself.

He doesn't. "This is it. I know it is," he says, rocking back on his heels.

I open my mouth, not sure how to respond. "Cool," I say, curling my fist around the necklace.

"So is there any way I can meet her? It can be subtle. Tell me where you'll be and I can just pass by?" Jared asks.

"That's kind of weird," Maddie says quietly. She's right.

"Uh, maybe," I say. My headache is ripping now. "Text me and we'll keep in touch. I definitely want to catch up with you, bro."

13

OSHUN

The sound of Kaat's feet pattering into my living room irritates me. She's a mosquito, sucking off my riches, buzzing in my ear. She hovers a few feet away, waiting for me to acknowledge her. I make her wait, instead admiring the various shimmering bracelets on my wrists, enjoying their weight, the way they twinkle in the light, the way they adorn my dainty wrists.

She clears her throat. She can't be less than thirty years old, but she has the confidence of a meek child. How did she get this far in life?

"You have a few interview requests," she says, looking at her notebook. "Uh... *NBC* and *InStyle Magazine*."

I shrug. "What's their angle?"

"NBC wants to do a feature on you and your new song, 'Candy,' rising on the charts. *InStyle* wants to talk about what you're going to wear to the Grammys."

"They don't need an interview for that. Just tell them."

"So you're declining the interview?"

I flop my hands down and glare at her. "I don't run from anyone."

"Okay, so that's a yes?"

"Sure, but I don't want to spend much time on it. I need to get a massage." I rub my neck, which pinches from dance practice.

"Right, right. And there's one more," she says, wincing. "Your publicist scheduled an interview with Dax Killis before the concert tonight, but I'll cancel it."

"The Star Whisperer?" I've heard of this guy and his so-called ability to get unusual stories that shake up people's careers—not to mention give them hours of free publicity from psychoanalyzing talking heads on cable TV.

"Yeah, but the record label told me to cancel it." She nods and then begins to turn away.

"Why?" I ask, irritated.

"He pulls secrets out of people, and we don't need that kind of publicity. They said that you shouldn't do it."

"I don't run from anyone. Let him try to crack me." This will be perfect; I will crush him.

Kaat chews her cheek. "But they said not to..."

I pick up a bracelet and turn it in the light of the sun. "Dax Killis is nothing but a fraud. I'll eat him for dinner."

14

MADDIE

"That's it, I officially hate LA," I say. The buildings are so close together in this stupid city that my navigation keeps taking us in circles. We're never going to find our hotel. "I'm asking for directions."

"No, come on, Mads, we can find it. We are *not* asking for directions." Jared rolls his eyes. I hate the way guys think asking for directions means handing over their manhood on a platter.

I slow my car and pull up next to a guy with a shaggy red beard and a USA baseball cap. He pushes a grocery cart full of blankets, coats, and cereal boxes.

"Maybe we can borrow a blanket if we can't find our hotel." I roll down Jared's window and the man doesn't look up. He shuffles slowly along the sidewalk, his gaze locked on the ground, just beyond the cart. "Yoo-hoo!" I yell.

"Mads!" Jared sighs. He tosses his head back onto the headrest, embarrassed.

The guy pushing the cart doesn't respond. Finally, I honk my horn. He jumps and looks at me with wide, crazed eyes.

"Sorry." I shrug and offer a fake embarrassed smile. "So, um, do you know how to find the Trip People Inn?"

"You're in front of it, lady," he says with his eyes still bugging out.

"What?"

He turns around slowly and points with a shaky index finger to the cinderblock building behind him. Bars cover small windows. A little pink awning hangs over a green wooden door and, sure enough, it says *TPI*. Ah. *Trip People Inn*. What a stupid name for a hotel.

An enormous guy wearing a bolero hat, and a plaid jacket stands across the street. He pulls a suitcase out of the trunk of his car and leers at me, dipping his Aviator sunglasses down to his nose and licking his lips with a long tongue.

Great.

I inhale and look at Jared, plastering a big fake smile on my face. I put the car in park. "Yeah, baby, that's what I'm talking about!" I say. "We're staying in the lap of luxury!"

A chocolate donut lies on the yellow linoleum floor. It just sits there in the middle of the lobby floor, upside down, while the motel clerk prints my credit card receipt with a cigarette dangling from his mouth. I cannot keep my eyes off the donut. Why doesn't he pick it up? The unshaven clerk, who smells faintly of old newspapers, doesn't seem to notice. If he were an animal, he surely would be a frog.

"I gotta use the john—real bad," Jared says.

"Bathroom is outside and around the corner." The clerk nods his head to the left but doesn't look up. Jared darts for the door of the motel lobby, and I catch a glimpse of his bobbing head passing through the high window.

The clerk turns to look at the wooden key rack behind

him. "I need to go in the back and get a key," he says, slipping behind a curtain and disappearing.

The door opens and in walks the bolero hat guy from across the street. He dips his sunglasses down again and looks me up and down from head to toe and back again. I'm guessing that must be his schtick, and so I flash a quick smile and look him up and down too—a trick I always rely on to put creepsters off balance: if someone gives you the creeps, give them the creeps back. Look them straight in the eye.

Bolero hat guy, however, seems to take my direct eye contact as an invitation to chat me up. "You cats here for business or pleasure?" He takes off his hat, revealing a balding head. Tiny beads of sweat dot his forehead, and he launches into a serious coughing fit.

"We're in town for the Oshun concert."

He laughs through his nose. "Her new single, 'Candy'— oh man." He smiles and shakes his head.

"What about it?" I try to ignore the fact that I drove cross country for an artist I couldn't care less about.

"The disco-rock refrain pretty much blasts you at full volume. It's cluttered. It has a decent melody, but it never relents. She sings the title over and over, like she's hoping it will be profound. Really, when you think about it, it's kind of that dread of wanting it to be good but listen after listen, you realize it just ain't. Thank God it's only three minutes long."

"Awesome," I say softly. He does not at all look like some sort of music critic, let alone someone slightly familiar with this new pop star Oshun.

"People love it or hate it," he says. Slowly, he shuffles back a couple steps and sinks into a chair, looking like a wilting flower in the shade. "Whoa, not feeling so hot."

"Oh, sorry," I say. "Anything I can do?"

"Naw." He waves his hand at me. "I'll be fine. Just a cold coming on I think." He takes off his plaid jacket slowly, struggling to get his thick arms free from the sleeves. "I hope the concert is worth the hype."

"Thanks," I say, turning away to look for the frog man clerk, who still hasn't come back with my key. I crane my neck to look for him behind the dingy gold curtain leading to a back room. The bolero man starts coughing loudly and I cringe at the ripping sound of it.

I hear a thud and turn around. The man lies on his side on the floor.

"Oh God," I say, racing to him. "Are you okay, sir?" I touch his shoulder, and he doesn't move. His eyes are closed. "Sir?"

I jiggle him, but his fat body is heavy and limp and lifeless. And I completely panic. "Help! Hey! We need help!" I yell to an empty room.

I think back to all my nursing classes. What do you do if someone is unresponsive? *Dial 9-1-1, dumbass!* I pull my phone out of my bag and, with shaky fingers, call for an ambulance.

"9-1-1, what's your emergency?" the dispatcher says in a nasal voice.

"I'm at the Trip People Inn in LA and this guy just collapsed." My voice sounds like it doesn't belong to me, ringing and high-pitched, stuttering along the air. I kneel next to his contorted body, a collapsed scarecrow. His bottom arm lies awkwardly kinked. I glance back over my shoulder to see if frog man is nearby, but he's still MIA. And Jared—did he drown in the toilet? Why isn't he in here? Can't he see we have an emergency? He should have some sort of friend alarm that just blares *Get the heck in here!* when I need him.

I consider running out to find him but I'm afraid to leave bolero man.

"Help!" I yell again over my shoulder.

"What happened exactly?" the dispatcher asks.

"Can you just send someone here please?" I ask. She is really pissing me off.

"Yes, ma'am. Can you please tell me what happened?"

"He just coughed really hard. He looked sick." I run my words together and my hand feels weak, like I'm going to drop the phone.

"And he's not responsive?"

"That's what I said!" Spare me the cross-examination.

"Does he have a pulse, ma'am?"

"I don't know. Can you send someone right away?"

"What is the address, ma'am?"

"I don't freaking know. Look it up!" I don't understand why this is so hard. My eyes bounce around the room. Donut. Counter. Linoleum. The guy's protruding stomach. I turn away. He radiates death.

"No problem. Please stay calm."

"I'm only going to be calm if the guy doesn't die."

"Okay, I need you to check if he has a pulse."

"Hang on." I tuck the phone under my chin, lean in close to the man, feeling really bad for thinking he was a creeper earlier, now that he may not even be alive. He smells like sweet, cheap cologne, sweat, and what I can only describe as cheesy man smell. I put my fingers along the vein of his neck, moving it over the rough stubble, waiting. I move my two fingers again. Maybe I need to move my fingers lower.

"Oh no."

"They're on the way. Please stay calm."

"I'm a nursing student. Of course I'm calm." But the reality is my hands feel like they're made of wet kindergarten paste, like *I'm* made out of thick, wet paste. I tug the hair near my scalp, unsure of what to do. I don't know what to do. He's a bomb, and I'll make him disintegrate if I touch the wrong wire.

"Miss? Are you okay?" the woman on the phone asks.

"Yes," I snap. It dawns on me what this means right now. What if I can't handle sick people or emergencies properly when I'm a nurse? This is all I've ever wanted. This is my path. I'm *supposed* to be a nurse. I'm *supposed* to help people. I am not a person afraid of anything. But here I am with paste hands. I *will not* be afraid.

I need to breathe. I take deep breaths, filling up my chest, exhaling completely, feeling it calm my nervous system like warm oil filling up my insides.

"I'm going to try CPR," I say, trying my best to sound authoritative.

"You didn't do this already?"

"No," I whisper, irritated.

"Okay, that would be good," she says calmly. I stare at his mouth and the little cracks on the corners and the tufts of hair coming out of his pear-shaped nostrils.

"Can you tell me everything that happened before he collapsed?" the dispatcher asks.

"No, I'm thinking about CPR. Give me a minute!"

"Okay," she says. "Do you need me to walk you through the process?"

"No." I say. *Yes* is the real truth, but I think I can do this. I learned it. I did.

I set the phone down next to me. *Okay. Press down in the center of the chest. Thirty times. Pump hard and fast at the rate of one hundred beats per minute, faster than once per second.* I do that. What's next... *Tilt the head back.* I lift the man's dimpled chin with two shaky fingers and then pinch his nose. I lean in close, taking in another whiff of his sweaty cologne. With a deep breath, I cover his mouth with mine and blow. I glance back at his chest. *Blow until you see the chest rise, Maddie.* Okay. I see it. *Give two breaths. Each breath should take one second.*

Panic bursts from my chest. "Nothing is happening,

nothing is happening," I say. "Shit. Shit. Shit." I pick up the phone.

"Miss? They're on their way. Can you please tell me what's happening now?"

"I don't know. He's just the same, not moving. He's not breathing." The moment swirls around me, making me feel light-headed before a single tendril of truth emerges. "I'm pretty sure he's... dead. Oh my God."

15

DAX

The star on the dressing room door is shiny and gold, and at least a foot in diameter. I wonder if this is the size of Oshun's head. I can't wait to peer inside and tell the world what this girl is really about.

"So," says Marsha, the publicist. Middle-aged, she stands a good foot taller than me and wears her black hair with severe bangs. Her face is painted with such thick makeup it looks like she used a spackle knife to apply the pink to her cheekbones. She leans into me, touching my arm, her eyebrows dancing. "Oshun is really excited to do this interview, even though her record label tried to cancel it. I bet you get so many stars asking you for interviews."

I nod, press my lips together and look at my shoes. I still don't get why everyone wants me to talk to them. The whole "Star Whisperer" thing is such a strange development, and wearing the title feels about as comfortable as scratchy Irish wool. It's not like I ever dreamed of being the go-to guy for unearthing childhood traumas from America's most over-paid, ego-tripping elite. Once, I considered myself a serious reporter. That person feels about a million miles away. One PR lady told me I had a way of seeing through people's skin. Maybe. I don't know. Guess I should just be glad my career is taking off, and I'm actually making some money.

I meet Marsha's steely blue eyes. "I'm glad they didn't cancel. *Beats* magazine wants the story, so yeah, I think it will be great play for her."

"We're highly selective about these stories. No *Rolling Stone*?" She presses her lips together.

I shake my head. "They don't have space for another cycle."

"Well." She sighs. "*This* is her dressing room. She's expecting you. Your photographer will be meeting with her later, correct?"

I nod and thank her. When she leaves, I send a quick text to Jared before knocking on the door.

At her dressing room. Headed in now.

He replies instantly. *Awesome. Tho she might change her mind once she gets a look at your face.*

Me: *Pop stars love me, don't you know? Call you later.*

Jared: *You rock.*

When I slide my phone into my pocket, it buzzes again. I pull it out and see another text from him: *Ask her about Ember?*

I put my phone back in my pocket. I probably *should* ask Oshun about Ember, just to put it all to rest. But I don't know. It ticks me off a little that Jared even wants me to risk my credibility by posing such a ridiculous question to a rock star. Maybe I'll just lie to Jared, tell him I asked. Or maybe, it'll be a last resort question.

I knock on the door. After a couple seconds, it swings open, and there she stands: Oshun, smelling of lavender and cigarettes and dressed in a leather halter bra, a Catholic school-type plaid miniskirt, and tall white stockings. Classic. Jared better hope this isn't his sister.

She wears false eyelashes and makeup that turns up, catlike, at the corners of her eyes, and her hair is bleached blonde and straight. Man, in person she's so much smaller than she appears in photos and on TV. She barely comes up to my chin, but her presence is six feet tall.

"Hey, I'm Dax Killis," I say, lifting the press pass dangling around my neck.

"I know who you are."

She doesn't smile, but raises her hand to shake mine. Her touch gives me an energetic zap, and I almost pull away. It makes the hair on my arm stand on end and triggers a really random, long-buried memory. When I was a little kid, I'd feel that exact same electric buzz sometimes, mostly at night. I'd lie in my bed, and I'd feel this presence, this vibe that told me someone was in the room. It was creepy at first. Then one night I saw a flash of something, like when you catch movement out of the corner of your eye. After a few seconds, I made out the outline of a little girl. She clutched a stuffed rabbit and told me how she'd died right outside my house decades earlier after she fell into a well. I listened to her talk and cry for a good forty-five minutes. That was the first time, this memory I'd long repressed. I saw ghosts for a long time after that. Almost every month. Then I just stopped seeing them. Or they stopped showing up.

Now, for the first time since then, I get the same vibe from some obnoxious teenager? Maybe there's a haunting in this arena. Maybe I'm still too wired from that iced quad I had after dinner. Whatever it is, it makes me want to cancel this interview right here and now. Instead, I step inside, casually scanning the dressing room, looking for clues or hints that might give me a better idea of who Oshun is offstage. Nothing extraordinary or telling. A vase of flowers. Box of chocolates. A poster of her album cover on the wall.

"Thanks for doing this interview," I say.

"Sure." Oshun smiles but it's completely phony. Her eyes are vacant. She's got to be high or something. She waves me to a black chair that's angular and modern and then perches across from me on a white leather sofa.

I twirl my pen in my hand and lean forward, resting my elbows on my knees. "So, Oshun, I'll just dive right in. Everyone's talking about you these days."

"Is that the case?" She averts her gaze to the floor and then looks up at me with those brown eyes. They look almost like they're glowing.

"You've sold two million copies of your *Seasons* album."

She doesn't respond, blinking slowly, demurely. An act. She certainly is gorgeous, and her skin looks so smooth, almost iridescent. It's as if she's not human. I can't look away from her.

I glance at my notebook. "Your 'Candy' video shows you topless, wearing pearls covering your, um, breasts? And in it, you're, uh, climbing over a pile of dead bodies."

She doesn't respond. She blinks.

"Pretty dark stuff for a young girl, wouldn't you say?" I sit back, waiting to see if this unsettles her. Sometimes being direct and a little controversial will just tear something loose from people, catch them off guard.

She tilts her head, playing dumb. "Dark?"

"The tone of your songs, the minor chords, the salty sound of your voice, the sultry lyrics... It's... great." I nod. Her voice really is awesome, but the rest of the presentation, the packaged-ness of it all-- that's just a shell. I want to know what's underneath. So does the rest of the world.

She doesn't respond. Instead, she lights a cigarette and

takes drag, blowing the smoke out in one long, breathy exhale.

I fan the smoke from my face and smile. "Really unique sound. Great reviews." I pause. "But the lyrics have some people scratching their heads." I flip to a page in my reporter notebook and read from it. "'I am magic of the earth. You are death that brings rebirth.' Here's another: 'Pain is the icing on the cake. Take it. Give it. Push it. Need it.'" I clear my throat. "Some people are pretty outraged to see a young girl be so, I don't know, unrestrained. There's that boycott a group of parents organized, and then a few stories on TV..."

There's a hint of a smirk that slides across her lips, but then she tilts her head and crinkles her brow in confusion. "If you want me to be a sex thing, that's not me," she says, blinking, wide-eyed and innocent. "My performances, my lyrics—it's art."

That's ridiculous and she knows it. Look how she's dressed. How she moves. This is a ploy. I can see it. I will let her fans see it, too.

I narrow my eyes and gaze intently at her, waiting for her to accept reality, to have some kind of response. I dip my head and bite my lower lip. This worked when I interviewed Booker and then Katerina Velensa and Max Duvine. All of them broke with the long pause and the incredulous look. They *want* to be authentic. They *want* to be out from under the thumb of their handlers.

It doesn't work with Oshun. She moves slowly to show her tanned leg and stretches, revealing all the eye-catching angles of her body. The thin, smooth leg. The skirt inching up to her hip. Her waist curving just so. Her breasts touching each other and protruding from her top.

Dude. She is so sexy and so completely manipulative; I can't help but let dirty thoughts race across my brain. Touching that thigh with my fingers, pulling her on top of me. My eyes flit to her legs, then back to her face, and then I can't help it, they bounce to her breasts and back down to her legs again. A buzzing sensation takes hold of my body.

That's it. I can't handle it. I've got to stay professional. Abruptly, I stand and walk over to her dressing table, picking up a hairbrush and studying it as if the black bristles are a fine piece of art—anything to avoid looking at her.

"So, tell me," I say, glancing back at her again. She tilts her head and coyly runs her fingers through a few strands of her hair. I look at the wall. "What do you think of the press you've received in the past several months?"

"It's great," she responds automatically, cheerful.

"But some people call you—"

"A whore," she says. Her top lip curls slightly at this. "But record executives call me brilliant. And my concerts are sold out. My music was iTunes' most downloaded of anyone this week."

"Cool. That's huge. Pretty big deal for you, because you're so young, so new. It's like you just came out of nowhere."

She smiles.

I press on. "That's why I'm here. I want to tell the real story of Oshun. Let people really understand you."

She nods again but doesn't say anything.

I need a new approach. First step, be her friend. Warm her up. Step two: get underneath her facade, make her forget she's being documented. I look around the room. This isn't going to work. There's no color here. No flavor. Nothing to riff off of.

"You and I should spend some more time together. You know, I'd like to see your house, do some of the things you like to do?"

"I want to get a tattoo," she says.

"Really? Perfect. When?" I pull out my phone to look at my calendar.

"Tomorrow. I need to get ready for the show now," she says, standing. "Great meeting you, Dax." The abrupt response makes me freeze, phone in hand. She moves to the door and opens it wide. "I'll walk you out."

Fumbling, I close my notebook and stand to follow. "Uh, okay. What time tomorrow?"

"Midday," she says. "Maybe we can have dinner after."

"Sure, sure," I say. She slips in front of me, leading me down the narrow concrete hallway backstage. "Sure, I'm looking forward to seeing the show tonight."

"Good." She touches my arm with fingers painted with black nail polish. It delivers that weird electricity to my body, and my hair actually tingles.

We pass a man hovering over a silver soundboard. Two men in T-shirts that say *Oshun Rising* carry large black suitcases full of sound equipment. The men gaze at her with jaws that hang open, and they practically bow to her as we pass.

She stops at the heavy metal door that marks the exit to the arena, then opens it. The sunlight from outside practically blinds me.

Suddenly I think of Jared: he's going to bug me about the Ember connection, and he'll be so bummed if I don't ask her and give her that crackpot necklace. This interview has been terrible, and I'm not getting Oshun to crack. What can I do? This is my career, dammit. I will not let some stubborn brat with a thing for pleather derail me. So on a whim, I pull out the necklace and my phone. The various-sized crystals look luminescent in the sunlight, reflecting various shades of light purple, amber, and rose pink. The gold nugget in the center is a little obnoxious, and I have no idea what she'll think about this.

"Uh, one of your fans—a good friend of mine—wanted me to give this to you. Said it was, uh, important...?" I laugh, feeling stupid. This surely is the last breath of my short-lived career. "Something about finding your way?"

Her face softens and she takes it immediately, running her fingers over the crystals. "Thanks," she says softly before linking it around her neck.

Then I open my phone to pull up the video. "And I know you've got to get going, but I wanted to ask you: Have you ever heard of the name Ember Trouvé?"

16

EMBER

The name zaps me, yanks me by the armpits and pulls me out of my dark underwater place where I have been floating submerged. Where the world's sights and sounds feel distorted and muffled.

"You okay?"

The man standing in front of me has thick black hair, brown skin, and a crooked nose. We're outside, somewhere warm. Palm trees. Salty air. *Where am I?* The smell of smog fills the air. Horns honk neon green. Pink and purple flowers overflow from the edges of garden planters. There are opal dots in my vision, and I assume it's the sound of ocean waves rolling, or perhaps wind in the distance.

He leans into me, lifting up my elbow, like I might fall down.

I actually do feel light-headed, as if I'm not entirely in my body, as if I'm watching this from a really faraway place. Another dream?

Then I hear my own voice, saying familiar words. "Hello, future self! If you're watching this, it means you made it."

I climb back to the surface. That's *me*. That's me from the video I made freshman year!

My arms and legs thrash to break the surface, to find light and air and clarity. The warm air again rushes onto my skin, followed by the roaring sounds of cars honking and conversations from people behind me. And I see it, the video playing on the guy's phone in my hand. It's the one I made when I was a freshman in high school, to be opened when I was nearing graduation. Euphoria fills me and my skin tingles. This video feels like a lifetime ago, when life was so *normal*. On the video, Mom bangs pots in the kitchen, and I show off her artwork in the living room.

Tears fill my eyes and a wave of heaviness moves in my chest. This is what I forgot. This is what Xintra told me I would never feel anymore, never remember: regret, guilt, sadness. But also, life, love, passion. My past, my future. *Me*.

All of a sudden, I'm aware.

I went to Trinity to escape the elephant on my chest. But the elephant wasn't just my parents' deaths and the guilt I carried for screaming and making the accident even happen. It was Mom. I never knew her, I never accepted her, and I was so freaking angry with who she was. *That* is why I lost my head in the car. *That* is why we wrecked the car. *That* is why they died. Turns out, I was just like her. More than I ever wanted to admit.

On-screen, the camera scans the weathered wooden bunkbed I shared with Jared, passing the pink and green tapestry on one wall. "So, self: Mom seems better right now," young Ember says into the camera. "Let's see. What's been happening lately. Last week, Jared threatened to beat up Alex for making fun of my most awesome silver duct tape costume I wore for Superhero Day last spring. Which, I suppose, gives him some big brother points."

I remember that day! When Jared stood toe to toe with

the six-foot meathead Alex. "But," I say on camera, "he is still freaking annoying and still Jared. *Gross.*"

The camera zooms in on the half-eaten sandwich on a plate on Jared's pillow.

I watch the whole video, hearing myself talk about recently going to a concert and singing onstage with Dad. And my body buzzes because I remember that! I remember that night I sang with Dad! The heat of the lights on my skin, the way the fans waved their hands in the air and screamed when I sang familiar songs.

On-screen, Dad pokes his head through my bedroom door with that goofy grin. Emotion gets stuck in my throat like thick peanut butter, and a flood of sunshine soon warms me as I hear myself sing that song I wrote for him. The sound is a buttery yellow color I haven't seen or felt in so long.

A tear trickles down my cheek, a briny stream. The corners of my lips turn up in a small smile, but then, it quickly dissipates.

Without any warning, I am pulled under the water again, drowning. The guy in front of me stares at me from the other end of what looks like a long black tunnel. I hear my own voice ripple in a faraway echo, a conversation in another room. My voice sounds familiar, but it's also unexpected— cold and brittle. "Well, her likeness is pretty striking. But that's not me."

I'm tugged under the surface again. Everything goes dark. I go dark.

17

MADDIE

The police buzz around the tiny motel lobby, and the frog man from behind the counter finally reappears. I run at him, throwing my hands in the air, furious. "Where *were* you? You went to get me a freaking key and some guy dies on the floor. What the hell?"

The frog man frowns and takes in the scene. "I left the room key at home."

I grimace. "You *what*?"

Two paramedics carry the black body bag like they're moving furniture, bustling past us and out the front door. I've never seen a dead body before, and I feel like the blood in my own body has somehow forgotten how to circulate. My fingers tingle and each breath feels shallow and difficult. Two firemen in heavy yellow suits thump behind the body bag and paramedics. Frog man watches with a gaping mouth.

"You just left," I say again, flabbergasted. He left me to futilely save a dying man.

"I had no idea this was going down," the man mutters, raising his hands in defense.

An arm wraps around my shoulder, taking me in, pulling me close. "What's going on?" Jared asks.

I spin around and glare at him. "How long does it take to go to the bathroom? Oh, wait, long enough for a guy to drop dead."

"Who's dead?" His eyes dart around the lobby. "What happened?"

"The creepster guy with the bolero hat. He stopped breathing." I shake my head, squeeze my eyes shut and press my fingers into my lips. I'm not going to cry. This. Is. Insane.

A barrel-chested police officer comes over to us, speaking softly and enunciating as he asks what happened. He asks what our conversation was and how long the man lay unresponsive. I answer all his questions and he nods continually, reaching out now and then to pat my shoulder.

"So did he have, like, a heart attack?" I ask.

He shakes his head. "The team is guessing he got HT55, the virus."

Jared and I exchange looks. "I tried to give him CPR. I breathed into his mouth," I say slowly. My head squeezes tight. Mom will freak. "Does that mean—"

"It means nothing. We've had a string of cases here in the city. It's blowing up," the policeman says. "No one knows how it gets passed."

"I breathed into his *mouth*." I repeat, staring at the place on the floor where he died.

"Maybe we should we move to another hotel?" Jared asks.

"You aren't getting your money back." That would be frog face hotel guy standing just behind us. "Unless you find bedbugs. One room had 'em last week."

Invisible bugs crawl across my skin. I turn around and glare at the clerk.

"It'll be fine," Jared says. "We paid for it, and we don't have many other options right now."

Great. We get to stay a hundred yards from where a guy just died. Where I just breathed into his mouth. In the place that might have virus germs swarming. And bedbugs.

Road trips are the stupidest thing ever.

Jared glances at his watch. "It's a quarter to five, Mads," he says. "We gotta bolt if we're going to get to the concert."

The concert? How can I even go to a concert after this? My fingers still tingle, and I am so shaken. I've lived through a real life zombie movie. I put my *mouth* on a dead body. How will I ever kiss someone again? I need to brush my teeth.

"Jared," I say. "I don't know if I feel up to it..."

It's a flash, but Jared narrows his gaze. Like usual, he quickly covers it up. "Oh, yeah, I guess you might be pretty wrecked." He pauses and shakes his head. "Naw, I can go alone. No big deal."

I'm the one who suggested we go on this little adventure, in spite of Mom's warnings. But heading out to a concert jam-packed with people who could very well be contagious, that's a little unnerving, even for bulletproof me. Still, if I sit here alone in this hotel, fear will creep under the door, crawl around my room, pounce on me—and seep into my skin forever. I don't do fear.

"Never mind," I say firmly. "I'm cool. We came. We will conquer."

I take our key and stride cooly to our ground-floor room, marked with a number four. The chipped paint makes the four look like a picture of a chair. I unlock the door and step inside the tiny room. It smells like bleach. That's a good sign, right?

18

TRE

Zoe's golden dress ripples at her heels, and she gestures to the Trinity House, leading a group of people up the grassy hill. A guy with dreadlocks walks behind her with a dazed look on his face, and he gazes up at the window where I stand, watching them arrive from the various vortex entrances from around the world.

Xintra stands next to me in the living room, arms crossed, watching. She points to a frowning girl trailing a few paces behind the others. "That one there, the young girl with short blue hair and a nose ring? Her name is Alexandria Winslette. But she likes to be called Blu." She touches her head. "You know, the whole blue hair thing?"

I shrug. "Why do I care? Her life is pretty much gone now that she's here."

"I suppose that's one way to look at it. Or if you're an optimist, you can say she finally gets a second chance."

I'm silent and sip the drink she made for me. It tastes like lemon and it's so tart and refreshing after being holed up in the dark for so long.

"Poor Alexandria," Xintra says, gazing at the girl. "Her

father left her family when she was eleven. Her older sister, Miranda, ran away after that. And for so long, it was just her and her mother. But then her mother had a stroke, and Alexandria had to push her around in that wheelchair for three years, the two of them homeless, sleeping under bridges, eating at those soup kitchens. She quit school—"

"So Trinity is supposed to be somehow better?"

"Yes. She's incredibly intelligent and has a knack for science," Xintra says. I watch the girl, vigorously chewing gum, hands tucked deep into her front pockets, looking up at the house. "I will upgrade her," she adds. "I think of it as one big human improvement project."

"Did she ask for that? Did *any* of us?"

"She came here, didn't she?"

"How would she know what she was getting into? None of us knew." I swivel around to face Xintra, glaring. Looking into those green eyes, I can't help but see Mom. It's unnerving, as if an invisible rope draws me to her. She must feel the same emotion about me, must feel *something* for me. I'm a trigger. I've got to believe that.

Her brow flickers and then she sighs. "Well, it may not sound appealing at first. You'll see, it's better than the pain."

"How do you even know these stories, know so much about these people? All of us?"

"My own psychic abilities are heightened here," she says simply. "I can see everything more clearly through dreams and astral projection. I also have hundreds of people out there—rebirthers—who help me. We find the lost. Pick them. Each has a purpose."

I look out at the group again. A middle-aged woman in a plaid button-down shirt and jeans walks up front, craning her head back and forth to take in her surroundings. She looks out of place.

"What about that lady?" I say with a nod of my head.

"Jackie," Xintra says. "She'll be a great sab. Sacrificial lamb."

"*That's* her gift?"

She nods and points to another guy with brown dreadlocks. "And Bo. The dreadlocks are misleading. The guy is brilliant and will be a great political plant. Really handsome, and when I turn him on, he'll be extremely charismatic."

She doesn't see us as people, just tools. I don't get why she's sharing so much information with me. After leaving me in the dark here for so long, it doesn't make sense. But curiosity cuts through my anger. "So why are they all coming at once?"

"I'm stepping up the number of recruits these days. These people here were overflow from those vortexes. Ember's high-profile disappearance kept people away from Trinity so I had to find other ways to keep the flow going."

I take a sip of my drink and think about what Xintra said to me earlier. "*This is destiny, baby brother.*"

I refuse to believe that's the case. If it is, then what's free will?

"Is this what you did when I came here? When Ember came? You stood here and watched Zoe parade us up to the house?"

She shrugs. "Sometimes. I've been busy."

"How do you even see what's happening out there? When we're out in Trinity? At the lake? How do you orchestrate all this?"

"Ah, that's why I'm in charge and you're not," she says with a smirk. "You'll have the chance to know my secrets. But you have to go through rebirth to find out."

"Forget it." I say this, but inside, I know my resolve has holes. I've been in here so long, stuck, frustrated, only to watch Ember leave, to be locked in that cell and bitten by a snake and then to experience the enormous power of Xintra.

Between outside and inside, I can't help but wonder if the decision I'm making is the right one.

"I have a feeling you'll see the beauty of my plan," Xintra says softly.

"Where do you go when we're all hanging out here in this stupid house?" I ask. "Why do you hide? Do you live in that basement like a freaking rat?"

"I prefer Hawaii," she says, smiling. "It's beautiful there. The ocean is so clear, truly unbelievable. The sushi is amazing. You'd love it. You could join me, you know."

"Why *me*? Why do you want *me*?"

"You're family."

Family? That's a lie. I know it. With that completely lame explanation, she turns and strides out of the living room.

The TV is still on, and a newscaster is talking about upcoming summer concerts. Just a few minutes ago, Ember was on-screen as the pop star Oshun, an entirely different person. My throat constricts. I always loved the way Ember was completely oblivious to her own beauty, and for that matter, her own intellect and strength. She had that soft, olive skin and the tiny bit of freckles across the bridge of her nose. Those hands that were bloody and cut—a sign of true perseverance. She was like a cool rain in the middle of the Sahara.

I physically ache knowing Ember's out there and I could be trapped here forever. If only there was a way to get out and reach her as that pop star, shake her and wake her up to who she really is.

"Ember is gone." Xintra stands by the top of the stairs, gazing confidently at me. "Be here, lonely and starved and pained, or go back out to the world. My rules."

19

OSHUN

I stand in the shape of a giant X, head down, legs spread apart, hands raised above my head. Now *this* is power, standing here onstage. It feeds an insatiable appetite in my bones.

The C minor chords weave a silky yarn of silver, charcoal grey, and black oil. My voice is salt and vinegar, sugar and cinnamon.

I stride across the stage and the crowd erupts into thunderous cheers. Silver stars explode in my vision. I sing like a fire-breathing dragon, glowing beneath the spotlight, tasting the euphoria derived from controlling the emotions and minds of thousands of people. I blind them with stardom.

When I finish my first song, breathless, panting, I thank the crowd, raising my hand in the air, listening to the roar of their cheers, viewing the sea of hands and arms and heads honoring my presence. I am their goddess.

"Thank you, thank you," I say into the microphone. "I gotta know something right now. Do you all like beaches?"

The crowd cheers.

"Is that a yes?" I ask, holding the microphone out to the

crowd. I listen for the response, a resounding "yeah!" that comes in waves of hoots and clapping. "Okay, I heard you. Well, I'm having a little party on the beach. In fact, the whole beach of California. I'll be hosting free concerts the week of June twenty-ninth. And you all are invited."

The audience erupts into massive murky grey and red applause. I smile.

The music for the next song comes on and my sinewy dancers move in from behind. We begin to twist and spin and kick to the rhythm in perfect unison. My voice belts out the lyrics to the song "Follow Me."

Goddess death, of black and lies
Fate is printed in your eyes
You are twilight's final haze
I'm on midnight's grandest stage
You will heed this temptation
I am Hecate's lunation
I am magic of the earth
You are death that brings rebirth

I scan the faces in the crowd. Many wear medical masks. Others brave the open air, pushing up to the edge of the stage to see me, touch me, feel my presence. The crowd is a waving blanket of skin—brown, black and white— of hair and clothing, flowing and moving to the music.

Then, I stop, flat-footed. A young man with dark hair and crinkly eyes stares at me, unmoving and distinctly different from the rest of my adoring fans. He wears a T-shirt with a picture of a piece of bacon, and looks to be in his early twenties.

My heart thumps like a kettledrum. It's as if he and I are one body connected by furiously pumping blood. He's so familiar.

Memories drip before me, obscuring the crowd, the lights, everything else. They explode in my vision: His shoulder jostling mine at a yellow kitchen counter—both of us small children, eager for a scoop of ice cream. Playing cards on the floor, the boy's face scrunched in frustration, both of us arguing over the rules. Digging in the dirt with small, rusted garden shovels. Driving in a busted pickup truck, plumes of dust flying around us, laughing uncontrollably, me holding my arm out the window, swirling it through the breeze.

My voice waivers, stalls, and I stumble over the lyrics. My hand limply holds the microphone, and I signal to my manager that I need to stop the concert immediately.

I know that guy. I know him. A name hits me square in the jaw.

Jared.

20

MADDIE

"You saw how she looked at us, right, Mads?" Jared's whole body is electric. People move around us in a mob, jostling us, screaming and shouting over the noise of the thousands of fans. "She got all weirded out, Mads. She looked straight at me."

I inhale. "I know Ember—*you* know Ember—and she would never go for this. Not in a million years."

I remember her lying on my futon and tearing apart the overproduced sound of pop music. "I hate the way they just sell their music with their bodies. Why not their talent?" Emby said. "Oh, and the fan blowing their hair as they sing in the music videos? I mean, come on." She stood in front of my window fan and rolled her hips in a ridiculously non-sexy way. We busted up laughing and I took a video of her, threatening to put it online.

"That wasn't her, Jared," I say.

"No, no, no," Jared says. "Remember how she used to press her lips together between lyrics? Oshun did that. I saw her."

"So? That doesn't mean anything." I remember how

Ember would get when she sang, like the whole world disappeared. One day, we sat on my loft bed in my room and she tried to explain how the colors absorbed her. A flute was silver. Her mom's voice was amber. She said it was her "Color Crayon Brain."

"Synesthesia sounds like a bong-hitting dream," I told her that day. "Crossed sensory wires in the brain? A total trip."

She shook her head. "It's not like that at all. It's medicine to me."

Someone in the crowd bumps me from behind. A flickering strobe light distorts the faces and bodies around me, sweaty and hot, pushing together as the throng of people files out of the arena. Bits of conversations and laughter swim in the air.

"That sucked, man," a guy with a baseball cap says, pushing past me. "Why'd she just end the concert?"

His friend with silver piercings in his nose shouts back, "We paid a hundred fifty bucks for these tickets. She should suck it up even if she's sick."

A woman who looks to be around thirty or forty passes me in the crowd with a surgical mask over her mouth. My shoulder blades squeeze together and a wave of nausea sweeps through me. I can't shake the memory of pressing my mouth over the cracked lips of bolero man, and my stomach twists. He's dead, and it's making me pretty freaking neurotic. Now I'm surrounded by people who may be sick, too.

I shake off the thought, wiggling my neck and shoulders loose like a boxer before a match. I don't live my life wrapped in bubble wrap, hiding under the covers because something bad might happen out there.

Jared jumps up and down in place as if he's trying to keep warm. I may be turning into a neurotic germophobe, while my dear best friend is on the verge of insanity.

"She might have looked at us like that because she was

going to puke, you know," I say, shuffling toward the arena's exit.

Once we get into the hallway that encircles the venue, Jared pulls my arm, taking me into a corner away from the crowd. "Hang on!" he shouts over the noise before dialing his phone, holding it up to an ear and sticking his finger in the other.

"Dax," he says into his cell. "She saw me tonight at the show, and she totally started stumbling onstage. The second she saw us, she stopped the show—dead in its tracks. It's her. I know it's her. What happened with the interview?"

The noise dies down, and I tug on his arm. "Speakerphone," I say. He obliges, putting the phone on speaker so I can hear Dax's voice, too. We huddle over the phone in a back hallway corner.

"That's weird," Dax says. "She stopped the show?"

"Did you ask her about Ember? Did you give her the necklace?" Jared asks.

"Yeah, I did," he says.

"Well?"

"Uh, she got weird. Kind of emotional."

Jared's eyes widen and his mouth gapes. "Holy—"

"Maybe she got emotional because Ember's disappearance *is* heartbreaking," I suggest. I hate being the one to rain on Jared's hopes, but this is going too far.

He ignores me. "Like what? What did she do?" Jared asks.

"I can't explain," Dax says. "She got really quiet and then her face changed, her eyes looked kind of glossy. She was *affected*. I saw a tear run down her cheek."

"No way. Oh my God." Jared pulls his hand through his hair. "Okay. This is good."

Dax doesn't say anything. Maybe because he knows, like I do, that this is going too far. We need to reel Jared back to shore.

"Are you getting more interview time with her?" Jared asks.

"Yeah, I'm going with her tomorrow to get a tattoo."

"Tattoo?" Jared asks.

"Yeah, it's what she wants to do. And it'll be great color for the story."

"Is there a chance we can meet her? You know, see if it really was me and Maddie that made her cancel the concert?"

"I don't know..." Dax says slowly.

"Please? I would owe you huge, seriously. And who knows? This could be a huge story for you."

"Let me see what I can do," Dax says. I hear it in his voice. He's doing what I've been doing for Jared, trying to satisfy those curiosities to help him let go. If only he knew how much worse we were both making it. Jared's going off the deep end, not getting better. I was so stupid to suggest this damn trip. What was I thinking?

"You're amazing," Jared says. "Man, I can't thank you enough. This is huge. This could be it." His voice gets choked and tears pool in his eyes. He shakes his head.

"Catch you later, bro," Dax says.

Jared hangs up looks at me wide-eyed. I bite my lip, wanting so badly to hope for Jared. But I just don't believe it.

"He's going to get us to meet her. I know it. That's the kind of guy Dax is," he says, reaching for my hand. The touch spreads warmth from my fingers to my toes. He's so inflated that if he were a balloon, he'd fly away. "It's good to know guys in lofty places." He grins and leads me out of the hallway and into the crowd.

"Well, if we can really meet her, this ought to be interesting," I say belatedly. "She might just be some crazy rock star who was high on something during the interview. I hear a lot of Hollywood people deal with mental illness, too."

Jared's smile slides off his face and he drops my hand. He

frowns and turns to me as we walk side by side. "You don't even want to find Ember anymore, do you? I mean you trash every ounce of hope I have."

"Jared, no, I—"

He slows his pace. "I thought you were on my side. That we were in this together." His voice burns.

"We are."

"Sure doesn't feel like it." He picks up his pace, walking ahead of me through the tight shoulder-to-shoulder crowd.

I trail behind, nervously twisting my fingers through the bracelet that Lodima gave me in the coffee shop. "That's not fair," I say, hoping my voice catches up to him. "You know how I miss her." Tears hit me by surprise, but I don't let them fall from my eyes. I reach for his arm through the crowd, and raise my voice so he hears me. "Come on, Jared. You know this is crazy."

He wriggles out of my grasp and walks, eyes locked straight ahead, like I'm a stranger. I trot up next to him, pushing my way through the crowd. "We've hit so many dead ends over the past two years. I don't want to be—I don't want *you* to be—crushed again if it doesn't work out. I mean, seriously, this is far-fetched, right?"

He purses his lips and pushes the metal doors to step outside the arena. "It's cool, Mads. You don't have to go with me to meet her."

"Let's just see what happens," I say. *I just want you back,* I think. *Why can't you give me back the Jared I used to love? The Jared that could live his own life?*

He shrugs and we weave through the mass of people to the car. But I can see it in his face. Her disappearance rules him. There isn't room for anything else.

21

TRE

The dizziness comes in waves. Not eating will do that to you. Of course, I ate some vile food, just to survive, when I was locked in the basement. But I still haven't shaken the weakness from the snake bite and Xintra's weird electrocution, either.

I sit on the bed in Ember's old room, resting, my hands feeling clammy and my face damp with cold sweat. Xintra is downstairs, and I have the rest of the house to myself. I pick up Ember's pillow and inhale, longing for her scent. But I only smell freshly laundered sheets. No Ember smell. I remember lying on this bed with her, kissing her neck, feeling her body against mine, consumed with desire. I clench my jaw, beat back the emotion and anger.

I search her old room, tearing apart the bed, going through the drawers and closet. I need to find those crystals that Zoe stole from her. I need to find a way out. We were so close before Ember gave in.

I'm going to get out of here. And when I do, I'm going to find Ember, break through to her.

I ransack every single room upstairs, overturning

mattresses, rummaging through all the closets and drawers. The crystals—I've got to find the crystals and Ember's notebook with all the weird Egyptian symbols. If I concentrate, I think I can remember what was written inside it.

My new plan is to completely upend the living room and kitchen, trash the entire house: drop vases on the floor, destroy the TV, break dishes and windows. I'm going to make Xintra pay.

But when I come down the stairs, I can hear the dishes clinking in the dining room and voices. "Peppercorn roasted pork with vermouth pan sauce," Zoe says.

"Oh my gosh, it's heaven," a girl says.

"Do you cook?" Zoe asks.

"No, but my mom did."

"Did? Why the past tense?" Zoe asks.

"She had a stroke."

"Oh no. You must feel so sad."

My body trembles and I clench my jaw, and suddenly, I'm seething mad. I remember how we all sat and ate dinner at this very table. Ember sat at the far end, talking about theories on reality. I thought she was beautiful when I met her, but it was her feisty intelligence that really knocked me off my feet.

Now she's gone. And I'm stuck here. Maybe forever. And the cycle goes on. More people who will play into Xintra and Zoe's trap.

I storm into the dining room, my hair hanging in my eyes. I catch a whiff of my body odor, after two weeks in that basement cell. "Hey, guys," I say.

The clinking of cutlery quiets, and the group turns to look at me.

"Everyone, I want you to meet Tre," Zoe says brightly. Her eyes bore into me, threatening me. She'll probably bomb the world for what I'm about to do.

They introduce themselves.

"Hey, I'm Matt."

"I'm Jackie."

"My name is Blu."

"Bo."

I can't help myself. I put two hands on the end of the table next to Zoe, take a deep breath, and grasp the white tablecloth with my hands and pull. Dishes fly toward me, crashing on the floor. Water glasses break, silverware flies through the air. The girl, Blu, screams and a couple of them gasp. They stand up quickly. Blu shakes a piece of meat off her lap, scowling.

"What the hell, dude!" the guy with the dreadlocks, Bo, says.

"It's all one giant trick. A mind game. A trap. Get. Out. NOW!" I yell, letting out all the rage that's been brewing inside me.

They glance at each other, fear coloring their faces. But it's not Trinity they fear. It's me.

22

EMBER

I paddle to the surface of my dark underwater place and open my eyes. I find myself lying down on a sofa. Bright lights make me blink. I'm in some sort of dressing room. Across from me sits a table with a mirror rimmed with bulb lights. Clothes and high-heeled shoes sit in piles on the floor.

Memories hover at the edge of my mind, and I reach for them but they dissolve like smoke. Jared. I saw my brother, didn't I? The color of music comes back to me in a rush, spinning threads of silver, charcoal, and slick black.

I recall the feel and sound of walking in high heels beneath the heat of spotlights, of singing a familiar song. The melody comes back to me, and I sing the words quietly to myself. *"Goddess death, of black and lies. Fate is printed in your eyes."*

I stop, inhaling sharply, knowing that this song is bad. Really bad. It's an ancient spell, calling on dark magic. I don't know *how* I know this.

I look at my hands, the black polish on my nails, and the tattoo of small black pyramids wrapping around my wrist.

Diamond rings adorn my fingers, and a shiny gold cuff in the shape of a snake wraps up my left bicep. Just like the one Zoe wore in Trinity. I can't breathe. I want to throw up.

What's happening to me? Is this real? I stand and run to the table with the mirror, and my face shatters into pieces as tears fill my eyes. That poster on the wall is really me. This is no dream. This is real.

"What's happening? What's happening to me?" I whisper.

A knock on the door startles me, and I sit up straighter, alert and wary. A voice calls through the door. "Oshun? Are you okay?"

Oshun? That name I loved so much in rebirth.

I'm a star. I'm famous. This was my dream to sing on stage. But this is not *me*. This is someone else in my body. Someone who is doing really bad things, though the memories of her actions remain fleeting as steam.

A feeling comes back to me, but it's so quick I can't fill in the lines. My hand touching a vial of some sort. A woman in a red business suit, placing her hand on her chest, unable to breathe. The picture vanishes.

I sink beneath the surface.

I emerge again, this time to the silver sound of running water. I'm standing in a hotel bathroom. My hands are wet and my face is covered in thick pink face cream. I drag my fingers slowly over my cheeks, and they press and stick on my skin, my lips, like I'm made of rubber. I lean into the mirror to study my perfectly plucked eyebrows and my unfamiliar thin nose. I inhale, and every muscle in my body flexes with the reminder that my body is not under my own control.

In the mirror behind me, I catch a glimpse of a ridiculously huge tub surrounded by tiles of white marble. Melted candles encircle it, and a wet hundred-dollar bill sticks to the wall in the corner.

I faintly remember a moment in time. Was that five minutes ago? Years? What happened? Candles flickered. Gobs of bills floated in the bathwater, and I pushed them around like boats on the surface. My laughter—from my voice—sounded distorted in the room.

I am reminded of the day my freshman year when Mom told me she could paint the future. I ate Doritos on the sofa and laughed—making bits of chips spew from my mouth—when she told me that. I thought she was ridiculous. "Will you paint me bathing in money? As a famous rock star? Maybe that'll be my future."

She rolled her eyes.

A chill runs down my spine, making the hair on my neck stand on end. I wonder if, somehow, I knew my own future. I wonder if I did this on purpose. I wonder why I refused to really see Mom for who she was or to even try to understand her. I just laughed at her, like everyone else in town. I wish I had paid more attention to her and her psychic gifts. Maybe then, somehow, everything would have been different. Or maybe this was destiny.

My breath catches in my throat, panic seizing me, squeezing my chest. I have to get out of here. I wipe the cream off my face with my fingers and race out of the bathroom.

I stop cold.

A body lies on the carpet, splayed as if he collapsed. Handsome with dark hair, he wears a crisp button-down white shirt and jeans. Blood drips from his mouth. My chest hurts, like someone just struck me with a baseball bat. What happened? What did I do?

I move to him, feel for his pulse on his wrist. Nothing. He's cold. Crap. Memories flash in front of my eyes but they move so quickly, it's like I'm watching a video on fast-forward. The guy—young, dazzling, handsome—laughing in my dressing room. His hand on my thigh. What else?

I can't stand here and try to find out.

I grab my leather purse—at least I think it's mine—and with high-heeled shoes in hand, I slip out of the room, hoping no one sees me, hoping no one knows I might have done something terrible to this man. Sweat beads on my face, and suddenly, hot tears stream down my cheeks. I can't breathe. I put on the shoes, fan my face with my hand, and talk quietly to myself in the elevator. *"You're okay. You're okay."*

I breeze across the quiet hotel lobby with white marble floors. The sound of elevator music twirls pale violet before my eyes. I ignore it and walk swiftly, looking straight ahead, avoiding eye contact. I've got to get home to Colorado. I have to.

A few feet ahead, in the middle of the lobby, a garden of delicate glass-blown flowers hangs from the ceiling and a guy stands with his back to me beneath it. His hands are shoved in his pockets and he cranes his neck to take in the unusual art on the ceiling. He's got dark hair and wears black skinny jeans and a black leather jacket. He runs his hand through his hair. He looks familiar.

Tre.

What are the chances? Maybe, somehow, he's standing right here in front of me, safe and whole, enjoying the beauty of the ceiling art in a hotel lobby. And he can save me from this crazy nightmare.

My heels click on the polished floor and memories flash back to me. The night we found clues in Mom's notebook about Trinity. We were supposed to escape. The moment we shared that last sweet kiss on top of the staircase. He told me that we would get out together.

I thrust myself forward and reach out and grab the back

of his leather jacket. As I do, he spins around to face me. This stranger. This stranger with dark hair and black leather and a bulbous nose and pockmarked skin. Who is, like, forty years old. Who is not Tre. Hope evaporates, and it must show on the outside, on my face.

"Hey, babe, you okay?" he says.

"Of course," I say. "I, uh, just thought you were someone else."

The guy's eyes look glassy and then they grow wide, like he was poked with a hot iron. "Hey! Hey! Are you that singer Oshun?"

I don't respond right away, stunned by the surrealism playing out before me.

"Can we have a picture?"

I lick my lips and nod without thinking. He and his two friends hold out their phones for selfies and I try to smile, but I don't think it works. My legs feel weak and I want to cry. The guy next to me glances at my chest.

One of the others, tall and skinny with a ponytail, continues to point his phone at me. He's taking a video.

"You okay?" the first guy asks. "You look sick."

"I'm lost. Please help me. I'm not who you think I am. Please." The words escape from my mouth in a sudden, jagged burst, and I don't even know what I'm asking for. Somebody in the world to help me?

Afraid, I turn away from them and run to the door of the hotel, hoping to find a cab or something to get me home. I hear the conversation between the Tre lookalike and his friends trailing from behind.

"Did you see her grab me?"

"Dude, text that picture to me."

"No freaking way."

"She was totally weird."

I push through the doors, and the warm air rushes onto

my skin. Conversations and car radios play in muddled indigo and lizard-green bursts. And slowly, the world becomes quiet again, darker and darker.

No! I scream in my own dark swimming hole. I sink down once again.

23

MADDIE

I squint through my thick black-framed glasses, the ones I only put on after taking out my contacts and when I'm not in public. It's just me and Jared. I examine the brown streaks on the walls of this cramped hotel room.

"Bedbugs leave these weird bloody streaks on the walls and behind picture frames," I say.

Jared lies on one of the double beds, looking at his phone. We didn't speak much on the way back from the show, but the more I pretend all is okay, the more I think he melts back to normalcy.

Dressed in sweats and a T-shirt, I walk around him on the bed, stepping over his body to get a better look at the wall behind him. The streaks run down from behind the hideous floral painting, which is bolted to the wall—*as if* anyone would ever want to steal it.

"If you see streaks, it's supposed to be a sign," I say. "A freaking bad one. We should leave our suitcases in the bathroom so we can see if any bugs climb in and out across the linoleum floor."

"You're overthinking this," he says.

"Uh, *no*, this place is pretty much a piece of crap," I say. "We should totally have put up your tent. I would rather sleep on the sidewalk in that than in this rat's nest. And this place costs like forty-five dollars a night."

"Fancy hotels have bedbugs, too."

I touch the wall with my finger and try to peer behind the picture hanging from the wall.

"Mads," Jared says, "you jump off tall cliffs into lakes and talk so much about exploring jungles, even though they have poisonous plants and wild boars and whatever else. How will you make it in Vietnam or Belize if you can't sleep in a dumpy American hotel?"

"I'll be fine in those places. Bedbugs don't live in jungles."

"You're being a freak," he says, not looking up from his phone.

"I think that was the wrong thing to say to the Bedbug Assassin." I grin and jump hard on his bed, making his body flop around and his fingers mistype on his phone.

He grins and pushes my legs so I land hard on my back on the bed. Lying prone, I kick at him and smile.

"I'm so comforted by the fact that I have the great bedbug hunter with me," he says, putting his phone down and smirking at me.

"Remember when you were obsessed with that guy the Crocodile Hunter?" I ask. "You used to talk in that really crappy Australian accent."

He puts on said crappy Australian accent and leans over to me, acting like the Jared I knew in middle school. "Here before me is the most dangerous, ferocious college girl in the world. Now watch me, as I poke-her-with-a-stick." He quickly jabs my stomach with a finger between words. I scream and push him away with my knee.

We wrestle on the bed, my legs wrapping around his waist, and I like the way it feels, our fronts pressed together, the warmth between us. He presses his head into my neck, his breath moving my hair, tickling my ear. This is fun, but it's also serious flirting. And it's sexy. And I love it.

I want desperately to pull his head toward my mouth, fling my arms around his neck, and kiss him, feel those crooked lips on mine, his tongue in my mouth. Our heads are pressed together now, our arms battling as I attempt to flip him over. But with one swift tug, he's managed to swivel me around so I'm dangling with my head and shoulders upside down off the edge of the bed. I laugh hysterically.

"Lava or surrender," he says in that stupid horrible accent.

"Never!" I gasp. The blood rushes to my scalp and I struggle to lift my head, but it's heavy like a bowling ball.

Slowly, he lets me slide down onto the floor, and I grab for his T-shirt and arms but they slip. He just grins and leans over me on the bed, smiling. "You wanted it."

My head and neck sink into the nasty brown carpet. It smells like major cat pee down here.

"Surrender! Surrender!" I scream. "Get me up!"

With a swift tug, he pulls me back up, and we pause. My left leg is still draped around his waist, and I sit partly on his thigh. We gaze at each other, looking directly into each other's eyes, breathing heavily. Our laughter peters out, and I feel it. That odd moment where the energy is so electric, and you want to kiss, and you feel like the other person might want it, too.

But it's just Jared. Right?

I bounce off the bed, bat him on the head, and run to the bathroom to brush my teeth. With the door closed, I gaze at myself in the mirror, my hair askew, dorky glasses with fingerprints along the edges, toothpaste foaming at my mouth.

You put your mouth on a dead man. You drove across the country on a suspicion that your missing friend is a crazy rock star. And in the midst of it, you want to jump on her brother in a cheesy, bedbug-ridden hotel. This is all wrong.

I shake my head and spit the toothpaste into the sink. I spit it out hard, as if to crush any thought of hooking up with a guy who should be my brother. How can I be feeling this way when Ember is still missing? Spit. Spit. Spit.

Back in the room, Jared clicks on the TV and climbs into the bed that's completely trashed from our wrestling match. I slide onto my bed, crisp and smelling of laundry detergent.

"Thanks for making me smile again, Mads."

"I missed your smile—even if it is kind of crooked and weird." I sit on the edge of the bed in the dark with him across from me. "I'm down to my last hundred dollars," I say, "so I think our little vacay needs to end."

I'm guessing that's about enough cash to buy some fast food, snacks, and gas to get home.

But Jared doesn't reply.

"You really think that girl Oshun is her, don't you?"

"My heart tells me yes. Definitely, yes," he says. "And Lodima? What about that? That's just too weird. I can't give up, Mads. Not now." His phone buzzes and he retrieves it from the nightstand. He clicks on a text message. "Dax is having dinner with her tomorrow. He says to meet them at the Lilac Restaurant at six," he says, looking up at me in the dark.

I don't respond, ticked that Dax is leading him down this road.

I can feel Jared's smile through the dark. "Looks like we're here another day. I'll put it on my credit card."

"Okay," I sing. Realizing I'm kind of being a snot, I add: "Bedbugs, get comfortable."

He moves across to my bed, leans in, and hugs me, wrapping his arms around my waist. My cheek presses against his

T-shirt. He's solid and warm and familiar, and the embrace makes my stomach flip.

"I have a good feeling about this, Mads," he says.

I bite my lip, keeping my arms around his neck, wishing I could keep him from crashing.

24

XINTRA

The carving of the ancient deity Weret Hekau looks alive. She sits upright in a chair and is the personification of supernatural powers, emblematic of me as a sorcerer.

I kiss her likeness on the stone wall before lifting up my hair and clasping a necklace around my throat. The pendant of the necklace is in the shape of an amenta, which looks like an umbrella with two uneven stems, and it rests on my clavicle. I let my hair drop like a waterfall.

The pendant represents the underworld, or the land of the dead. The magnetite, ferberite, and siderite inside it contain the magnetic properties necessary for accessing the vortex's power and keeping the connection to my rebirthers out in the world. I begin the low-pitched chant that takes me through astral projection, and soon the ghostly fog rises from the dirt floor.

In the haze, I can see all the rebirthers out there doing my work, moving by the hand of my sorcery. Eventually I see Oshun, unaware of my influence over her decisions, poisoning the crowd, organizing the event on the beach where thousands will die in the tsunami of chaos I will cause.

It's all for the good of the earth. Eventually, the history books will show this.

I inhale sharply when I see Oshun examining herself in a bathroom mirror. My back straightens. It's not my creation of Oshun reflecting back, but Ember. She's crawling through the holes in the chakras.

My body trembles, anger coursing beneath my skin. I am here to save the world, to elevate the superior race. If Ember emerges, she could undo everything.

I spin around, knowing Zoe is watching me.

"Tre is causing havoc again," she says quietly, gazing down at the hem of her robe.

So is Ember.

"Oh?" I knew in my bones Tre would be a problem. He's defiant, but he's family. I've got to show him that my way is the right way.

"I calmed the storm at the dinner table, but he's still disobedient," Zoe says.

"As usual," I say. "Punish him on the outside. Send a sab."

"I think we should destroy Ember. The ultimate consequence."

"That may be necessary. The hole in the chakra is growing and she's seeping to the surface. Her consciousness should be stuffed down in the toe of her body. Why is it not stuffed? Why is she seeping through?" Rage makes me tremble.

"She's different than the others," Zoe says. "You know she heard me play the piano in the ballroom when she was here in Trinity and she... saw a vision of me. She brought back... um... strange memories that I didn't understand."

Those memories were of Zoe's pre-rebirthed life as Nisha, a girl my father plucked from Chicago. Zoe should never remember the details or feelings of those things. It's too confusing to the rebirthed and can cause uncertainty. Uncertainty breeds chaos. Ember is more dangerous than I thought. Just like her mum, Dezi. Always the rat, gnawing on everything good.

"Ember and Tre are stronger than the rest," Zoe says. Her words make my skin grow hotter, and my insides shudder.

"My father and I worked long and hard here," I say, my voice like fire. "Dormant souls never waken."

I open a heavy book lying on a stone table. Its cover is worn leather, and the size is tremendous, the length of an unfolded newspaper. I turn the pages depicting constellations and stars and planets until I come to the Venus Friday constellation. Dezi saw hope in that constellation, and so do I. I see hope for my destiny, the Dark Day, when all the planets, spirits, and vortexes come together and I will see my destiny complete. Those who control the weather control the fate of the world.

I look up at Zoe. "I'll deal with Ember. As for Tre... bring out the hangers."

25

OSHUN

Dax clenches the handle on the car door as I swerve through traffic on the highway, honking the horn as I go. "Wow, you know your way around," he says.

"Sure." I drive with the dexterity of a race car driver, seeing ten cars ahead. I anticipate the mother talking to her child in the back seat, the guy picking his nose in the fast lane, the old woman swerving a bit—and I weave around them easily. My brain works far faster than most.

"I'm surprised you choose to drive when you have limos that can take you around."

"I like control."

He lets out a nervous laugh, and I step on the gas to pass a candy-pink Volkswagen on the highway's blind curve. The speedometer on the Porsche inches up to 125 miles an hour. And I swerve back into the right lane, narrowly avoiding a head-on collision with a semi in the left.

I turn on the stereo and roll down the window, letting the air blow my hair wildly. I play my own album, *Seasons*, turn up the volume, and sing along. Dax watches me with a small smile. He won't break me. I dare him.

"So, uh, tell me how you got to where you are, Oshun." He turns the volume down.

"Well," I say, smiling. This is what he wants. This is the story. The tragic sad story of my rise to fame. "It's the most amazing thing."

"Yeah?"

"My real name is Sarah Shiles," I say. "You probably know that. I grew up in Queens, but my parents died when I was only two. I was taken in by this neighbor, his name is Spencer." I stop talking, bite my lip, letting my words choke me though I don't know exactly the experience that causes me to tear up. The details of my story are hazy.

His gaze is heavy on me, like it's going to smother me. I blink quickly and pinch my lips together and continue. "But Spencer, well, he was... abusive," I say softly, "for years and years, and so, when I was fifteen, I decided I could do it on my own. You know, live on my own."

"What was that like?" He crinkles his brow.

"Hard," I say, shaking my head and gazing at the road ahead. I pause dramatically. "I slept on the sidewalk, over the air vents to keep warm, worked out deals to stay in other people's apartments. On the floor. I stayed at a homeless shelter for a while."

"Oh? Which one? A buddy of mine, Brandon, works in a homeless shelter in Queens."

I know this is what happened, but the details are muddy in my mind. "Uh, I don't know," I say quickly.

Through my peripheral vision, I see him jot a note about this in his notebook.

"Was it that one called Restful Nights on 150th Street?"

I shrug. "I don't know. But I found a way to persevere. You know? I sang on the street corner, with just enough money to buy dinner. And then a record company executive, Sal James, just happened to hear me."

We stop at a light and I glance over at his scribbling. It's kind of irritating, seeing him write down his thoughts, taking note of me. I see the name *Sal James* on his notebook with a question mark.

"And the rest is history," I say, exhaling a smile. There. He got down deep, he's found my ugly past. Now I can have the three-page glossy spread that will make my fame double, triple, even quadruple. People will buy my records. I'll bathe in more money and I will poison the strong, keep the weak as our slaves and sabs. It's brilliant. Pride pulses through me like a heartbeat.

"So you just got a recording contract, just like that?" He frowns.

"It's like they were waiting for me. To serve a higher purpose."

"Oh," he says. "Okay, what does *that* mean?"

He's supposed to just write down my words, not parse them. I frown and flip my hair over my shoulder with the back of my hand. "My art. That's what I mean."

"Can you elaborate?" He gazes at me, waiting for more. But I just smile, showing my white, perfectly straight teeth. I look back through the windshield, and the stoplight changes to green. I hit the gas.

A block later, I pull up next to a building with a red awning below the name *King Tattoos*. A red neon sign out front also advertises piercings. I put the car in park. "Let's go."

Inside, the small shop smells like a doctor's office and the skunky scent of marijuana. A skinny girl in a tank top and jeans sits on a stool, her skin shaded in blue, green, and red ink. She pierces a young blonde's tongue. Not three feet away, a short Asian man with a long face sits on another stool, leaning against a wall covered with paper drawings of dragons and spiders and thorny roses. The sound of the tattoo machine buzzes red.

"I want a tattoo."

"You need to fill out paperwork and show an ID," the man says. He doesn't stand up.

"Why?"

"You look young. Teenager young. Gotta ID everyone to be sure you're not a minor. Law says anyone under eighteen needs parental consent." He uses two fingers to call me over to the corner of the shop.

I go to him, opening my wallet and pulling out a thousand dollars in hundred-dollar bills. "Here's my ID," I say.

He looks at the money. "How much."

"A thousand."

"Would you like to make another transaction?" he asks, raising his eyebrows.

I nod and look over my shoulder at Dax. "Be right back," I sing.

I follow him into a back office that smells garlicky, like Chinese food, and contains a desk cluttered with papers and a coffee cup that says *Inked Butts*. He opens a mini fridge and pulls out two small vials that look like they should be in a hospital. Perfect.

He leans into me, pressing the vials into my hand, and whispers. "I made these up special for you," he says with a wink. "More snapdragon. Just one drop in a drink. Shows up clear. Undetectable on any autopsy. The Russians use the same shit."

"Awesome," I say, jutting my hip into his body. "I'll make it happen."

The man leans in close, taking a whiff of my hair, and I smile, bat my eyelashes. I carefully slip the vials into my purse, decorated with leopard skin and diamonds. I take out two silver coins: one is embossed with a pyramid that says

Trinity Forest on one side, and the other coin says *Hamakulia Volcano.*

"Please give these to special customers," I say. "You'll know who."

He nods, takes them, puts them into his pocket, and stands up taller. "Let's get you inked, little lady," he says. He barges out the office and shouts across the shop to the blonde up front. "Her ID says she's old enough. Get her covered."

The skinny girl walks over to me. Her top lip looks like the top of a shower curtain, lined with a series of four small silver rings. "So what kind of tat you want?"

"Give me some paper."

She gazes at me for a second, unimpressed, before sauntering over to a pile of paper on a shelf and tossing me a sketchbook across the counter. "We got flash on the wall you can pick from." She jerks her head over to the wall covered in paper designs.

I ignore her and take the pencil and begin sketching on the paper. A guy in the back of the room lies on a chair, grunting and then moaning. It shows up a yummy orange in my vision.

"I want this on my back," I say, handing her the paper.

The sketch depicts a pyramid with a delicate eye at the top. Just like the pyramid on the Trinity coin.

The blonde nods slowly, examining my artwork. "You sure about that?"

Dax leans over my shoulder. "What's that?"

"It's, like, the dollar bill sign or something," the girl says.

"No, it's not the dollar bill sign, you idiot," I say.

"The Eye of Providence," Dax says, nodding.

"Uh, it's the Eye of Horus. Don't you know anything?" I correct him, pushing the paper into the girl's hands. "Make it the size of a large dinner plate."

"Ancient Egyptians and Romans believed the evil eye

means some pretty bad shit," the girl says with a shrug. I'm surprised she would know this. She looks stupid.

"Gods and goddesses used it to punish those who became too proud of their achievements," I say. "They destroyed them with its power."

"Yeah," says Dax, "but didn't the Greeks believe it was a sign of good luck? You know, protection against evil?" He takes a seat on a stool by the wall. "It's a symbol that there's a greater power watching over you. Protecting you, seeing good deeds and bad."

"What's with the pyramid?" the girl asks. "Egypt? Trinity something or other?"

I don't respond.

Dax studies the designs on the wall. "That's a pretty big tattoo. We'll be here forever. How about something smaller?" He points to a picture of a small star on a square page. It's purple. It looks like a stick-figure star with a circle around it.

I don't say anything.

"That's a duat. Egyptian symbol. But it's like you. A pop star," Dax says. I can see him waiting for me to acknowledge him and his knack for ancient hieroglyphics, but instead I only stare at him.

"You never smile," Dax says.

"I have no idea what you're talking about." My voice has forced cheer.

"I mean, you smile, but not with your eyes."

I suppose that's true. I'm hollow. Yet I don't know any different.

"This is going to take three hours or so," the girl says. "Just outlines of this picture? No color?"

"No color," I say.

I stand up and go to a reclined chair, pulling my T-shirt over my head, undoing my bra. The girl doesn't blink but Dax quickly looks away.

I lie facedown on the padded chair, which feels more like a table. "You should get a tattoo, too. That would be awesome," I tell Dax.

"I already got one," he says. "It's an angel."

The girl puts foam on my back and begins pressing something along my skin. I catch a glimpse over my shoulder of a razor; she's moving it across my back.

"I said I wanted a tattoo, not a goddamn shave. I'm female. I have no hair," I snap.

"We do it with everyone. Got to get every bit of hair off. Even the peach fuzz on the *females*."

I shut my eyes again. "So, Dax, tell me about this angel."

"I guess it seems a little cheesy. But when I was a kid, I thought I saw dead people."

Quickly, I flick my head to meet his eyes, which look like brown sugar. He looks younger this evening, I suppose, than he did earlier. "Why are you telling me this?"

He shrugs and lets out a small laugh. "Don't know."

The girl wipes off the shaving cream and retrieves a Xerox copy of my design. She sprays my skin with a cool lemon rub and presses the paper to my back. The high-pitched tattoo machine begins to buzz.

Without warning, a sharp pinch zaps me between my shoulder blades, like the point of a knife pressing into my skin over and over. I like it.

"So dead people, huh, Dax?" I ask. "Tell me more. Like, what was it like to see a ghost?"

I wonder if this is why I can't see his aura. It's like he has this block against me, plus this ability to see the unseen. He must be like me.

"You'd think it'd be creepy, and I guess a couple times it was. But..." He trails off.

"But what?" White pain moves down my back. I drink it in.

"I think a lot of the ghosts were drawn to me. I called them lost angels." Dax rustles his T-shirt, pulling it over his head, before moving in front of me. He turns his back to me, revealing a tattoo above a bony brown shoulder blade: a picture of a girl with rather large wings, sitting with her knees folded inward and her head tilted down in sadness.

"Is that what the ghosts looked like to you?" I ask.

He shrugs. "It's more of a feeling, you know, like when you just feel like someone is watching you. Sometimes, I could see a faint outline of a body, a curve of the cheek, a leg. Sometimes, the really screwed-up ones actually crawled, slithered in weird forms across the floor."

I close my eyes.

"I never really told many people about it," he says. "I could tell they were near because I could hear voices, like conversations in another room. I talked to them. They'd tell me their stories."

"Stories?" the girl interjects.

"Yeah, like guys who died trapped in gold mines. Little girls who drowned in wells. Broken women who lingered too long in the physical world before following the light. Pretty depressing. Especially when you're just a kid."

"Why'd they tell *you*? Like you're some sort of ghost whisperer?"

He shrugs. "I just listened." He chuckles. "They seemed to just disappear, float off. Finally content. Off to a peaceful place I hope." He pauses. "Now you think I'm a complete nut."

"No." *I don't actually.* I shut my eyes, wondering what he sees in me. I try to remember myself as a kid, but the memories are fuzzy. It's as if I've just always been me, Oshun, the pop star. Everything that came before is unclear. How strange.

"So tell me, Oshun, when did you start singing?" Dax asks.

I see a memory of Dad, messy brown hair, jaw jutted, strumming the guitar, his gaze a virtual stroke of my hair. My soul glows.

"I used to sing with my dad when I was six—" I say, but immediately I know those are the wrong words. Not my memories.

"I thought you said your parents died when you were a toddler and you were raised by a neighbor until you ran away at fifteen?"

"Ha," I say, trying to make up something on the fly. I don't open my eyes because he'll know I'm lying. "Um, yeah, I'm like you. I used to sing with my dad's ghost."

"Okay, so what did Spencer say about that?"

"He didn't know," I lie.

Do I even know my story? I always thought I did. But now, I'm confused. Last night, something got to me when I saw that guy in the crowd. Jared was his name, and he came with a flood of memories. But they weren't mine.

The thoughts drift through my mind, and noises and voices and pain and touch become dull and muted.

Later, I open my eyes to see a soft smile on Dax's face. No one has ever looked at me like that. Or at least not from what I remember.

"You must have fallen asleep," he says. "At first I thought you were trying to avoid my questions..."

I smile. "No."

"You're probably the only person in the world to sleep while getting a tattoo." He hands me my T-shirt and turns away, and I turn around to see the tattoo across my back in the mirror. A piece of plastic is taped around the drawing of the pyramid with the eye. My skin is swollen and red. Dax snaps a picture of it on his phone.

I don't even really know why I wanted this tattoo. Why I felt compelled to mark myself like this—and with this design. I know it's part of the Annunaki, but I don't even know what the Annunaki is, or why I'm determined to fulfill the group's agenda. It's like a fog is lifting and descending at the same time.

"So I hope you don't mind, but I invited a couple of big fans to dinner tomorrow," Dax says, nodding and gazing down at his notebook. "It'll be great."

"What?" I flip my hair and glare at him. "I thought it was just you and me."

"It'll look good for the story. Since you had to cancel the concert and everything. People are probably pissed. You need some good PR."

I consider this for a minute. If it helps him play up my story, I suppose it'll be good. "Whatever," I say. "Just make sure they're not super lame."

I pay the tattoo girl behind the counter another two thousand dollars cash and then sit on the edge of a sofa while Dax uses the restroom. I put the crystal necklace he gave me back around my neck. Something tells me I shouldn't wear it, but I'm drawn to it like a moth around a night-light. I need it.

The light in the waiting area is dim, and a pile of books sits on a coffee table. The sofa smells like corn chips, and a guitar leans against the wall. I go to pick it up, then sit back down and strum a little, coming across an A minor chord. A familiar song plays in my mind. I slip a little, feeling as if I'm falling into a trance.

26

MADDIE

Jared's high. Not high-high. But he's the happiest I've seen him in so long.

"We're in freaking Los Angeles. One of the weirdest, coolest, most vain, most vibrant cities in the free world. We gotta explore," he said first thing this morning.

Immediately, I grab a pair of shorts and a T-shirt and we get in the car. We spend the day window-shopping the boutique shops in Manhattan Beach, and we eat Thai food at some cute little restaurant that smells like lemongrass and ginger and has painted wooden masks on its yellow walls.

Later, Jared turns up a peppy reggae song as we drive to the beach. I put the car in park and turn off the ignition, and we race down the concrete steps to the hot sand. Jared smiles, and his energy is like caffeine to my soul.

We run and put our feet in the water, standing side by side. I watch the white water gush over our feet and then pull away, drawing away sand and leaving our toes in deep holes in the beach. The sound of steady, thunderous waves feels like the sea itself is breathing, and the rush is spellbinding. I feel as if I will fall into a trance if I stand here long enough. I'm overcome with the peace of it.

"I feel like I should live by the water," I say. Maybe I'll move to the beach after graduation. Maybe I'll just quit school and move to LA now.

"It'd be awesome." Jared nods.

After a few turns of the tide, our feet are buried so deep in the sand, I have to reach out and grab Jared's shoulder so as not to lose my balance.

"It's so crazy that one day we're in Leadville and then *bam*, we're standing with our feet in the ocean," I say, leaning on him. He puts his hand on my elbow to keep me from falling, and the touch sends a tingle across my skin and makes my heart flutter.

He held me up like this once before. In eighth grade, when I broke my toe and he helped me get to my mom's car in, like, five feet of snow. He volunteered to carry my books to class for a good two weeks after that.

That year, Ember and Jared's house was my solace. That was the year when things were so tense at mine. Dad barely showed his face because he was trying to get his engineering business up and running, and Mom obsessed over gluten-free food and meditation apps, trying to help my little brother, who threw emotional tantrums all the time. It consumed her, and it drove me crazy to hear how her language had changed.

"I feel sad when you throw your spaghetti on the wall, Hunter," she'd say quietly at dinner. I was infuriated that she didn't grab him by the scruff of the neck—kids have scruff, like puppies, right?—and toss him in his room for the rest of the school year. Instead, she pored over parenting books and watched self-help videos and worried and stressed and pretty much didn't see me or anything I did. I was invisible to her for that year.

Jared and Emby's mom was all depressed and weird at the time, lying around in her pajamas, painting creepy pictures. But their dad, he was cool. I still can't believe he's gone. All the Trouvés but one. Gone. I remember how Jared and Ember's Dad would play guitar on the patio after he got off work at the motel, and we'd sit in Ember's room, lying on the bunk beds, talking about which movie stars we'd kiss. Jared was always there. He was somehow part of us, a comfortable shadow. A shadow that I didn't really see clearly until she disappeared and both of our hearts broke. Now, he's no longer a shadow but a clearly defined piece of me, someone who's always been with me, and all the endearing things about him are printed in neon in my mind: the way he holds the door for me, the way he puts spiders outside instead of smashing them with a shoe, the way I can actually hear his voice when I read his text messages. I realize I want him here. I *need* him here with me. I need to dig him out.

"I'm glad we took a road trip to see this," I say, nudging him. "Ha ha. Get it? Oshun the person? Ocean like the water?"

"Me too," he says, turning to look at me. His face is just a couple inches from mine, and his hazel eyes look brighter in the sunshine. I want to press on the dimple in his chin, just below those crooked lips.

"Speaking of which—we need to get going and make sure we're on time for dinner," he says. "I am so freaking excited, Mads, because this may be it. I might finally get my family back—or at least Emby."

I exhale quietly, bracing myself for the moment he embarrasses himself and Oshun looks at him like he has three heads. I hide my thoughts, squatting down to pick up a handful of sand and let it spill onto the ground. I tried to fix Emby, but I couldn't reach her, and now she's gone. I don't want to lose him, too.

When I rise, he reaches out a finger and gently traces my nose, dragging it like a feather, down over my lips to my chin. An electric spark jumps between us, and sensation shudders through me.

His eyes look like swirling golden fall leaves in this light, and they lock onto mine. A flaming knot tenses in my belly. I wonder for a moment if I might love this boy. My best friend. It's a dangerous experiment that could explode in my face. If we're more than friends, we can never go back to being the same.

"What if it doesn't work?" I'm talking about Oshun as Ember, but also about me and him.

That tiny crooked smile moves onto his face, and he slowly takes my hand in both of his, holding it up near his mouth, squeezing. Once. Twice. Slowly. He gazes deep into my eyes. All of it: his nearness, his touch, makes my breath quicken. He drops one hand, reaching for my other one, clasping my wrist and drawing me closer to him. We look at each other for a long moment, our noses an inch apart, his hot breath tickling my mouth.

"It will work out," he whispers against my lips. "It has to."

Both of his hands drag along my waist, and he presses his lips against mine. The spark I felt earlier erupts into a full-fledged wildfire.

My lips move with his in this kiss, a dance both familiar and electrifying all at once. He places a warm hand on my cheek, and everything intimate and perfect about our friendship detonates inside of me. I grasp his T-shirt with one hand and drown in the minty taste of his mouth, the softness of his lips, the warmth and tenderness of his hand on my cheek. I'm hyper aware of every sensation. The brush of a little stubble from his chin. The squawk of seagulls behind us. The breeze blowing a few strands of hair against my skin.

Then: the footsteps and chattering of two really annoyed older women.

"Today's kids."

"No decorum."

I open one eye to catch two gray-haired ladies walking past in white sneakers and windbreakers. I glance at them, flash an embarrassed smile, and then look out at the water, then at the sand and to my feet. When I look up, Jared is just as close as he was before, grinning.

27

TRE

My head is going to fall off. It's heavy, it aches, and blood thumps in the roots where my hair meets my scalp.

I open my eyes and jerk with a start at the realization that I'm hanging upside down in a room with flickering candle-light. This is as shocking as waking up and finding out you're falling out of an airplane. My spine cracks and my ankles cut into the edge of a metal cufflink; they're shackled to the ceiling of a dim room. My hair brushes against the dirt floor. I squirm, flapping and swinging. I twist and a deep roar fires from the pit of my stomach.

How did I wind up here, hanging upside down? I got caught under Zoe's trancelike spell again. Trinity. That's how. It takes you, moves you like a chess piece. I still don't understand it.

"Hey!" I scream, the sound so loud it scratches my throat. Dread feels like it suffocates me, and I struggle to do a sit-up and reach my ankles. Heaving and grunting, I manage to climb up just a few inches before my body flops back down. I'm so weak.

Then I feel her. The familiar flutter of her robe. She

carries a sort of staff in one hand, and a candle in the other. Her feet squeak on the dirt as she squats down to my head. Her breath is rank, and I can feel it blow into my face. My hands are free, so I swing to take a punch at her. But an electric shock bites into my muscle mid-strike, sending excruciating stabs through my bicep and shoulder. My body spasms, and I scream in agony.

"For being so smart, you're a slow learner, baby brother," Xintra says.

I seethe. "Get me down!"

I feel as if I have seams that are breaking one by one in my neck and gravity's threatening to pop my head off my shoulders. "Don't you know hanging upside down too long can kill a person? It can cause a brain hemorrhage!"

"Why do you think you're hanging chained to the ceiling?"

To kill me. This is how she's going to do it. Frantic, I shake, wriggle, and reach for my feet and the shackles above. She stands and watches, breathing loudly through her nose. I struggle, grunt, and yell, until finally with one thrust, I touch my toes, grasp the thick metal brackets, my body bent, and hang on to the thick shackles. I can't get them off my feet. Finally, frustration and exhaustion—and gravity—snag me, and I collapse again into my upside-down position.

"I need a key. Give me a key," I say, my voice now calm. "Please. You're my *sister*."

"Join me, as family. It won't get any better than this."

"Why do you want me to join you?!" I scream the words instead of ask them. Anger cuts me like a knife. "Why?"

"Because I love you."

I will die here with a nutjob sister. I breathe deeply and close my eyes, considering how I can use her need for a family to my advantage. But she has her own agenda.

"It's like we're kids," she says. "We're playing Mercy, the game. Do you plead mercy yet?"

This is *all* a game to her. My life, everyone's lives, and her weird wicked and electric power. I can't imagine she will really kill me, let me hang for hours like this, but she's twisted enough to enjoy torturing me. How long can I endure it?

I hang in silence for a few beats. The pain in my head and spine throb, my ankles feel numb. I could die this way. I could. Maybe it's not a terrible way to die.

"Fine, be that way." She stands and her electric presence fades, as does the candlelight and the footsteps. She leaves me in the dark.

I close my eyes and wait for death. I fall into a strange mixture of dreaming and memories, ephemeral, like flipping through a photo album. I think of Mom in her 49ers sweatshirt, yelling at the TV during Monday night football. Dad, buying me a motorcycle, pulling a wad of cash out of his pocket. Dancing to punk music in front of the Berlin Wall with my buddies, throwing big pieces of concrete onto the ground. Sinking deep into my seat at the back of biology class, trying to blend in with the color of the walls. My first kiss with Cindy Bromstine behind the bushes in fifth grade. Riding my motorcycle with Lilly's arms around my waist, laughing.

Ember.

Falling in love with Ember, watching her hobble to the cliff in those dirty clothes, grumbling under her breath, determined to climb it. The way her voice sounded sweet like honey; you just wanted to alternately devour and savor the sound—and her—like a decadent dessert. I always wondered what that big *wow* would be like when you finally feel it— finally feel in love. We stood beneath the overhang in the rain together, reading that notebook, feeling hopeful in Trinity for the first time in so long. Profound gratefulness swept through me. The feeling hit me like an avalanche, and I knew.

It. *Love.* The thing that makes you feel like you'd do anything for that person, that you'd lay your life down for them. Maybe you don't even *fall* in love; you just tumble, like gravity itself pulls you. You have no choice in the matter. When it happens, you're in deep. I think of her face and the way her mouth felt so soft. Her long fingers and the small of her back, her silky olive skin and her dark waterfall of hair, the way it curled in little ringlets around her temples. The way she wouldn't give up on climbing that stupid rock wall, even with a half-broken ankle. The memories twirl in my head, morphing into a ream of strange, flowing colors.

Then it dawns on me. The only way to save Ember.

"Hey!" I yell. "Hey—I made a decision!"

I wait for an answer for several minutes, but no one comes.

I wake suddenly, sucking in a large, gasping breath. A chain clinks once, twice, and then I drop to the ground, and the most awful pain bursts into my head and neck. A candle flickers in the dark. Xintra has unclipped my chains, and I lie on the ground, my legs and arms and fingers numb. I can't move. Her bare feet with painted red toenails, stand near my nose.

"I thought for a while there that your head was going to turn into a cherry," Xintra says with a giggle. She puts her hand over her mouth to stifle the laugh. "But I like your head. It could serve you. Well, serve *the world* really."

I glare up at her, but I don't lift my head. It throbs, and the rest of my body feels like a pot of oatmeal. Sticky and heavy and clumped in strange places. Slowly, I manage to scoot back, away from her foot.

"Are you done screwing with me? Don't you have a world to take over about now?" I rub my head with my hand. Even my hair tingles. I sit up slowly, squeezing my neck and hands, trying to get feeling into them again, massaging away the ache.

"Not *me*, the Annunaki."

"You keep saying that. Why?"

"It's our people, Tre." Her voice sounds light, friendly. "I'm so glad you asked."

She squats down to the ground to sit next to me. I could get up and run away, but I have nowhere to go. As long as she or Zoe are close by, the power of their presence usurps any free will on my part. My stomach twists. God, I'm starving, and so thirsty.

"We hold DNA from beings from the sky, from another planet. When we came here, we were considered gods by ancient civilizations. We taught them architecture and gave them technology. We helped them build Stonehenge and the great pyramids of Egypt. How else do you think mere men could build pyramids standing four hundred and fifty feet tall with two million blocks of stone that weighed as much as fifty tons each? The geometry alone is perfect. Right angles that align with the four points of the compass."

"I know all the theories about aliens and the pyramids. So save me the history lesson and conspiracy theories."

"Then you know that some of our people went back to their planet, and some intermingled with humans. The DNA stayed, and destiny has called for us to rekindle a pure race, one of all Annunaki."

My ears ring and my vision remains blurry. I don't want to talk about this, but I'll humor her, challenge and engage. That's better than hanging upside down. "We're not pure," I say. "Right? I mean, you've got human DNA—regular people in your blood. Me too."

"We've met in secret for generations, managed to become high-ranking leaders of the world, influential business and media stars."

"Not *you*. You're not important."

"Ah, but the puppet master is the one you don't see. The one pulling the strings to the one-world government that will culminate on the Dark Day."

"That sounds pretty cheesy. Did you make that name up? Dark Day?"

She doesn't bite at my taunting. She stands. "It's been prophesized by the stars, by my ancestors. And once we discovered the power of the vortexes... well, it's starting to happen." She extends her hand to me, to help me stand up. I take it, and her fingers are long and strong, and her hand is soft.

"You were made for this, little brother," she says with a quick whap on the back.

The slap stings my skin and makes my knees buckle. I've got no feeling in them, and they're starting to become bones. I think of her Hawaiian house she just darts off to, I think of Ember out in the world—not herself anymore. I can't sit here and watch it. I have to do something.

I gaze into my sister's green eyes. They're so clear, I feel like I could walk right through them. "Fine," I say. "I'll join you."

28

EMBER

I strum the guitar without thought. It's as if my hands have a mind of their own. I sing a familiar song, somber and defiant. It fills my soul like a warm bath.

There's a secret in this candy-covered place
And we've eaten up the lies to be erased
In this prison, there is frustration
Keeping us here 'til we break
We've been dining like the food would never end
Played in beauty made of lies to be best friends
I say that something's gotta change
I need it but I only seem to bleed
Then I scream out loud/ Oooooh
They'll pay the world for it/ Oooooh
Yet I must get out/ Oooooh
Oh I'm in the trap
And it steals from me
I can feel me slip now
But I will be tenacious
Trinity will tempt you
By promising to help you

Beauty and lies run thick as thieves,
That's what I'm learning this time
It may try to steal me
But oh, my light will heal me
Yeah, fire is tenacious

"What's that?" The voice makes me snap open my eyes.

That guy with brown skin and black hair stands in front of me. The one who showed me a video of me from high school. My back burns like someone cut it. Something buzzes in the air. The cool, smooth wood of a guitar rests in my lap. I look at my hands holding it.

Who is this guy, and where am I? A man in a black tank top hovers over a person on a table. He moves a small bit and I see a tattoo machine in his hand.

"Candy-covered place? Is that a new song?" That guy in front of me shoves his hands in his pockets.

A thin girl with piercings on her face holds up her phone to me. She must be videotaping me. It smells like pot and my old neighbor's house, where she let her really big, shaggy dogs sleep on the sofa.

"The sound is different for you." He carries a yellow notepad and has a nose like a sickle. He sits down next to me. I feel light-headed and confused, and it must show on my face. He leans in and touches my shoulder. "You don't look well. Are you okay?" He turns and waves at the girl behind the counter who still holds up her phone, recording me. "Hey, that's enough. Give her some space. You're like the paparazzi."

The girl, who looks like a little goth elf, frowns and puts the phone down.

"I guess it's got to be intense being watched by everyone all the time," he says to me. "You've got to have that fire inside you in order to do this job."

Fire inside. Memories flood me. Lying by the lake, which was smooth like glass. I looked up at Tre, his dark hair wet and pale blue eyes shining. I could see every single eyelash. *Tre.*

"I love the fire inside you, Ember," he said. I remember the electricity of his kiss, and my insides swirl, as if I'm feeling his touch once again. I remember the taste of his mouth, the feel of his biceps and his stomach, my insides hot, his hands entangled in my hair, the feel of his skin beneath my fingers. A shiver runs through me, and a feeling of pink love and deep loss sweeps through my bones.

I'm alive, but I've lost control of my own free will. Nausea twists my stomach and tears poke behind my eyes. I abandoned Tre. I wonder where he is. Is he a shell of a person, like me? I have to find him. I set the guitar down and stand up, looking for the door.

A TV on the wall across from me airs the evening news. On-screen, a beautiful girl, perhaps Asian or Indian, delivers the news, looking into the teleprompter. I watch her mouth move. Her head nods robotically, but her eyebrows don't budge. She looks so familiar. Then I recall that Tre pointed her out while we were in Trinity as some *smoking hot* girl who was in the house with him before she got spacey, disappeared, and showed up as a broadcast anchor on TV named Megan Snow. I remember feeling kind of jealous that he thought she was hot. I *should* have been terrified of what she became.

The story shows B-roll of a girl—blonde hair, gap-toothed smile. Beneath her face reads her name, Tonia Davies. Megan tells the story over the scene. "Horror movie actress Tonia Davies is accused of making explosive comments on Twitter about Jews and African Americans, triggering violent riots at theaters and death threats prior to her new movie's debut."

They show a clip of Tonia running through a house,

zombies chasing her. She climbs over broken furniture and screams.

Oh my God, that's Lilly. I know it.

She looks only slightly different, but no one would recognize her because she's been missing for so long—decades — and she hasn't aged. Her face looks unusual, ghostly, or something. Kind of like Zoe's did.

The guy stands. "So you want to head out to meet those guys for dinner?"

"No," I blurt, shaking my head swiftly. I don't want to eat dinner. I need to run back to Trinity, *do* something.

"No?" His voice shifts from friendly to icy. "Jared and Maddie will be so bummed. They were looking forward to it. And so was I."

I swivel around to look at him. A hint of a sneer crosses his face.

"Jared? Maddie?" I repeat.

"Yeah, they're big fans. And I thought this would be good PR. I guess if you don't feel well... But I really wanted more time. I mean, you fell asleep during your tattoo, so we didn't get to chat as much as I hoped, for the story." He tries to lighten his words with a breathy laugh and a tilt of the head.

"Tattoo?" I ask. The skin on my back stings and feels achy. "I got a tattoo?"

He frowns with an incredulous expression, as if I've been on a different planet. When, in fact, I really have been. Tears fill my eyes, and my skin feels like it has shrunk a size. I've been living and moving in the world without my knowledge, my consent, my awareness.

"Come on, Oshun," he says.

That name again. Oshun. The name I loved in rebirth, amid Zoe's hypnotic voice.

"Is the tattoo on my back?" I reach for it with my hand and jump from the sharp pain of my wound. Then, gently, my fingers feel tape and plastic. Panicked, I glance around the room, desperation choking my words. "What happened?"

"Uh... this?" the guy shows me a photo of a black triangle and eye spanning the width of my shoulder blades to my middle back. Just like the Trinity coin.

I gasp and put my hand over my mouth, tears rolling steadily now down my face. "Really? It's huge."

"You wanted it."

I'm walking around as someone else. It's as if I'm sleep-walking, stepping into someone else's life. A faint memory hovers at the edge of my mind. Jared. I saw him. He was wearing a bacon T-shirt. Where was I? Where was he?

"Jared and Maddie," I whisper slowly.

"We're having dinner at the Lilac? The guy's name is Jared Trouvé and the girl is Maddie something or other. They're from Colorado."

The words strike me like a hot poker. My heart pounds and excitement brims, and I grin. "Yes! Yes!" I nod quickly. "Let's go. Now. We have to go now." As I dart for the door, I catch a glimpse of my unfamiliar body and face in the mirror. I hardly recognize myself. I wonder if *they* will even recognize me.

I plan what I'll say, as I push open the glass door to the tattoo shop and step into the sunshine. I'll have to convince Jared that it's me and tell him things only he and I would know. Like when Mom would make that awful cream chip beaf thing on toast for dinner because she didn't have any money and we called it "shit on a shingle," and then we'd sneak out the window after bed and walk to the gas station and mooch old hot dogs off that cashier. What was her name? Gretchen! She had the funny snaggletooth.

I'll remind him about the time we short-sheeted Dad on his birthday, and he sprained his toe when he jammed it and then fell out of bed. And Mom made us his personal servants the next day to make up for it.

I'll remind Maddie about how we thought if we put seashells under our bed, somehow our nighttime wishes would come true, that we'd someday live by the ocean. And I'll remind her of the time I gave her the Heimlich in fifth grade after she took a bet she could swallow a whole Twinkie —but then choked.

I'll remind them of how bad I feel about the hospital after my overdose and how I refused to talk to them. And I'll apologize. And I'll hug them. Jared will smell just like he always did—a mixture of menthol and cedar. Maddie will probably smell like licorice and shampoo.

That guy is talking to me in the parking lot, but I don't hear him or comprehend what he's saying. His voice is white noise. Car exhaust floods my nostrils and the coffee-colored sound of rushing traffic floods my senses. I have to get out of here. I have to find Jared and Maddie. My mind spins frantically. I've never been so close to home.

Home: the word tumbles inside like a bowling ball down a flight of stairs. Loud. Clunky. Dangerous. Totally, completely unexpected.

I take a step to run, but I have no idea where to go, where I am. I stop in the middle of the parking lot, heart pounding, desperate to find them, not knowing where to go, or where I even am.

"Your car is over here," the guy says slowly, clearly baffled by my dazed behavior. He points to a red Porsche.

"Oh," I say, trotting to the car. I stand by the passenger door, waiting for him to unlock it.

"You want me to drive?" he asks, leaning in toward me. "Are you feeling okay? You sure you're up for dinner?"

"Yeah, yeah," I say quickly, realizing this must be my car. I need to be in the driver's seat so I can floor the gas and get to them. I can't let anyone else drive my life anymore. "Yeah, I'll drive. We have to go. Will you please give me directions?" I run around to the driver's side door.

"Please?" he repeats. "I've never heard Oshun say the word *please* ever." He laughs.

I feel as if that's true. That somehow, this person moving through my bones is a total and complete bitch. It makes me want to apologize to the world and sink down in embarrassment. But I wouldn't even know who to apologize to, because I can't remember jack.

"Open it please?" I flap my hands like a bird.

He nods to the door handle. "Keyless entry."

I jerk open the door and climb into the driver's seat. This car is nicer than anything I've ever been in before. Cream-colored leather seats and a black-and-orange glowing dash.

A flash of light blinds me for an instant, and I jump with a start at the sight of two cameras just inches away from the car window. A cameraman with a shaven head chews neon-yellow gum furiously and then raps on my window with his knuckles. "Oshun! Oshun!" he yells.

It's as if they're beating at the door with their successive flashes and shutter-clicking. My chest tightens and I frantically press the "Start" button and gun the engine.

I stare at the gearshift for a few seconds, considering how to put it into reverse. Two more photographers descend at Dax's side. The car jerks backwards swiftly, then I gun the gas forward toward the busy street.

"Damn," he says. "I know you must be used to it by now, but for real? Vultures."

"Where do I go?" I ask urgently. "Tell me. I have to see them. Oh God. I need to see them now."

"Uh, left?"

"Good, good," I say, pulling out into the street, yanking the steering wheel and slamming my foot on the gas. I drive, not knowing where I am, who I am or what the hell has been happening to me. But I feel a sliver of hope that I'm going to get my life back. I have to get to Maddie and Jared.

After a few stoplights, though, the world taunts me, wavering like water. The sky and the pavement blur together. The edges get fuzzy, and I know what's about to happen.

This cannot happen. I'm slipping. *No. No. No.*

Then, the world moves farther away, as if I'm being swept from the shore by a horrendous current.

"No!" I scream, but my voice is no longer mine. Again, it has no sound. I'm muffled in that underwater place. I paddle and kick in the deep water, but it's not enough to stay above the surface. *This* is what rebirthing is. I made the mistake of just letting go, just watching my life float away, like a leaf down a blackened well. Now I'm a prisoner, living in the deep recesses of my own mind. I'm invisible.

29

MADDIE

Lit candles sit on shelves, slowly dripping wax like molasses, trickling and then hardening on the walls of the Lilac Restaurant. Bottles of wine line the top of a wooden bar, textured with worn white paint. Rusted birdcages hang from the ceiling, housing dangling lights. The smell of sautéed fish and garlic make my stomach growl.

Jared and I are alone together, the first to arrive for the big dinner date at this rustic, chic restaurant. He sits close to me and leans in, kissing me softly. The touch delivers another zing to my stomach, igniting everything inside me, and I desperately want to pull him into me and underneath this table. If I weren't so hungry, I would suggest we go back to my car where I can properly enjoy his lips without the audience of hipster richies.

Jared pulls back slowly, smiling, and I swear, the word *euphoria* is written across his forehead. Maybe he's excited about us. But really, he's pretty amped about meeting Oshun.

"What should we say to her?" he asks. "Maybe I'll just tell her I miss her." He takes a sip of water and then turns, digging his eyes deep into mine. On one hand, I feel like kissing Jared was the best decision of my life. But then there's that crazed look in his eye, that hint of insanity brimming at the edges. The edges of my best friend who is so much more than just a best friend.

"Hmmm probably not." I flash a quick, fraudulent smile, tapping my fingers. *Tap. Tap. Tap.* I telegraph my nerves.

At the next table a woman with long, shiny blonde hair and tanned skin wears an expensive white blouse that bares her shoulders. A man dressed in slacks and a crisp white shirt is with her. I glance down at my tank top I thought was so cute the other day. It looks so average and dull. The girls in this town are all so tanned and perfect and plastic, with faces dipped in makeup troughs. Funny how just a couple hours ago, I was ready to pick up and move here. Now, I can't wait to leave.

"Okay, so what do you propose we say?" he asks.

"Something like, 'Hey, I love that part in your concerts where you pretend to shoot people with guns.' And then after a minute, I'll throw in, 'And he thinks you're really his sister hiding out as a superstar.'" I put a piece of bread into my mouth. "Jared, you do realize this is insane, what we're doing? I mean, the search, the posters, the talking to news reporters, that was one thing. This is a whole other level of desperate craziness."

He shrugs and takes another anxious sip of water, his eyes flitting around the restaurant over his glass. He sets the glass down. "We'll just ask her about her life, and she'll break. We'll take her home." He draws a finger down my nose, again, traces my lips with his fingertip.

My breath quickens, and my gut folds into a knot. "Yeah," I whisper. But inside, I'm screaming, *No. No, Jared. Your hopes are about to be dashed.*

A few minutes later, Oshun and Dax come around the

corner, and my pulse quickens. Jared may be on the verge of being locked up in the loony bin, but we are also meeting someone famous. That's a first.

Oshun is short with straight blonde hair, dressed in a worn-looking red T-shirt with an open back, a short leather skirt, and tall silver boots. She wears tons of makeup, and her lips are a velvety red. I stare at her, stunned, because it's as if the air shifted when she walked into the room. A buzz wraps around my head. She sort of looks like Ember—without the hair color, of course. It's like I'm looking at a twin, but at the same time, she seems so *different*. She walks with shoulders pulled back, her chin turned up, eyes wide like she's some sort of innocent Barbie doll. Ember would have hated this girl. She probably would have been insulted that Jared is even questioning whether she might be Oshun. I can imagine Ember's voice in my head now. "Don't you even *know* me?"

Dax's shoulders are slumped forward, like he spends too much time texting and on his computer, and he's dressed all swanky like he was the other night, with a hipster checkered button-down shirt, rust-colored jeans, and white-sole Vans. "Hey! You made it," he says.

I still feel that weird buzz in my head. Oshun's eyes swirl brown with a hint of gold, and almost look hollow as if they stare straight through us. Jared's mouth gapes a little. He runs his hand through his hair and kind of stammers. "Uh, hey, yeah, hey."

Dax gently puts his hand on Oshun's upper back and extends an arm out to me and Jared. "Oshun, these are two of your biggest fans, Jared and Maddie."

It's so clear we are not at all fans. We don't fawn over her for autographs or ask for photos. But she doesn't seem to notice. Oshun dangles her hand, as if Jared would kiss her ring finger or something. He shakes her hand limply.

"Hi," I say.

"Nice to meet you." She nods deeply.

"They were at your concert last night."

"Did you enjoy the show?" she asks. Her voice is higher than Ember's.

Jared swallows and flashes an uncertain smile. "Well, the concert was great until you got sick," he says. "You feeling better?"

Her nostrils flare and her lip curls up in almost a sneer. Whoa, that is so not Ember.

"Yeah, I feel great," she says.

Jared can't take his eyes off her. He's sizing her up. I'd say a little like a psychopath. I elbow him.

"Sorry." He chuckles and looks away. "I don't mean to stare. You just look so much like my sister. She went missing three years ago."

Oshun doesn't blink for an instant; she looks a bit like a robot. Then she purses her lips. "Will you please excuse me? I need to use the restroom." She walks past me, and I notice a large pyramid tattoo on her back. It's red on the edges and looks fresh.

In ninth grade, Emby and I drew pictures and planned what tattoos we'd get after graduation. She wanted something in each corner of her body, symbols that represented earth, wind, fire, and water. "I'll write the words *ignis intus* here." She pointed to the right side of her rib cage. "It's Latin and means 'the fire within.'" She touched her back. "And then here, I'll put an upside-down triangle, the symbol of water in alchemy. And under my left arm, I'll do wind. The words *I rise,* a quote from a Maya Angelou poem. And then I'll put a tree with roots on my left ankle. You know, earth."

I thought it was so cool. "You're more like your mom than you think, Ember."

She grimaced and then smiled. "Yeah, I guess I like the

symbolism and definitely think my tattoos should have good mojo."

I look at that horrible pyramid on Oshun's back. This is *not* Ember. I lean into Jared. "She is so freaked out by you," I say in a low voice, laughing through my nose. He needs to reel in his stalker face.

Jared ignores me and directs his attention to Dax, who now sits across the table from us. "She's acting funny again. It's her. I know it's her."

Dax shrugs. "Yeah, she *is* acting weird. When I told her we were meeting you two, she kept saying she needed to get to you. She even said *please*." He chuckles. "I didn't think the word was in her vocabulary."

"Really?" Jared asks. "What'd she say?"

"Just got into a rush to see you when I told her your names. But then after a minute or two, she went right back to being über-bitch Oshun. So hey—the magazine is picking up the tab for dinner. Get something good." He looks at the menu for a second and then up at us. "So where are you guys staying?"

"Wait," Jared says, leaning across the table. His voice is thundering. "You're saying she was excited? Did she act like she knew us?"

"Dude, don't get too amped." Dax holds up his hand. "Did she act like she knew you? I don't know. Yeah, kind of. She's just... eccentric I think."

I need to change the subject. "Our place is okay. I think we had to pay extra for the crackheads who hang outside our door." I don't tell him how I'm reeling after witnessing death for the first time before the concert, how I put my mouth on said dead guy's lips for CPR and how he had the virus. Just thinking about it all makes me feel like I want to heave.

Something brushes past me and I turn around to find

Oshun walking by to her chair across the table from us. She smiles, and her skin still has that weird glowy look to it. When she was onstage, I thought it was just the lighting. Maybe it's her makeup.

Ember would be older now, but this girl looks young. Why am I even thinking of this? Analyzing her like Jared? It's not *her*, but my gut keeps poking me, begging the questions, trying to convince me otherwise.

"So do you like LA?" Dax ask us. "I mean, this is the first time you've been here, right?"

I wait for Jared to answer, but he's just staring at Oshun like he's watching TV.

"Yeah, the city is cool I guess," I say, injecting forced cheer into my voice. "It's the first time I've ever seen the ocean."

I purposely try not to look at Oshun. Plus, something about her makes me feel warm and fuzzy inside, like being swallowed by a cashmere sweater. My gaze flits to my water glass, then to the candles burning behind her, the top of her hair, and to Dax's eyes.

"Sorry I stare," Jared says, laughing, seeming suddenly aware of what a weirdo he's been acting like. "You just really look like my sister."

She tilts her head and smiles serenely—but not with her whole face.

He squints and examines her. "The nose is different. The lips and the... body... are different. But the way you tilt your head, the way you frown, lean forward when you speak. Your mannerisms—they're spot on. Your voice is identical, too, though I'm not sure she would sing the kind of songs you do."

He laughs nervously. "Not that your music isn't *good*. But the resemblance between you and my sister is crazy. She'd be older now, almost twenty, not as young as you. But I had to meet you. It's like you two are twins. Pretty funny." He shakes his head and smiles at his plate. He takes a quick drink of water.

"I say everyone has a twin in the world," Oshun says. "It happens." She shrugs and looks at the menu. "It's nice to meet my fans. It's rare if I get to see them face-to-face in such an intimate setting."

Anxious, I scan the menu. It's a big jump from Applebee's. *Jumbo lump crab cakes. Crispy pork belly. Yellowfin tuna poké.* The waiter, a tall man in black pants and a white button-down shirt, comes to me, waiting patiently for my order.

"I'll have the crab cakes," I say, handing him the menu.

I pull out my napkin and place it gently on my lap when suddenly, Oshun is right there next to me, squatting down. She leans in without warning and hugs me tight. "Oh my God, I can't believe you're here," she whispers. Emotion twirls in her voice. "I missed you guys so much."

She sounds so much like Ember, it sends a chill down my spine. She leans into me with a fierce hug. Surprised, I pat her shoulder with two uncertain taps, gazing at the hardwood floor.

She lets go of me and turns to Jared and gives him an intense embrace too. Their hug lasts a long time, like a few seconds too long. What's happening here?

"You look so good," she says, holding Jared's hands tightly in her own.

Jared swallows and his eyes widen, looking glossy. He glances at me and Dax.

She offers a loopy smile to me, and then she takes my hand, tugging slightly with each of her words. Her eyes look different, more like Embers—a cup of dark coffee. "I thought of you all the time," she says. The words make my eyes pool with tears.

Is this Ember? Or is this some freak show girl just trying to mess with us? I'm so confused. I stare at her for a couple seconds, waiting for more, biting my cheek. I glance at Jared. His face is frozen in shock.

"What?" I ask. "What do you mean?"

Jared leans in toward us and whispers, "Ember?"

Oshun's demeanor swiftly shifts, morphing back to that of a stranger with an enormous toothy grin. Her back straightens, she pulls her hands away, and even her eyes shift back to the golden swirl. The hairs on my arms stand tall, and a warm, pulsing rush of *something* runs over my skin. I can't get over how I feel in her presence.

She stands slowly, confidently, beaming and backing up a few steps. She sits down across the table again. "Tell me more about your sister. It must be so hard for you."

My body feels weightless and soft, and I can't take my eyes off her. The waiter's voice snaps us all back to reality. "Some bread for you," he says, placing a basket of warm, crusty rolls in the center of the table.

Disturbed by what just happened, I scoot my chair back and stand up. How horrible she was to screw with Jared— and me—and then put simply on that star demeanor like nothing bizarre happened.

Jared stays under her mysterious spell, and eventually turns his head to notice I'm standing.

"What is this—some kind of cruel joke?" I say, directing my gaze to Dax and then Oshun. I can't help it. I spit the words. "You find out about Ember, and then what, just put on this little charade? She's gone, and fortunately for you, you just happen to look like her and sound like her, too. Too bad you're not half the person she was."

Oshun gazes at me, unfazed, blinking slowly with those eyes that remain treacherous, swirling pools.

Jared frowns and reaches a hand out to me. "Hey, Mads, it's cool."

No, it's not. I throw my napkin on the table. "I'm going

back to the hotel." I pause for half a second, waiting, hoping he'll come with me. But he just sits there, looking at Oshun. I shake my head and move through the scattered tables, emotion and confusion rattling me to the core. "This is ridiculous—and disgusting," I mutter.

I hope Oshun hears me. What a complete psychopath.

30

XINTRA

I lead Tre down the hallway, sucking in his aura, still green and dark purple—signs of the residual strength of his spiritual soul. But the edges of it are spindly and cracked, yellowing like old paper. Opportunity.

"Let's go relax," I say softly, exhaling the perfume of numbness, of death. This is typically Zoe's job, but I indulge in it tonight because this, right here, is a special case. My brother. Finally.

We come to the wooden door for the Bath House, and I lead him inside, watching a small smile turn up the edges of his lips. He will finally be mine.

I instruct him to undress, and he folds his arms over his chest. Bloody defiant. Then after a second, he sighs and yanks his T-shirt over his head with one hand. I turn away to light the candles around him on the ground, sprinkling bore tusk and snowberry and then the thistle branch. I repeat the mantra that leads him to let go, allowing the spirits to poke at his skin, climb beneath the fingernails and the epidural layer, squeeze into the tears in the chakra. The ultimate preparations for my control.

"You will shed your skin. You will find the light inside," I whisper, my voice echoing off the stone walls. I instruct him to move to the edge of the water. The bath is hot, a mixture of sulfur and sage stirring from deep within the earth's core.

"Lie on your back," I say, and he does, floating in the water.

I open a small jar of scented sandalwood oil, brushing my fingers through the mixture and onto the carving of the duat on the wall, the stick-figure star enclosed in a circle—a sign of the dead. I murmur the words under my breath, "Come, ye dead, and open the skin, let this one marinate in my command."

The power courses through my body from my toes to my fingertips, and an electrical pulse hums. The glorious voices of the dead.

I leave him, floating in the trance, and shut the door for his ritual to continue alone in silence.

Zoe sits obediently in a stone chair in the corner of the cabal room. "Tre is in the Bath House now," I say. "I'll rebirth him tonight. Prepare the room."

"He's only been in the pool this one time, though," Zoe says.

"I have a deadline."

"Are you sure?" she asks. "I'm afraid we're rushing the rebirths. What if what happened with Ember happens again?"

I have little patience for her newfound insolence. Nothing will stop this. I have a destiny to fix and save the earth.

I sneer. "There is the risk of chakra leaks, but the stars have destined this. The Dark Day is coming and I need rebirthers and all the energy of the universe to get this done."

"But there are other planetary alignments needed to ensure everything happens appropriately," Zoe says.

Ever since Ember pulled on the chords of Zoe's former

life, she's questioning me, doubting me, her job. My trust in her is eroding. If need be, I'll replace her with Tre.

"I thought you were the best my father created. Am I wrong, Zoe?"

"I'm the best, your highness."

"In one hour, call on the others and bring Tre in," I say. "I need him out in the world. Now."

31

OSHUN

I watch the girl, Maddie, through the window of the restaurant. She walks toward her car, mumbling to herself and pulling keys from her purse. For some strange reason, I want to run to her, yet I feel like I'm swimming against a swift river current and being swept away from the safety of shore. Drowning. Something inside me is swirling, unfamiliar, and it's terrifying. I've got to push it down, keep it at bay. If not, somehow I know everything will be ruined.

Maddie pushes a few strands of hair behind her ear, and the gesture strikes me as familiar. It's something she does when she's nervous. Just like the tapping of her fingers. Is that something inside me, telling me this information? An intuition? Or am I making this stuff up about Maddie, my biggest fan?

I shake my head and focus my attention on Dax, the reporter I must charm. *Turn it on, Oshun.* No one beats Oshun. I own the media.

I sit at the table, perching delicately on my chair, shoulders back, batting my heavy eyelashes and nodding in feigned interest.

Dax asks me about the sound of my album, and I answer automatically. "I think the reggae beat in 'I Want Your Skin' really resonates with fans. It's an innovative sound."

Jared nods absently. Outside of being mesmerized by my looks, he doesn't seem like much of a fan, and I'm a little annoyed that Dax didn't connect me with people who truly fawned over me, who I could indulge with big favors, like surprising their dying sister in the hospital. That kind of shit sells records.

Instead I get the nasty Maddie, who left in such a huff, and this Jared guy, who shoves his mouth with noodles, pushing his eyebrows together when I pause.

"So is it hard for you to get out to restaurants like this, now that you've got hit songs?" Dax asks.

"Oh sure, the paparazzi follow me all the time," I say. "But my home is my solace. You saw that I bought a place on the cliff overlooking the ocean? So funny, it matches my name. I love it there, because I can really sit and contemplate life and how I want to someday help poor, unfortunate children."

"Oh? How so?" Dax asks.

This is my chance. I'm not only wicked awesome onstage. I can be a savior to all the sad people in the world. Jared gazes at me, his eyes studying every gesture, every feature. It's a little unnerving, but I guess I'm getting used to it; that's how most people look at me. They're memorizing these interactions so they can tell stories to friends about me for years, even decades.

"I haven't figured out how I'll help yet. I'm thinking maybe shoes. Yeah, like, a lot of them need shoes." I glance at Jared and see his mind go someplace else. A thought crosses my mind: *It's the look that drove Dad crazy. The Checked-Out Daze he'd go into when he was getting a lecture about driving too fast or breaking curfew.* I stop midsentence, confused. How on earth would I even know that?

"But I'm sure people need me, need hope," I recover. "And I can be that hope... as long as they buy my album!" My laugh is high-pitched and glittery.

Dax pays the bill even though I make a ridiculous amount of money, but all this will be a great story for him. Something he can go on and on about, telling other people he bought Oshun dinner. So I let him pay the six-hundred-dollar tab and we walk out to the street.

We stand there on the sidewalk, and I tell Dax how he needs to go to my Oshun Beach Party. I smile and slap him on the shoulder. He didn't break me, dig underneath my skin. I won. I always win.

I turn and hand Jared a voucher for a free plane ticket to Hawaii, an idea sent via text earlier from my record label. "It's my treat to special fans," I say.

His face lights up a little as he takes it. "No way."

"Yes way." I wanted Dax to see this. See how I can charm fans—even lame ones like Jared—and send them on amazing vacations. Even if this is more of a permanent vacation for him.

Jared turns the ticket over in his hands, hesitant. "Wow, I don't know what to say..."

I smile, flip my hair, and wiggle three fingers—my signature good-bye wave—and then leave him on the sidewalk.

Just before I climb into my Porsche, I drop a coin on the sidewalk. It's subtle and the sound is like breathy shattering glass. A flash of metallic silver in my mind. I know Jared will see it in the streetlight. I know he'll pick it up. I know he'll see our symbol, the pyramid with an eye. And I know then that he'll squint to see the words beneath it: *Hamakulia Volcano*.

Inside the parked car, Dax buckles his seat belt and blabbers on about the tuna he ate, while I gaze at Jared in the rearview mirror, smiling. What a scrap of a person he is—the aura around his head is torn and breaking off in pewter and sand-colored chunks. He's shattered. He'll love the soothing feel of the coin, the idea of being numb, of falling into the vortex. We'll make better use of that body than he will.

The coin. His magnetic key to enter.

32

MADDIE

I watch *Ghost Hunters*. Then *Christmas Vacation*. Then *The Tonight Show*.

Finally, Jared walks in the door. He doesn't make eye contact but instead just takes off his sneakers and tosses them on his duffel bag.

I don't move or look away from the TV when he walks into the bathroom and shuts the door. He has no room to be pissed at me. In fact, I should be the one who is ticked because he didn't leave the restaurant with me, as a united front.

He comes out of the bathroom, walks straight to his bag and then takes off his button-down shirt. I watch him undress, eyeing his thin frame and smooth skin. I see him so differently now that I've kissed his lips, now that I've pressed up against his body and let his hands trace my hips and ribs. I want that again, and I half want to jump off this bed and tackle him now. But his mood forms a giant cactus barrier around him.

"Well?" I ask.

"Well, you missed a mighty fine dinner."

"That's it? What'd she say?" I ask. "What happened?"

"She's a freaking nut." He plugs his phone into his charger and acts as if he wasn't completely convinced, hours ago, that he had found his sister.

He drops a coin and a rectangular piece of paper into his duffel bag.

"What's that stuff?" I ask.

"Nothing."

Nothing. I strain my neck to see and catch the name American Airlines on the paper. I want so desperately to return to those moments before Oshun showed up at the restaurant, where he was buzzing and looking into my eyes, kissing me softly. I want to crawl into his bed and lay my head on his chest. But he's shutting me out again.

He's shoving everything under the rug just like he did when his parents first died. It wasn't until Ember's disappearance that I was pulled underneath that rug and into his world. He can't kick me out now. I'm already there, caught up with the cobwebs and dust and bits of cereal. I'm there with him.

"Is that a plane ticket?"

"Yeah." He nods absently, moving around the room.

"To where?" He better not leave me and make me drive all the way home alone. Maybe this whole more-than-a-friend thing freaked him out. My pulse quickens; every muscle cinches up inside my body. "Are you flying home instead of going with me?"

"No," he says.

I want him to tell me more about both that coin and the plane ticket, but he doesn't explain anything further. "Well... what did you guys talk about?"

"She was pretty pretentious." His eyes still don't fall on me. "She talked about her music and being rich."

Part of me wants to ask him if he felt the way I did when

she was kneeling by me, holding my hand—warm and furry inside. But I don't.

He takes off his pants and strips down to his boxers. Quickly, he pulls on a pair of athletic shorts. I drink in his arms and the skin on his flat stomach above his shorts. I watch him click off the light and climb into the bed next to me.

Well, this is it. Oshun isn't Ember, and now, the topic of his sister is officially a dead conversation. He's moving on, just like I wanted. But this darkness feels heavy, like dirt piled on a grave.

"So tomorrow we go home?" I ask.

"Yeah, sure," he says.

I crawl under the covers, lying on my back for a few minutes, not sleeping. I can't help but feel disappointed, too. A part of me had hoped that Oshun *would* be Ember, or lead us to her somehow.

Jared's phone rings and he grabs it off the nightstand and sits up on an elbow. "Hello?" He bolts up straight, his voice urgent and loud. "Ember?"

I can make out the faint sound of a female voice on the other end of the phone. I flick on the light and sit up, confused. I frown and wave my hands. "Ember?" I whisper urgently. I take a deep breath. Ember is calling! Oh my God, she's alive! My heart races, and I'm dying to know what's being said on the phone.

Jared doesn't look at me. He shakes his head, the whites of his eyes showing, and spurts words like they can't come out fast enough. "You're what?" he asks, then pauses. "Who? Where are you?" Finally, he looks at me with an open mouth and holds up the phone. "She just hung up!"

"That was Emby?" I ask. "Call her back! Are you sure it was her? What'd she say?"

He looks at his phone. "Crap, it says 'unknown caller.'" He

stands up and slips on his shoes. "We have to find her."

"What'd she say?" Frustration builds inside me.

"She said she was stuck. That she needed me to call the police. That she was being brainwashed. She said she was at Oshun's mansion."

I inhale and hold my breath, the excitement dissipating like a popped balloon. This is all a giant joke. Some cruel person out there just trying to mess with his head. Maybe that Lodima lady, or someone who heard our conversation in the coffee shop.

"Jared..."

"She said she was at Oshun's mansion."

"Hmmm," I say, chewing on my lip.

"I don't know where that is." He starts tapping on his phone. "I've got to find out."

"Famous people keep that stuff totally private." *For a reason,* I think.

"I'll ask Dax. Maybe he knows where to find her. He can call her publicist." He taps on his cell phone. Then he stops and stares at the wall, thinking. "But... if her publicist is brainwashing her, maybe we don't want them to know."

I stand up and put my hands on Jared's shoulders, firmly squeezing him, shaking him. "Jared!" I plead. "You've got to stop this. Oshun is *not* Ember. She's not. And whoever called you is just some sick person."

He shakes my hands off him and his voice is so harsh it makes me cringe. "I *know* this. I feel this in my gut. I heard her voice. Are you with me? I mean, what was today on the beach? Am I some game to you? Or are you and I really in this together?"

My heart stretches in two different directions. One is falling in love with my best friend and everything that is Jared. The weird way he crinkles his eyes when he talks. The quirky habits like the way he keeps all of his old shoes— a collection that comprises more than twenty tucked inside a drawer—and even the way he likes to sleep with blankets in a ball instead of making his bed. I love how he and I are connected by Emby, how we were woven together. But now, I gaze at him in disbelief. Have I fallen for a guy who might seriously be losing it? Whose despair has driven him to delusions?

I flap my mouth open and closed, completely speechless.

"We've got to call the police," he says. "What if she's being held by some creepy dude, you know? We can't just go over there alone." Jared groans and shakes his phone. "Nothing on Google. How do we find her address? How?"

The idea of Ember being held against her will and tortured or raped makes my stomach twist—just like it always has. That's the worst part about all of this being unresolved—not knowing, and picturing every worst-case scenario as a result. We've scoured every possible lead for three years now. Maybe we should pull on this one thread, see where it takes us.

Jared paces, hitting his forehead with the palm of his hand. He looks like he's truly gone off the deep end. If I turn away from him, he's alone. And us? We're inevitably done. I will have lost Ember *and* Jared. I think of the way he kissed me earlier, and a shiver runs through me. I tap my fingers on my thigh. *Tap. Tap. Tap.*

Screw it. I'm along for the ride, at least for now. Maybe I can bring him to his senses—or at least be here for him when he's crushed yet again.

"Let's go." I slip on my plaid Tom's shoes and my glasses and grab my purse and keys off the dresser.

"Okay." Jared exhales and stands up taller and then talks nonstop as we leave the room, neither of us entirely sure where we're headed.

"I knew it! We found her. We did. But we have to move

fast. What if something is happening to her right this very second? Something bad?" he says.

My stomach rises to my throat. "No. No. We'll find her."

He's a giant stew of panic and hope and fear and joy. I clasp his hand and give it two quick squeezes. "Hey," I say softly.

He stills and we look each other in the eye for a moment, that connection back. Then he looks at his phone again. "I'm calling 9-1-1." This time, he puts his phone on speaker. For the second time this week, I'm talking to a dispatcher.

"9-1-1, what's your emergency?"

"My name is Jared Trouvé and my sister, Ember Trouvé, went missing three years ago. She just called me. She says she's being held against her will, brainwashed. That she's really the pop star Oshun. I don't know where she lives, but we need to send a squad car there as soon as possible. Now. Really. It's serious. I'm afraid she's hurt."

"Okay, sir, could you please slow down?"

He looks at me, taking a deep breath.

"Okay, sir, so you're saying your sister went missing and you think she's pretending to be a pop star?"

He nods swiftly, exhaling. "Yeah," he says. "And it sounds crazy but you have to believe me." His voice runs on, high, like one of those little windup toys spinning in circles on a table.

"Okay, sir, how do you spell her name?"

"T-R-O-U-V-É. Ember. Her name is Ember. She's in Oshun's mansion but I don't know where that is. Can I come with the police? She might be able to open up if so?"

"Sir, I think you're going to need to come to the police station to handle this situation."

"What? No, you need to get there as soon as possible. Now!"

I wince, feeling so incredibly embarrassed for him. This is

someone messing with him.

"I'm sorry, sir, but this is better handled with a report."

"Where's the police station?" he asks.

"You'd need to go to the Los Angeles Sheriff's Department in Malibu."

Jared glances at me, discouragement coloring his face. "Can you just send someone there now?" Jared pleads. "I'm terrified for her."

"Please come fill out a report."

He hangs up the phone and screams, throwing his head back on the headrest.

"Are we really driving to Malibu?" I ask.

"We have to," he says.

I nod and inhale deeply. It's true. How can I not check out every single lead, no matter how crazy it sounds? I want her back just as badly as he does. I put the car into drive, as Jared reads directions to the sheriff's department like we're cutting the fuses for a bomb. We weave around cars on the four-lane highway, which is surprisingly busy for midnight.

"I can't believe we have to drive to the sheriff's department a freaking hour away," he says. "This is a huge waste of time." He bangs his fist on the passenger window. "Argh!"

"They just need to see that we're not freaks," I say. But maybe they *will* see that he's a freak, or at least a delusional brother drowned by loss. What will they do when they find out?

He looks out the window, rubbing his forehead.

"You *do* know how many weirdos she must attract?" I say.

He ignores the question. "So she said she was being held against her will. Who? Who is holding her? I'll search her manager's name. Maybe her record label?" He taps on his phone, running Google searches. "I can't find anything. How is that?"

"Famous people can control their private information." I

shake my head.

"I'm calling Dax," Jared says. "I don't care what time it is." He puts his phone up to his ear and gazes out at the night sky, filtered by city lights. "Dax," he says suddenly. "I know it's late, but I got a call from Ember."

I can hear Dax's voice even though the phone is on Jared's ear. He's groggy and half-asleep. "What?"

"Ember called me! She said that she needed help, that she was being brainwashed. Then she hung up."

"Really? Oh my God, that's huge," Dax says.

"She said she was at Oshun's mansion."

Dax pauses. "Uh…"

"Can you tell me who her manager is? You know, people who control her schedule and everything? Do you know where she lives? The police won't go over there."

"You sure that call was from her?" Dax asks.

"Honest to God, something's going on." Jared gazes out the window and then turns to look at me while he talks. "We wondered if you could find out where she lives and, you know, like, who her people were?"

We. The royal *we.* I'm being lumped into crazy status here. I guess I *am* an accomplice. I am, after all, the one driving to the police station so my childhood friend can deliver an off-the-wall story to a police officer in the middle of the night.

A BMW cuts me off and honks, a reminder that I'm distracted, driving fifty miles per hour in a sixty-five zone. I press on the gas and listen carefully to the conversation between Dax and Jared.

"Yeah, sure, bro," Dax says. "I can call her in the morning."

"Can't you call her now?" Jared asks.

"Man, I gotta wait 'til tomorrow. But if there's truth to it, sure, that would be a good story."

"Do you believe it?"

Dax hesitates. "I don't know. She says some unusual things, does some strange stuff. Tell me what the police say."

"They're going to think we're stalkers," I say loudly.

"Well, no doubt," Dax says with a little chuckle. "I'll do my best to help you out."

Jared hangs up, and we drive for a few moments in silence.

"When I see her, I'm gonna have so many questions," he says. "But really, I just want to hug her."

I let myself imagine what it would be like if this really were Ember and she really were to come back into our lives. We'd pick up where we left off. We'd hike and watch reruns of the *Buffy the Vampire Slayer* on Netflix. Maybe we'd see some concerts. All of it feels so hopeful and yet so out of reach.

When we pull up to the white one-story sheriff's office, Jared jumps out of the car and races to the door, and I trail behind. We step into a small room with a counter beneath a glass window with its shade drawn. It looks like a closed ticketing booth.

I knock on the glass once, but Jared rings the silver bell on the counter multiple times like an impatient child.

I grab his hand, squeeze. "Dude, composure," I whisper.

He nods and takes a deep breath. I drink in his lips and a ping-pong ball rolls around in my stomach. Just a few hours ago, his lips were on mine, and now I'm not even sure what we are.

The shade flies up and I jump. A bespectacled woman with dark hair, pinned back tightly, leans forward and presses a button to speak through an intercom. "How can I help you?"

"My sister has been taken. Brainwashed. We think she's

Oshun the pop star."

Oh man. The words of a lunatic. Plus, he's saying "we" again. Crap.

The woman stares at us for a moment, glances over her shoulder at the clock, which says one fifteen in the morning. She pinches her lips together, swallows, and then nods. "Do you need someone to talk to, sir?"

"Yes!" he says, placing his hands on the edge of the counter and leaning into the glass. "I'm not crazy. Neither is she. And look, I know it's a weird time but she just called us and said she needed help. We don't know where Oshun lives, but we need to help her."

The woman gazes at us for a long time. "Do you know how many people come in here claiming things about Hollywood stars?" Her face is slack and she doesn't wait for our reply. "Last week, we had a guy come in and tell us that Britney Spears had stolen his dirty underwear and his prized high school trophy collection."

I stifle a smirk.

"We've been looking for Ember Trouvé for three years, since she went missing in Colorado," Jared says. He pulls up a photo of Ember from senior year on his phone. "See? She was seventeen. She vanished."

The woman nods and her brow crinkles. "I'm sorry to hear that."

"And look." He pulls up a photo of Oshun saved on his phone and places it up against the glass. It clinks and the woman jerks her head back. "Notice the similarity?" he asks.

The woman looks down at a piece of paper. "Your names and driver's licenses, please?"

Jared fills out paperwork, and I try to stand in solidarity but can't bring myself to say anything. I'm not sure how long I can ride on his crazy train.

We wait in plastic chairs for forty-five minutes while the

woman types on her computer and talks to people on the phone about this. Jared stands up and knocks on the window. "Can't you just call the police in Colorado and get a car out there to her house? This is wasting valuable time."

The woman, with her slick-backed hair and her narrow nose and pointy chin, glares at him and continues her phone conversation. I rest my head on the wall next to me and doze until the woman's voice on the intercom snaps me to attention. "We'll check into it. You can go home now. Goodnight."

"Wait—I was hoping I could go out there with the police?" Jared says.

"No, sir. Please go home, and we'll let you know if anything comes of it."

Jared stands up, takes three steps to the counter. His body is tense. "*Who* is checking it out?"

"We have an officer leaving here soon, sir."

My eyes feel hot and bleary now, and the time and the lack of sleep is starting to catch up with me. I want to go to bed.

"Okay, okay," he says, his disposition suddenly shifting to be more amiable. "Thanks."

Jared leans in gently to whisper in my ear, sending a tingle down my neck. "It's cool, Mads. I'll drive. You get in the car with me and sleep."

"Okay," I mumble, my eyelids heavy. "They're going to check it out?"

"Yeah," he says. "It's fine."

We walk to the car, and I climb inside. I feel a wave of relief. If that really was Ember, the police will be on their way. And if it wasn't—and of course it wasn't—then we'll be able to sleep, knowing the police checked it out. Maybe they'll be able to pinpoint who made the crank call. I lean my head against the passenger window, and the hum of the engine rocks me to sleep.

33

TRE

The heavy wooden door creaks open, and someone in a long dark robe stands in the doorway, a silhouette framed by the hallway's dim light.

"It's time." The sound of Zoe's voice makes my skin buzz and my brain feel foggy. "Please emerge from the water."

I walk toward the edge of the pool in the waist-deep water, the steam hissing around me. The relaxing purr of this place still tickles my skin and my mind. I can see why Pete liked the Bath House so much. You're in the darkness without sound or weight, and it feels like you're floating through space without a body. It's a total trip and a little addicting— especially if you're trying to forget or run away from your problems.

But I'm not running away. I'm running *to Ember*. The rebirth is the only way out, the only chance I have to find her again. The flickering candles lend an eerie vibe to the circular room with gray stone walls, and in the dim light, I towel off slowly, as if all my muscles have slowed and are less under my control. Robotically, I pull on my jeans and a white T-shirt.

Now, I'll go upstairs and take a nap in the sun, avoiding all those other newcomers oblivious about their fate. I could whisper more warnings to them about Trinity, but it wouldn't matter. Whatever I say to them is moot. They can't get out. Neither can I.

A few more times in the Bath House, and then rebirth. This is the only way.

I go to Zoe, still standing in the doorway, and she touches my arm. A glowing buzz of warm electricity floods my synapses. "Now is the time for rebirth, for you to shed your skin, Tre," she says softly.

Now? A flash of doubt crosses my mind. When I'm out in the world, I wonder if I'll be able to cling on to a piece of myself and really keep control. And while my heart is sure this is the right way, rebirth, my mind questions whether I'll even be able to reach Ember once I'm out.

Yes, I tell myself. Rebirthing is the only way. The only way to Ember.

I let Zoe's nearness drown my mind in a silky, numbing feeling and she leads me down the meandering, dark hallway. The only sound is our footsteps. Eventually, we come to a room that looks like a candlelit, soggy sewer, and Zoe lets go of my arm.

Without her touch, I feel a little more lucid, more like myself. Xintra stands in her red robe in the center of the room, gazing at me. Smug. Poised. About fifty people wearing dark robes file in behind her, coming from what looks like a long tunnel.

My pulse quickens. This is the same kind of scene I saw when I was in Berlin, when I crouched down and peered in the window of that old stone building. Robed people were chanting in some sort of candlelit ceremony—just like this. This is what Mom tried to keep me from when she freaked out and put me on a plane back to California.

All the pieces of the puzzle fit together now. Mom knew about this group, maybe even about Trinity Forest. All this time I've been here in this stupid house, stuck. It wasn't by chance. It was purposeful. Xintra wanted me here. I wonder if Mom even knows that her own daughter is here, doing this, leading this horrendous operation.

I take a step back from Zoe and Xintra but play it cool. "You didn't tell me you were having a party. I would have dressed up more," I say, pointing to the robed people. Their chanting grows louder.

Xintra gazes at me, disapproving. "I'm going to enjoy this," she says.

"Sure, great, but first, I have some conditions," I say, tossing my jaw toward her and crossing my arms over my chest.

"You're not really in a position to make demands, baby brother."

"I'll do this for you. I'll be the family you never had," I say, watching Xintra's neck straighten just a couple centimeters. "Because you felt rejected, didn't you, when she didn't come looking for you?"

Her expression slides off her face and is replaced by a steamy glower.

I pause and bat my hand. "Sorry. What am I saying? *My* mom rejected you. And so I'll be there for you, *sister*. But I come with a price."

"Oh, is that so?"

"I want to find Ember. You have to put me in the world near Ember."

A hint of a smile flashes on her lips. "Ahhhh, love conquers all? Isn't that sweet." She releases a drop of dark liquid onto a flat stone placed on the floor beside me. The liquid sizzles when it lands.

A pulsing energy in the room makes me feel light-headed,

and the robed people begin to chant louder and faster. The sound floats, as if it's wrapping around my chest, squeezing, making my body feel weak and my heart quicken. The bodies shuffle through the room to encircle me.

"You'll find plenty of other girls who will be drawn to your power on the outside. But sure, of course. Ember. My word is gold."

"Good," I say. "Mom would be happy to hear that." Her face falls again. "And it makes me happy, too, because I want to be your partner here. Family you never had."

Wicked delight returns to her face. She knows I'm playing her, but I don't care. She has wanted me to succumb to rebirthing for so long now, and here I am. But I'm going to get what I want in return.

"Step into the circle." She tilts her head, holding a drop of liquid above another stone. It drips, then hisses on the rock.

My scalp tingles as if my skin literally is slowly sliding off my bones. I try to shake it off, blinking my eyes quickly, but I still feel warm and sleepy. Zoe steps forward and wipes something on my temple with two fingers.

Again, that flash of hesitation slaps me. But I have to take the risk. I have no choice. I'm trapped, and Ember needs me. I take a deep breath and do as instructed, moving into the center of a ring of sizzling stones and robed people. I clench and unclench my fists. The steam from the liquid on the stones rises and a metallic waft fills the air. The liquid must be blood. My blood. I remember the cut Zoe made on the palm of my hand early on when I got here and how, under her cloudy spell, I let her collect blood from me. It feels so long ago.

The humming becomes a haunting, hallucinogenic sound, distorting the steam from the stones into gaping char-coal ghosts. Xintra's red robe flutters, the deep color of blood.

I close my eyes and an invisible pulse wraps around me like a cocoon.

34

OSHUN

A gruff voice crackles on the intercom. "Miss Oshun, the police are here to see you."

The noise wakes me from some sort of trance, and I sit on the sofa in my mansion, with no clue how I got here. Why would the police be here?

"Sure, send them up," I say finally. I go to the mirror, apply some lipstick, and run my fingers through my hair. Something inside me is growing more forceful, like a tide, and my body trembles with this knowledge. I run my fingers over the crystal necklace still strung around my neck.

A few minutes later, wearing a silky pink robe, I crack open the door. Two police officers are standing on my porch. "Hi?"

The taller, younger officer grins and scratches his head. He adopts a serious look before clasping his hands behind his back. His eyes still burst with excitement. He's starstruck like everyone else.

His partner, a shorter man with a belly that pours over his belt, looks unfazed by my celebrity. "Miss," he says. "We have a report that you're being held against your will. Is that true?"

I grimace and laugh through my nose. "Is that why you woke me up in the middle of the night? Why would you even say that?" Really, though, for some reason, I'm not surprised to hear this claim. The words sound familiar.

I catch movement on the road beyond the black wrought-iron fence that cuts my property off from the street. It's a young man, lingering by the fence, watching us intently. I squint. It looks like that guy Jared I had dinner with, and the sight of him snaps hope in my heart—a feeling that surprises me.

I turn back to the officer. "No, everything is fine. I'm fine, and I *was* sleeping." My voice is a thousand knives.

The two police officers exchange looks, and then the squat man bows slightly, a reverence that belies extreme nosiness. "Mind if we have a look around?" He pauses before attempting to step through the doorway.

I snort at him and block his way. "Why?"

"Just curious, unless you have something to hide?" He pokes his head to see beyond me. He's a gawker and wants to see how beautiful my place is. By the looks of him, the guy must live in a barn.

"What do you want to see?" I ask. "You *do* know that you're asking for a private tour in the middle of the night."

I look up again at that guy at the fence, and my body softens. A pang of desperation floods me—a feeling that leaves me feeling confused and unsteady, like I'm standing on a rocking boat.

"Just a look around," the short one says.

"No," I say. "I told you I'm fine."

"Miss Oshun, we understand you called Jared Trouvé from your cell phone a couple hours ago, asking to be rescued and that you were being held and brainwashed."

"What?" I spit the words, and my eyes shoot back to the guy outside my fence. "I never called him. That's a lie." The words tumble out of my mouth hard and fast, but for some reason, I feel like it's true. That maybe I did call him.

"You're not being harmed in any way?" he asks. "You can tell us."

"I told you, I'm good," I say, clipped. I begin to shut the door on them.

The squat policeman reaches out to keep the door open, craning his neck one last time to see inside my palace, and I can tell by the look on his face that he just caught a glimpse of my ten-foot tall black statue in the entrance behind me. It's a sculpture of a man with a demon face and bald head, wielding a spear overhead, four human skulls at his feet. I love that statue.

He clears his throat.

"Well, if you need anything," the squat one whispers, "please call." He hands me his business card and nods quickly.

For some reason, I feel like I need to ensure this guy doesn't come poking around my house again, asking questions. So I touch his arm and watch his body melt. His shoulders droop, and his cinnamon eyes gaze deep into mine. His secrets pulse in foggy color around his head, rising, falling, bending and breathing like steam in a cool breeze. In it, I can see his truth: He cheats on his wife with a woman named Thelma. He spent his wife's money gambling online.

"Sure, sure," I say. I release him, and his body snaps back to its arrogant tilt. I lean into him, whispering in his ear. "Tell Thelma hi," I say softly. "Hopefully you hit the jackpot online soon."

The color drains from his skin, like water swirling down a sink, and his eyes widen slightly.

"Our secret," I whisper with a wink. I point to Jared, who now paces in the street, hands in the front pockets of his jeans. "Oh, and that guy, Jared? He's, like, totally obsessed. So if anything, I might need protection from him."

The police turn around to look at the street, their posture erect at the sight of him there.

"What the..." the tall one says.

"He must have followed us," the other one says.

"So, yes," I say. "I'll need a restraining order. He says I look like his dead sister, and he's been harassing me. He's the one you need to investigate. And if you bring him here again, I'll sue your ass."

The two officers nod and walk to their cruiser.

Jared yells from the street. His voice is agitated. "Hey! You're not getting her out of there? Hey!" He points at me. "That's my sister, Officers. You've got to get her out of there. She needs help."

I gaze at him with conflicting feelings stirring inside me: revulsion and love—and a pang of heartbreak. I want to run to him, hug him. But I'm not his sister. So why do I care for him at all?

"Ember!" His panicked voice swirls in black spots. He will ruin everything. I don't know why I know that, but it's got to be true.

"Hey, guy, let's just have a talk in the vehicle," the tall officer shouts, walking down the driveway toward him.

Jared shouts back to him, and I take a step forward to hear what he's saying. "She was taken, Officers! She's been missing for years and she called *me*. Did you check her phone?"

That last sentence changes everything. The tall officer turns back to look at me. "Miss?"

The short cop stands near the police cruiser, still appearing uneasy. He rubs his balding head in nervous fits. He waves his hand at his partner, telling him to drop such questions.

"Miss Oshun, in order to put this to bed, can you please

show us your cell phone?" the tall one asks, coming back toward me.

"Whatever," I say, sneering. I go to the living room, pick up my phone off the sofa where it was sitting when I awoke. I hand it to the officer. He looks at the recent calls and raises his eyebrows with surprise.

"Mind if I call this number?" he asks.

"What number?" I ask, leaning over his arm to look at the phone. It's a 970 area code. "Whatever. I don't care."

The policeman dials the phone number. Jared's hand flies into the air and I can hear a distant ring on his phone. "My phone! It's ringing! See?"

I feel like I've been hit in the face with a frying pan. I didn't call him. Did I? Why would I do that? How would I even know his number?

"Care to explain, miss?" the tall officer asks.

A phony smile spreads across my face. "Yeah, I suppose I did call him. I asked him to stop harassing me. But it didn't work, obviously."

Jared yells to me in the distance, calling through hands cupped around his mouth. "What have they done to you, Emby?"

Emby. The nickname moves across the air and burrows its way under my skin. I reach for memories I never knew I had. This boy throwing dirty socks at me from a bunk bed. Eating cookie dough underneath a slide at a park with that girl Maddie. A woman with splattered paint on her cheeks, talking about painting the future. Mom. *Whose* mom? Not mine. She died when I was a baby.

I touch the doorframe to keep my balance and watch wordlessly as the police walk toward Jared. On the other side of the fence, he pleads with them, but I can't hear what he's saying.

With my arms crossed, I watch the tall one walk him to a

dark car and the short one waves to me before climbing into his police cruiser and reversing down the driveway. My mind clings tight to my identity, my Annunaki agenda, while my heart reaches out to grab the guy being pulled away by the police.

35

MADDIE

There's shouting, and I wake with a start. I'm alone in my car, and it's dark except for flashing red and blue lights. Definitely police lights.

I wonder if Jared got pulled over. I spin around to gaze out the windows. We're in some kind of residential area with tall fences, thick green shrubs, colorful flowers, tall palm trees... and mansions set high on grassy hills.

Jared is talking loudly to two police officers by a wrought-iron fence. "Just check into it. That's all I ask," he says.

Crap. Oshun. He went to her house.

I unbuckle my seat belt and open the car door but stop when it's clear Jared is giving in, walking back to the car. He climbs into the driver's seat and shuts the door with a thud.

"Did you follow the police to Oshun's house?" I ask, flabbergasted.

Jared sighs and nods. "Yep, and we're being escorted off the premises because now they think I'm a stalker."

"Jared!" I whine, throwing my head back onto the headrest. "Why didn't you just let them check it out and take us back to the hotel?"

"I thought maybe she'd see me and, you know, feel safe enough to open up." A pained smile crosses his face as he starts the car and turns it around in the street. The police follow behind us with the headache-inducing flashing lights. "But"—he sighs—"she said I was some obsessed fan, and now she's getting a restraining order against me."

I wince. "Wow."

"She called *me*," he says. "The police asked to see her cell phone and sure enough, the last number dialed was mine."

My chin spasms and I jump in my seat. *"Really?"*

She really did call Jared just to toy with him. How screwed up is that? I jut my jaw. I want the world to see what a true psychopath she really is. How cruel she is. "Well you *have* to tell Dax that she's the kind of person who would do that to someone who's been through so much. Unbelievable. He needs to know."

He grips the steering wheel tighter and suddenly, anger busts from him like steam from a boiling tea kettle. "What if she really likes this life and she just wanted a new identity? Maybe she didn't even want to be Ember anymore." He raises his eyebrows. "I mean, she lives in a freaking mansion by the beach. She travels the world. Sings onstage. It's what she always wanted." He shakes his head and tosses his hand in the air. "And she's got people, like, falling over her. She's rich. She's *famous*."

I shake my head. "No," I whisper. If we indulge this idea that Oshun is really Ember and she doesn't want to be found, it's twisting the knife once more into his heart.

"It really was her, Maddie. I've got to figure out how to get through to her."

I don't know what to say anymore. I'm so tired, so worn out from humoring Jared in these ludicrous fantasies. I had hoped maybe this would be the moment he'd let go, move on, and come back to reality. But the way things are looking, he's either going to fall to the bottom of the graveyard of despair or get thrown in jail.

I touch his shoulder. He doesn't respond. Instead, he looks at the road ahead. The flashing lights continue to blink until it's hard to even see straight.

I swivel around to glare at the police cruiser behind us. "Come on!" I shout at the car. "Give the lights a rest. We get the idea."

"Have you ever heard of something called split personality disorder?" he asks.

I shrug. "Maybe in psych class."

"Look it up for me?"

My body tenses. I draw in a long inhale, as if trying to pull in enough air and energy to be here with him anymore. But I do as he requested, finding a description of it on a mental health website. "Okay."

"What are the symptoms?"

"Jared..."

"What are the symptoms?" he repeats, more forcefully this time.

"One of the symptoms is mood swings. Um, headaches, amnesia, time loss, trances, violence, and voilà, acting like you have different personal identities. What are you trying to say?"

"Or maybe"—he talks to the road without answering me —"maybe it's drugs. She did OD on heroin before she disappeared. I bet this is drugs. Can you get split personality disorder from drugs?"

I shrug and flop my head back on the headrest, closing my eyes. I want this to stop.

He shakes his head. "No. On the phone, she said she was being *brainwashed*. If she was really kidnapped..." He stares at the wall. "Maybe it's Stockholm syndrome."

"What?"

"I learned about it at school. It's where you start to feel compassion for your captor, fall in love even. Maybe that's what happened to her?"

"God, Jared."

"Well, if that's the case, I can't go home. I have to figure out a way to get the cops to take me seriously. I've got to figure out how to get to her."

I look at him, stunned. I can't leave him here to stalk Oshun. "How are you even going to afford to stay here?"

"Open a crapload of credit cards?" He shrugs.

"Jared," I whisper.

"I'm calling Dax. Maybe we can get him to write something that draws attention to this. He witnessed how she was with you and me at the restaurant. She was... weird. Even if it was just a for a quick minute." He smiles and touches my arm. My skin tingles with his touch. I turn my head to look at him, and my heart expands a couple inches.

He's smiling—and I love that smile.

"I'm glad you're here, Mads," he says. "Everyone else, they just kind of faded away. But you're like... a rock."

I smile, but it's meager.

I'm tired of being a rock. I only seem to sink the people I love.

36

DAX

My computer glows in the dark. Hunched over on my bed, I contemplate how I'm going to start this story. The pressure squeezes my temples. I'm the Star Whisperer. I have a reputation to live up to.

But unlike the others I've interviewed, Oshun hasn't cried, she hasn't opened up about what's underneath. She's only kept me guessing. I type a sentence on my screen.

Oshun is a grade-A psychopath.

I delete it and think about Jared, running to the police station in the middle of the night, worried that Oshun really is his sister. I open up the pictures he sent me of Ember on my laptop, and then I put the pictures of Oshun side by side next to them. They're eerily similar. I get why he thinks this. But *come on*, seriously.

A text pops up on my phone from Jared. It's funny how you just think of someone and they message or call. Or maybe that's just me.

Went to her house. She denied it to police but they found her cell phone. She did call me, Dax. Something's up.

Missing girl shows up as rising pop star? If true, this

would be a huge story—bigger than all the others. Everyone will want me even more.

The cursor blinks at me, ready, asking for the words to come. I type a sentence.

Oshun, the pop star, isn't what you think she is.

Delete. Another sentence.

Three years ago, a girl named Ember Trouvé disappeared. Now, you can pay $150 to see her reappear onstage.

Delete.

I suck. I hit my head with the palm of my hand and stare at the cracks in the ceiling. I'm such a freaking fraud. Why did I ever want to be a writer, anyway?

I flip through the pages on my yellow notepad and review my notes from Jared, from my conversation with Oshun in her dressing room, at the tattoo shop, the notes about the weird song she played on her guitar, the way she cried as if she didn't know she had gotten a tattoo and urgently wanted to see Jared and Maddie—and then acted as if they were strangers at the restaurant. I can't shake the feeling that there's something beneath Oshun's persona that's not entirely visible to the world. She was so interested in my ghost stories, and there would be moments where the color of her eyes looked like they changed with her mood. They were almost a rich shimmery brown, fierce, like a sandstorm that could spin and suck you up and take you to another land. But at the same time, they could look empty, hollow, and, in a way, spooky.

I think about her skin, too. She's too *perfect*. Like she's been sprayed with some sort of ethereal glow. Probably expensive makeup and lotions that only rich people can afford. Or maybe it's the plastic surgery. Surely she's had plastic surgery. Most of them do.

But I've interviewed celebrities before. This girl... she's

different. I shake my head. A guy shouldn't write a big story at four in the morning—and without real facts.

I don't like her, but somehow I'm drawn to her. Maybe it's just curiosity. But man, I've got to believe it's something else, too. That first moment we met and we shook hands in her dressing room, there was a zap that ran from the palm of my hand to my fingertips. Maybe it was only me, feeling amped about interviewing such a hot star. Or... static electricity.

I pace the room, stepping over piles of dirty laundry, and then kick a soccer ball against the wall back and forth while I think. *Thump. Thump. Thump.* There's more to her. It's the same weird feeling I had when I talked to those ghosts as a kid.

There was that time when I was five and lying in the dark in my shared bedroom with my brother. I sat up and screamed in bed. Mamma came running up the stairs and into our room, worried I'd fallen out of bed or something. "What is it, honey? What?" she asked, wiping the hair from my sweaty forehead.

"Mamma, there's a man in the corner!" I shouted, pointing. He wore farmer's trousers, held a long shotgun at his side, and his face looked melted.

Mamma stared at the corner, disturbed. "No one's there, honey, you're just having a bad dream."

I shook my head, frustrated, and pointed. "He's there. I can hear him breathing. He's hiding in the shadow."

The next day, I overheard Mamma telling my nana that she thought I'd seen a ghost. She suggested selling the house, but I didn't want to leave my friends and our neighborhood, so I stopped telling her about the spirits. Eventually, I learned how to make them leave by asking them questions, trying to make them feel better, because they were pretty sad or mad when they showed up.

But Oshun is no ghost. And yet there's something about her that *exudes* dead spirits.

The steps creak outside my apartment. One of my neighbors is finally home from the night shift. If this story is crap, that's where I'll wind up: working the night shift at the local bakery. So, no big deal. I can just write a story telling readers that I see ghosts and Oshun feels like one, too. A crazy laugh escapes my chest.

There are so many people to interview. The Leadville police. Her manager. A missing person's advocate, maybe an expert in brainwashing. Some sort of psychologist. My buddy about the homeless shelter. The music exec who apparently discovered Oshun. Plus I'll have to do a deep search on the name Sarah Shiles to dig up any information about the backstory that may or may not be true. I scribble a list onto a notepad.

All of it feels fishy. She never gave authentic details about her past. She didn't even know what homeless shelter she stayed in. Wouldn't you remember where you stayed for a year on the streets?

I rub the nape of my neck. The stress headache is on fire. This can't be some superficial story about another pop star who has a penchant for fast cars and tattoos; this is going to be an exposé. Bigger than any of my other stories. This is going deep beneath Oshun's skin. She may not have revealed her secrets, but I can still dig.

I tap out an email to my editor, outlining what I've found. *This could be a huge story, Ben. I'll be pounding it out tomorrow.*

Google will be my friend for research, and in a couple hours, I'll start making the phone calls. And I need to see Oshun again. I need more time with her.

37

OSHUN

Now, I can put my finger on what it is about Dax's voice that feels so good. It's a soft red color that bobs in my vision like little fuzzy strawberries. Dark on the outside, sweet and light on the inside.

"I didn't get enough time with you," he says, standing on the doorstep of my white stone house. The sunlight shines into his face and he squints. He's got bags under his eyes like he had a long night, but he's smiling, eager to talk.

"Sure," I say.

We move through the open marble foyer, past my demon statue. I've always loved that statue, but for some reason today, it makes me feel like ants are crawling on my skin. Dax studies it and writes something on his notepad.

I take him out to my patio, beside the infinity pool. The water silently pours over the edge, as if it drains right into the ocean below my home. I lie back in a patio chair, put on a pair of sunglasses, and watch the waves flood the beach. It looks like the world is being tipped on its side and then back again, rolling the sea back and forth.

"I could sit and watch the tides forever," he says, reclining in a chair next to me. "Tides are just about the only thing that are predictable in the world." His laugh is the color of fresh peaches.

"I love the ocean, too," I say.

"Is that why you chose it as your stage name?"

"Perhaps." I don't know why that's my name. But hearing it feels hypnotic, like a soft gauze is being delicately wrapped around my whole body.

"The ocean's beauty is beguiling. It's unpredictable. It's seductive." I turn to him, knowing my intent here on the earth, feeling it in my bones. "It's also dangerous."

He raises a single eyebrow and nods before gazing again at the uniform waves rolling across the sandy beach. "So I wanted to talk a little more before I write this story. I guess I felt like somehow, you're *different* than other pop stars."

"Of course I am." My chest inflates.

"There's a video that's gone viral online," he says. "It shows you in some hotel lobby with three guys, and in it, you're telling the camera some strange things." He looks at his notebook and reads the quote verbatim. "'I'm lost. Please help me. I'm not who you think I am. Please.'"

I don't remember that. He looks to me for a reaction, and I'm not sure what my expression shows. I'm assuming it's something like a deer in headlights. I don't answer him.

"What did you mean when you said that?" he asks.

"I don't remember that."

He pulls out his phone and clicks on a video. I watch myself on-screen with a bunch of men who are held rapt by my presence. But I'm not really there. I look bewildered by the attention. It doesn't look like me at all. But in my heart, I know it's my body. My voice.

"Maybe it's just someone who looks like me," I say. "An imposter." Dax does that deep gaze thing again, like he's waiting for a crying spell or reaction, but I turn my attention to the pool. "Next question?"

"Um. Okay. Also, I did a little research and found some inconsistencies," he says.

"Oh?"

"Yeah," he says. "There's no record of anyone named Sarah Shiles born around the time you say you were born. There's a woman who is, like, ninety-seven, who has that name. But no one else. Is that *really* your name?"

That *was* my name. Right? Every memory of my pre-Oshun life is as if I'm looking through that hypnotic gauze, incomplete and distorted. "No... I'm not who you think I am," I mutter.

"No?" he asks.

My own words and admission take me by complete surprise. I have no idea what I just said. "I mean, yes."

"Who are you then?" He sits up.

"Sarah Shiles," I say. "I told you. But I'm complicated."

"You just said you're not who I think you are."

"I was joking."

"Ooookay," Dax says, smiling. "Do you, um, see anyone about being *complicated*? You know, a doctor, a therapist? Any kind of condition you haven't discussed with me?"

"No." I want him to stop his questions, get off my patio, get out of my house. I want him to drive home and write his stupid story, get it over with. His words will be forgotten in a matter of days and the magazine pages will line the bottom of someone's birdcage.

"Right," he says. "Okay. So, yeah, and about the homeless shelter you mentioned. You don't remember which one it was? I have a buddy who runs a biggie there, and he says he doesn't remember you coming by. They kept a log of everyone who checked in over the past five years. Your name isn't on it."

"That doesn't mean anything." I say this, but I'm defending a story I don't even know—or sure I believe. These blackouts, blurry memories, and rushes of confusing feelings tilt my world, and something soft and light and unfamiliar is dripping out.

"You sure you didn't have some nickname or something?"

I shake my head. "There are 8.4 million people in New York."

"Listen," Dax says finally, with a sigh and a shake of his head. His eyes are sincere. "You had the police come here last night. I know this. You said some strange things the other night at the restaurant—just for a minute with Maddie and Jared—and you were confused at the tattoo shop. What I'm trying to say is, if there's anything going on, I'm here to help you. You just seem like there's something else you're not telling me. Something big. I mean this as a friend, not just as a journalist." He reaches out to touch my arm, still resting on the chair. A tingle surges through us. Weird.

I let Dax study my eyes for a long time and don't try to manipulate him with my energy. The way his brown eyes are soft and gentle, it makes me realize that people haven't looked at me with that kind of genuine sincerity in so long.

Except Tre.

Tre? The thought rattles me, and a memory, indistinct on the edges, flashes in my mind. A boy with dark hair and striking sky-blue eyes smiles at me in my head.

Dax blinks and shakes his head quickly. "I can't explain, but it's like I'm seeing something else..." He pinches his lips together and looks at the ground. "Never mind."

"Seeing something else beneath my skin?" I finish for him. I, too, am seeing the same thing. And it's confusing the hell out of me.

He sighs a quick laugh. "Yeah. You read my mind."

I need to change the subject. "So you're from Colorado

originally? What did you write about there? Probably not this sort of stuff."

"Yeah," he says taking the bait and leaning back in his chair. His body relaxes. "When I was freelancing for the *Boulder Daily Camera*, I wrote a lot about water rights and the Colorado River."

"Oh, yeah, all those dams really cut the river's flow, triggering all that animosity between Arizona and California." But I know nothing about this. I have no idea where this information comes from. I was a homeless girl on the streets of New York and now I'm a star wrapped in diamonds and furs. I'm so confused and I push away the panic that's starting to jam up my throat and knot my stomach.

He stares at me, stunned for a second. "Yeah, you follow that stuff?" I nod and blink.

Engaged, he leans toward me, smiling. "The river serves thirty million people in seven states," he says. "Isn't that insane?"

I turn away and look at the ocean again, pondering how an invisible force controls it, energy from the earth guiding every wave, every drop of water, every gravitational pull. If the ocean has a conscience, it doesn't even know what's controlling it. It just does what it's supposed to do. *Like me.*

Dax squints at me, writing something illegible in his notebook. "What about Jared? He says you called him in the middle of the night, saying you'd been brainwashed. Is that true?"

"I called him only to tell him to leave me alone. You introduced me to a stalker."

Dax inhales. "Well, I wouldn't say... that."

"I need to go," I say, standing up. "I have a party I need to get to."

Dax rises slowly and claps his hands on his jeans. "Okay.

Well, anything else you want to say before we wrap up? Anything at all?" He gazes directly into my eyes.

"Nope," I say, turning and walking swiftly ahead of him to the front door. I want him gone. Ever since I met him, he's made me feel inside out.

Then a strange feeling overwhelms me, an ominous one, and I stop with the open door in my hand.

"Well," I say, "one thing: good-bye. I want to say good-bye, because I don't think I'll be around much longer."

38

MADDIE

The air feels thick and salty. A sea of people lounge on the beach, picnicking under bright, colorful umbrellas. A group of men sits on a concrete wall and they nod their heads to the bass of reggae music. A man in tight spandex shorts rushes past me on a bicycle, and the breeze from his movement flutters my hair and blouse. It's my last glance at the ocean before we head home.

Jared's phone buzzes. It's a text from Dax, telling us that the story about Oshun is out in *Beats* magazine. Jared looks at me with raised eyebrows before clicking on a link to read it. I hold my breath, wondering what Dax got her to say.

Jared and I take a seat on the concrete wall and huddle over his phone. A photo of Oshun's face is at the top of the page. The dark, smoldering cat eyes and parted, glossed lips. An animal. Her blonde hair is a wild mane. Above it, the headline: *Lifting the Lid on the Head of Pop Icon Oshun.*

He scrolls down to the story.

Oshun, seventeen, may be the latest enigma in the music business. She lives on an enormous beachfront mansion, has a smash hit—"Follow Me"—prospective Grammy nods, and a controversial debut album. The pop star claims to be nothing more than a fortu-itous child, but her lyrics belie that youthful innocence, alluding to witchcraft séances and sexual violence. Her "Candy" music video shows her topless, covered only by a handful of strands of pearls, climbing over dead bodies. But perhaps the biggest contradiction clouding Oshun's rise to fame is her striking resemblance to Ember Trouvé, a teen who went missing in Colorado three years ago. The pop star says she grew up homeless, panhandling on the streets of New York before being discovered and hitting it big. When confronted by the idea that she may, in fact, be Trouvé, she initially indicated that it might be true, only to later deny it. Is Oshun facing an identity crisis?

Jared twists open the cap of his Mountain Dew. He takes a swig and looks up at me with raised eyebrows. "Crazy."

"Makes her sound like a freaking lunatic," I say, shaking my head.

I can't believe Dax really went there, staked his reputation on the idea that Oshun is really Ember. He'll never get an assignment after this, and in fact, it surprises me that a maga-zine the caliber of *Beats* would even print this.

We read the rest of the story.

The story of Oshun's rise to fame first started to shake loose a few days ago, when the young singer abruptly canceled a sold-out concert in Los Angeles, angering fans who gathered in throngs outside the stadium, chanting for her to return to the stage. An open letter to Oshun online, signed by thousands of fans, demanded a refund or a rescheduled concert date to be set. Oshun said she was feeling ill and needed to stop the performance.

But one concertgoer, Jared Trouvé, had another wild theory about the star's sudden stumbling and disorientation. "She saw me. She looked at me and fell apart onstage," he says.

Those words might sound like a fantastical theory by most accounts, but Trouvé attended the concert in the eighth row because he claims Oshun looks suspiciously like his missing sister,

Ember Trouvé, who went missing three years ago outside of Leadville, Colorado. Trouvé's features are slightly different, and the missing girl had dark curly hair. But the teen was a singer-song-writer and her voice sounds eerily similar. (See the video of Ember Trouvé, here.)

On a fluke, I decided to ask Oshun about this theory backstage before that same concert. When she viewed a video of the young Trouvé playing guitar and singing a song for her deceased father, Oshun cried and became disoriented. Then she replied, "Well, her likeness is pretty striking. But that's not me."

Later, I invited Jared Trouvé and his friend Maddie Olson—Ember's best friend—to dinner with Oshun, hoping they could reconcile this strange missing-person account. Oshun initially appeared amused by the mistaken identity, but then dropped to her knees before both of them, whispering that they looked so good and how much she missed them. Then, as if nothing bizarre had happened, she went back to her regular conversation.

The switch infuriated Olson, who stormed out of the restaurant, but the pop star appeared unfazed. Later that evening, police were dispatched to Oshun's Malibu mansion after Trouvé claimed he received a desperate call from the star claiming she was "brain-washed and being held against her will."

Oshun says that she called Trouvé to tell him to stop stalking her. Police never pressed any charges against Trouvé, but escorted him off the premises of Oshun's home when he followed them there after submitting his report.

Whatever the case, it wouldn't be the first time Oshun has dealt with an infatuated fan. Several months ago, twenty-six-year-old prison inmate Steven Bekhn reportedly got a tattoo of the pop star on his left leg and started writing fan letters to Oshun, telling her that she was his wife and that the two would soon die together.

"These fans can be over the top, and it's not surprising because Oshun is on top of the charts," says Jett Rogers, a music analyst who follows the pop industry. Last week, her Seasons album went platinum, hitting more than 500,000 unit sales.

Oshun continues to deny any connection to Ember Trouvé. Instead, she tells a different story of her pre-pop-star life and her road to stardom. Her story starts with her as a young girl named Sarah Shiles, whose parents died and who, after her subsequent caretaker abused her, ran away at age fifteen. For years, she lived on the streets of New York City and in homeless shelters. That's where famed record producer Sal James discovered her, she says. When asked for details about that day, she says it was a sunny day and she was in Times Square, playing guitar. Says Oshun: "I was amazed that my life could go from rags to riches in one day."

But when reached by phone, James's memory is less clear. "Yeah, I discovered her. Sure. Sure. Chicago. Some theater production?"

James declined to answer any more questions about Oshun's rise to fame.

In fact, a public records search of the name Sarah Shiles shows only one result: a woman who lives in Montgomery, Alabama. She is age ninety-seven. When pressed on this fact, Oshun said, "I'm not who you think I am," but then confirmed that, indeed, she is Sarah Shiles and was only joking about that comment.

Recently, a video of Oshun in a hotel lobby went viral. In it, she talks to a group of men and then gasps the following into the camera: "I'm lost. Please help me. I'm not who you think I am. Please."

Oshun later implied that the woman in the video wasn't even her, but an imposter. The man who took the video, Brett Huffington, said it was indeed Oshun. "She just said that weird stuff and walked off."

"She's just eccentric," says Rogers. "That's her allure. That's why she's brilliant."

Rogers went on to list of a number of other stars who had erratic behavior but who dazzled onstage, markedly changing the music of their generation. *Britney Spears. Amy Winehouse. Kurt Cobain. Janis Joplin. Jim Morrison.* He then added, "*Of course, all but one of those stars are dead. And they were involved in drugs. Died young. Really young.*"

Oshun's publicist proclaimed the star is fine but has yet to reset her tour dates. Questions still linger about her erratic behavior and her mysterious past.

Is Jared Trouvé indeed a crazed fan, a brother engaged in a desperate search for his missing sister? Or is Oshun hiding some-thing behind the curtain? Trouvé, who has spent two years searching for Ember, organizing manhunts and working with investigators, says he won't be dissuaded, though Oshun has issued a restraining order against the twenty-one-year-old grocery store clerk. At the end of our interview, Oshun said she didn't think she'd be around much longer, hinting that her career may flame out, but fans of the popular singer want the show to go on.

"He made you sound kind of crazy," I say.

"I don't care." He tosses his head quickly. That makes me worry.

Another text from Dax pops up on Jared's phone: *This just went viral. Thought you might be interested. Someone recorded Oshun playing this song at the tattoo shop.*

Jared clicks on a link below it to a YouTube video. The lyrics are different from the kinds of songs she sings onstage. The words say something like, "*Trinity will tempt you by promising to save you.*" It's a dark and depressing song, but it sounds pretty. It sounds like Ember.

When the clip ends, I look at Jared, my pulse quickening. "Trinity. She sings about Trinity."

"Trinity Forest?"

I shrug, wide-eyed. "*Our* Trinity Forest?"

"I don't know, but it makes me wonder if we should go there?"

I sigh and hand the phone to him and stand up. An ocean

breeze tickles my skin. "Jared, come on. You've got to stop. Seriously. You're starting to—"

"What?" He glares at me. "I'm *what*?"

"It feels like... you're losing it," I say quietly.

He stands, holds my hands with both of his, and I see the little golden flecks in his eyes. "Mads, just do this for me. Just this last thing. Let's drive back, go to Leadville, and stop by Trinity. Just check. That's it. Promise. I won't drag you in with me any more after that."

I sigh, studying his face, genuine candor coloring his expression.

"I'll cut you loose," he adds. "Promise."

I don't want to be cut loose. But I do want off this crazy train for sure. I bite my lip and nod, and he leans in close, touches his nose to mine, and kisses my cheek softly, moving his lips slowly to my mouth. My insides flutter, and I can feel my skin flush. He puts his hands on the sides of my face, enclosing us into the kiss, into our own intimate, private world. My entire body is on fire.

He pulls away and grins. "You're my girl, Mads," he says, then takes my hand and we walk back to the parking lot. Sirens blare down the street.

"Trinity is a pretty scary place. Shouldn't we call the cops? Ask them to investigate?" I ask.

"Ask them to investigate on a hunch, after all I put them through? After all the calls and pestering in those months after she disappeared?"

"Yeah, you might start a collection of restraining orders." I always said the Trouvés are made of rubber. They get knocked down, they bounce up, and keep fighting. Jared holds tight to that tradition.

We jog back to my car and climb inside, off on another road trip, another spontaneous adventure. Me and Jared.

This time, I'm not into it. This time, I'm worried. But I can't leave him out in the cold.

He must see it on my face, because he clasps my hand tight, and when I swivel around to look over my shoulder to back up the car, his lips are on mine again and my body quivers with the kiss. It's soft but intense, and Jared's energy is pure fire.

"Let's go," he says.

We gaze at each other, breathless. It's going to be hard to drive.

39

DAX

I can't write fast enough. "Wait, slow down, slow down," I say before shaking a cramp out of my right hand. I lean across the table at the café. "So you're only eighteen? *And* you've invented some devices, and you're buying MeToo, one of the biggest tech companies in the world?"

Damien Pratt nods and leans back in the booth, an arrogant tilt to his head. He looks like a rock star with his dark hair, goatee, and faded black T-shirt. He runs a hand through his hair, showing a long scar on his bicep, like someone scraped the skin off his arm.

"I've heard of plenty of teenage startup founders, but what's your story? How did you do that?" I ask.

"Well, you're young, too, Dax." He smiles but it's sort of a sneer. "How did I get here? My sister built the tech a few years ago with some researchers, and now I'm stepping up to close the deal and run the show."

Nepotism. No wonder he's so arrogant. I nod and scribble in my notebook. I'm still not sure I want to write about this guy. His tech sounds like science fiction—creepy, and not at all in my wheelhouse. But I don't want to turn down a good story.

I don't ask another question right away, letting a long pause fill the air. My silence makes people talk, which is usually how I operate. Those long pauses always get filled with secrets and surprising revelations.

Damien takes the bait. "Hell, the young and beautiful rule the world," he says, lighting a cigarette with a cupped hand. "People want to be us. Bathe vicariously in the fountain of youth. We've got the power, the influence, the brains."

I write this down, still in disbelief people can really be so brazen and talk like this to a reporter on the record. He gives off a vibe that's familiar. In a way, it reminds me of Oshun: arrogant, rude, powerful—with a strange energy. When I shook his hand a couple minutes ago, it gave me that same crazy electric jolt, just like when I met Oshun. Maybe I need to get to a doctor to see why that's happening to me. Maybe my nerve endings are off.

"Okay, so tell me if I'm understanding this right..." I say. "MeToo will now make an implantable chip that promises to allow people to get rid of their smartphones and all their devices?"

Damien nods and sniffs. "Yup, the chip is connected to another chip in the brain for always-on communication."

I grimace. "The brain? Is that even safe?"

"Sure, sure," he says. "It's based on old tech, implantables, the stuff we've used for years to treat things like Parkinson's, strokes, and other neurological diseases. The FDA fast-tracked it so we could get it out as soon as possible."

"What's the rush? There's no medical emergency or deadly disease you're solving."

"We've got to get people off their phones. We've all got neck problems. We never look up when we're walking around. People are getting into car accidents trying to read their texts. With devices, you lose them, you're always spending money updating them. This way, you're *part* of the Internet. It's no longer the Internet of Things. It's the Internet of People. Imagine sending a text just by thinking it. Seeing pictures on Instagram with a voice command. You're driving and you get the weather delivered right to your brain."

"That's crazy," I say, shaking my head. I'm no tech reporter, but this is pretty far out there. "How does it work?"

"The iPhone changed everything, shrinking components, driving down prices and allowing us to put more computing power into a chip than ever before. You'll still be able to use your phone. But it's like an iWatch without the watch. It's all voice. Turn off your lights at home by just asking your wrist to do it. Send a message, check voicemail, see a photo. It's all there."

"Come on. I mean, will people really want to do this? Does it really work?"

"Sure does," he says. "Like I said, the feds gave it the okay and now we're ramping up fast. We thought you could be the one to actually write a first-person story about getting the implant and how it works out."

My reaction is incredulous. "You *do know* that I write about media and music. Not tech."

"Yeah, but your feature on Oshun, well, that caught the attention of some important and powerful people. And, we picked you. We thought you'd be the perfect reporter. You *earned* it. It's your payback for lifting the lid on Oshun."

It makes me chuckle that he thinks writing about MeToo is some sort of prize for doing the piece on Oshun. But the compliment does pump a little more air in my head. I can't get cocky or I'll lose my touch.

"So, are you in?" he asks. "Want to give it a whirl? I'll get you hooked up today and you can have an implant by the day's end."

I pause for a minute and look at this guy, chewing the side of my cheek. He's mysterious and, like Oshun, I want to be around him, even though he seems like a royal jerk. Maybe this means it will be another big story. And I'm so tired of being addicted to my phone. But this... it's just too creepy.

A waitress takes my plate and refills my water. I smile and thank her.

"I don't know," I say, taking a sip of the water. "I think I'll pass and keep my old-school phone."

Damien shakes his head. "Bad choice, man. You're missing out."

I laugh. "Sorry, I've got a ton of people asking for interviews and I can't be doing injections. It'll mess up my mojo."

"It only takes about five or ten minutes," he says. "And the chip just sits on the surface of your skull. Not deep in the brain. But hey, I wouldn't want anything to happen to you. Or your mojo." Damien's face shifts; he clenches his teeth, and his eyes, outlined by dark lashes and brows, shift from a glimmering ice blue to a shiny titanium. It completely freaks me out.

After a moment, he perks up and looks out the window and then points at something across the street. "Well, look at our luck! There's a free vaccine booth right there across the street. To protect against the virus." He raises his eyebrows and turns to me. "You gonna get one?"

"I've been meaning to."

"Well, today is your lucky day," he says. "Let's get you a vaccine."

40

OSHUN

I order a cocktail—everyone serves me even though I'm underage—and I drain it in one gulp. I savor the taste, like spicy honey, and scan the crowd at the rooftop party. A tall girl with cinnamon hair stands next to me, and for some reason she feels familiar, but I've never met her. She's talking to my manager, Kip, a handsome guy with long blonde hair pulled back in a low ponytail. He talks about his penchant for expensive cars and chasing eclipses. I barely hear his voice, which hammers in my mind the color of dead leaves.

We're surrounded by the rich and powerful. Hollywood types and politicians. Many of them are also Annunaki. I don't know why I know this, but I can see their dark energy rise above their heads like clumps of black ashes and rolling storm clouds.

"So many rebirthers," the redheaded girl next to me says, reading my mind. She wears a petulant expression while scanning the body of a nearby girl. She tilts her head and scratches her ear, slowly, and I notice a thin scar running the length of her palm.

"Yeah," I say. I know the term *rebirther* like I recognize the word *person*, but if you asked me to define what a rebirther is exactly, I couldn't explain. All I know is that I belong to them, that we're better than ordinary people in the world, and that we have a plan.

This is the first time I've actually considered this: how I know certain things, why I know them. It's as if I was dropped into my place in the world with memories, but trying to see them clearly is like looking through a smudged window.

"Did you see the whole waitstaff is wearing masks?" Kip says.

"Like that's going to help them," the girl says. "We're the only ones immune to the virus." Her voice is syrup and the color of honey. I turn around and take a good look at her. She has a high forehead. Defined cheekbones. She radiates power and influence and is built like a statue, chiseled and hard and unbreakable.

Valerie Monsette from my Missing Persons notebook.

Confused, I clear my throat and give a quick shake of my head, hoping I didn't say the words out loud.

Yet a memory comes clearly to me now: I'm sitting on the floor of a bedroom, pressing clipped photos of missing people into a spiral notebook, writing their names in ink pen. Their faces come into focus: the Howdy Doody look of Ben Alackness. The intense gaze of Phil Sei. The rose petal lips of Laurie Parker. The chiseled cheeks of Valerie Monsette. The faces of the missing.

Another memory: I saw those same people later, standing in a dark room wearing hooded robes.

I shake my head.

In glimpses through the crowd, I think maybe I see Phil Sei across the party. He stands next to the ice sculpture of the goddess Baphomet. That can't be him, is it?

Then my gaze lands on a guy with dark hair wearing blue-grey sunglasses and a loose-fitting white dress shirt.

My head turns inside out, and my skin feels as though it's on fire.

"Do you know that guy?" I ask the tall redhead, pointing at the boy.

"Damien Pratt," she explains. "Runs MeToo. They're making implantable chips. He's a new rebirther. Super wicked psychic, too."

Tre.

"You okay?" the girl asks, wrinkling her nose.

I nod absently. She sneers and puts the cherry from her drink into her mouth.

For some reason, I want to run to this guy, throw my arms around his neck, and kiss him. That's not me. That's what other people want to do when they see me.

Still, I'm drawn to him like a like he's a missing piece of me. I move toward him, squeezing between people, feeling their sweat and heat and the splashes of cold drinks on my skin. I can't take my eyes off him. Two young girls fawn over him, placing their hands on his jacket. He wears a bit of facial hair on his chin, and his dark hair flops over to one side.

I know this guy. It's deep inside me, imprinted on my soul.

I stop in my high heels, tottering as I'm bumped and pushed aside by strangers. Some guy comes up to me, touches my arm, introduces himself as Chet, and eagerly launches into a spiel about a movie he's doing. The jade-color sound of his voice is muted and I cut him off. "Go away."

I'm running through a forest of memories in my mind. Jared cheering for me at a cross-country meet. Riding horses with Maddie by a stream. Mom leaning over a plate of spaghetti and laughing. Dad hovering over a math textbook with me. The accident. Trinity. Lilly. Pete. Zoe. Xintra. The crystals.

Tre.

I'm running so hard that the memories swoosh past me in

a streaming blur until finally, I come to a clearing. There's a reason my Sarah Shiles memories are cloudy; there's a reason why I've been blacking out. I'm not only Oshun, the pop star. I'm someone else, too. Someone with a past, with relationships, with a story. Pain and love and memories.

My name is Ember. I'm that girl who disappeared. I know this in my heart. Something tears loose from me, and a rosy-pink color fills me from head to toe. I exhale, break out of my dark underwater prison, and stretch out into my own skin.

41

EMBER

I'm me. Really me! And in front of me is really Tre. His perfect lips and ink-black brows. His hair, less like a punk rocker, more like a guy of my generation. He wears rounded blue-tinted sunglasses. Awe sweeps through me like a rushing river current.

I glance down to see what I'm wearing. Neon-green puffy miniskirt, neon-green heels, and matching bra top. Not much. So I'm at a party, dressed like a freak. My fingers graze the hard, rough edges of the necklace around my throat before I glance down at the various colored crystals.

I feel like I'm going to burst as I dart toward Tre, pushing people out of my way. People whisper in waves.

"Is that Oshun?"

"That's her."

My attention stays fixed on Tre. He looks so cool, so important. He takes off the sunglasses, puts them on the lapel of his hipster suit jacket, and something in the way he moves, he looks *different*. His skin, visible in glimpses between people's arms and heads, has the same shimmery look that Zoe's had—the way it makes him look almost inhuman. The closer I get, it's clear his eyes are different somehow, too. Still pale blue with dark lashes, but they look liquid, like two deep holes. The realization gives me pause, and I hesitate for half a second before reaching out between a couple people to touch his arm.

"Tre!" I say, trying to keep from bursting at the seams, my whole body abuzz. I can't believe both of us are now standing here on the outside of Trinity, that both of us made it out alive.

He doesn't respond, but I get close enough to throw myself at him in a forceful hug, looping my arms tight around his neck. "Oh my God, you're alive!" I gush. Emotion wells inside and I'm giddy. With hands cinched behind his neck, I pull back, grinning, to look at his face.

He has one arm wrapped around my waist, and it slides down to my butt and then grabs hard at one cheek.

I pull back and smile hesitantly. "Uh... okay..."

He sneers at me. "Hey, babe, nice to meet you."

I tilt my head. "*Meet* me?" I say. "You *know* me!"

His face is absent of Tre's softness and personality. The women around him are melting in his presence, gazing up at him, entranced with loopy smiles. He has the same power that Zoe had—maybe he's even stronger. Perhaps I have that same power—or at least, Oshun does.

"Looks like you got the wrong guy." His voice is no longer chocolate. It's blood red. "I'm Damien Pratt. You've probably heard of me. I run MeToo."

It's as if the name itself kicks me in the stomach. He's been rebirthed. Of course he's been rebirthed. How else could he be here at this party? Out of Trinity, alive? But just hearing him say that foreign name crushes my hope.

"Oh," I mumble.

No, I tell myself, *it shouldn't matter.* I was rebirthed, and

I'm standing here, completely lucid. He can get there, too. He must. I'll make him.

He turns away to nuzzle the blonde next to him, whispering something in her ear. She giggles. My face heats up and jealousy swims through me. It takes everything in my power not to punch her in the face. But after a moment, the girl on his arm pouts and leaves him. He turns his attention to me, his eyes lingering on my breasts.

"I know who you are," he says, a smirk climbing up his face.

My heart soars. I knew it. I knew he would remember!

He takes a step closer and holds out a hand to shake mine, holding it close to his body. "You're Oshun, right? His eyes lock onto my breasts again, and I hesitate before grasping his warm hand. I gaze at him towering above me, an entirely different person.

"So you don't *remember* me?" I swallow. Being so close to him, just inches away, sandwiched together in this crowd of people, I'm dying to touch his face, kiss his lips, throw my arms around his neck and scream with euphoria that I'm actually next to him again. We're not in Trinity.

He shakes his head. "I've seen you on TV, and we talked about you at the last meeting." His eyes dig into mine, and I feel that electric chemistry that we had in Trinity, but this time, it's even more intoxicating, more dangerous, than before. It's animalistic and delivers a pulsating feeling throughout me, as if my skin is melting hot.

"I'm Emb—" I stop myself. I have to play along or I'll lose him. "I'm Oshun."

"We've established that."

"Oh." There is so much I want to say to him. So much I want to get through. I want desperately to tell him I'm here, inside my own body, *back*. I want to see if there's a glimmer of him in there, too. I'm pushed by someone on my left and I stumble, then recover. I can't think straight with the pulsing gooey feeling rippling and massaging my brain.

I recall what that girl said earlier about his company and how it made some kind of implantable chip. I have to figure out a way to talk to him, to keep him here, until I can figure out how to get him back. "What does your company do?"

"We make microscopic sensors." He reaches out and takes my arm with one hand, and my skin tingles. Slowly, he turns the soft side of my wrist faceup and then takes his other hand, runs his finger down my arm. The move is slow, juicy and sexy, and my knees go weak. "It's injected beneath the skin, and the chip allows people to call up information, connect to the Internet, and communicate—all by voice." He drags the finger up my arm, over my shoulder, up my neck and cheek to my temple. He places two fingers there on the side of my head. Then taps gently. "It all ends up here."

That fluttery feeling races through me, and I involuntarily move a couple inches closer to him, swept up in the slushy intoxication, the quiver of his touch, the proximity of our bodies. He presses his lips into a small, sexy smile, and his eyes smolder.

"Sounds cool." My voice sounds like a cloud.

"It's the hottest thing out there. We're giving away free injectables in June. Just in time for your big Oshun Beach Party."

"Why?" I'm half listening to him, eating up the blood-red color of his voice, which swirls in waves in my vision.

He tilts his head down, skeptical, like I've had too much to drink. "You know *that*, babe. We'll be getting as many people as possible to wear them before the Dark Day." I stare at him, trying to connect the dots of the conversation, but they float all over the place. He leans in, whispering, his breath tickling my ear. "You know, control the survivors, their whereabouts, their movements, their health after the genocide?"

"Yeah," I whisper, nodding slowly, feeling almost as if I really *am* drunk, not knowing what on earth he's talking about. My face feels limp in his presence, and I want to attach myself to him, glue my body to his. The pulsing feeling is so sensual, so warm.

Someone approaches him from behind, rattling him with a gregarious hug, and Tre turns and laughs. The sound of it is unfamiliar and reminds me of the memory of my own twisted laughter inside the tub in the hotel bathroom the other night when I was Oshun. When I was bad. Really bad. Killing people, doing evil things—for Xintra.

With my trance broken by this thought and his friend's interruption, my body goes cold. I knew that Xintra was up to something wicked. But genocide? Tre would never have gone through with rebirthing if he knew this is what it was about.

He needs to be reminded and wake up. Like I did. But even if he *does* remember who he is, who he *really* is, will he even forgive me for leaving him behind? We were so close to escaping together before I blew it. Before I abandoned him. Is that why he went through the rebirthing? Without me, did he give up?

The noise from the party surges a liquid copper color, and I take in the smooth faces of people with long lashes and perky noses. Thin, strong, beautiful bodies. Some dance, a guy and girl kiss, and a girl in jeans snorts cocaine off a table-top, her long brown hair dragging through leftover sushi. My stomach roils. This is so screwed up. I've got to get out of here. But I want to bring Tre with me.

With his friend now gone, Tre's attention returns to me. He takes a long drag on a cigarette and follows my eyes as I gawk at the people at the party. "You can spot those of us that are rebirthers, right?"

"Yeah," I say absently, taking a step back from him, trying

to avoid the mind-melting effect he has on me. Panic clenches my muscles. How do I stop this? How do I extract Tre?

Gazing at his profile in the dim light of the party, I can't help but think he's so beautiful. I want nothing more than to feel the heat from his body, to wrap him up and take him home and apologize for giving in to rebirthing. I want to live happily ever after.

But when he turns to look at me, I see his expression, and the feeling vanishes. He's an imposter. He's Damien.

"What a kickoff for the countdown to the big day, wouldn't you say?" He exhales smoke into the air and leans in closer again. "The tsunami and the hurricane should hit the coasts simultaneously next month. Then the tornadoes take care of the middle of the country, and when the earthquakes hit the gas lines? Bam! It'll light up massive urban forest fires. Then after that, the rest of the world."

An uncomfortable fire burns my skin. I need to get him away from this place, remind him of who he is.

A faint black fog hangs over his head, moving in clumps like ashes, pulsing, breaking up and dissolving before forming new clouds again. This is not synesthesia. This is Crayon Brain on crack. This, I think, is some kind of dark, malicious energy I'm watching that's emanating from his body. Why can I still see this even though Oshun is gone? *Is* she really gone? It feels like all the furniture in my brain has been shuffled around, and I'm not sure where anything is in the world anymore.

Damien gazes back at me with those same intense eyes, and he reaches out a warm hand, pulling me closer to him. I lick my lips and turn my head away, eager to avoid the toxic spell of his presence.

"Come with me," he says, turning and leading me by the hand through the crowd of people. I follow, not wanting to let go of him, of this chance, but afraid of where he's taking me.

Xintra must know by now that I'm not under her spell anymore, that I flushed Oshun away. Or at least I hope I did.

He leads me to a quiet spot away from the party, behind the ring of white catering tables, at the far end of the roof. He lets go of my hand to sit on the ledge, with his feet dangling off the side of a building that must be at least thirteen stories tall.

"Sit," he says, patting the spot next to him on the metal edge.

I move slowly and sink down next to him, wary. The breeze blows my hair, goosebumps tickle my arms, and the tall building shifts slightly, giving me a disorienting feeling of weightlessness. Below, it looks like toy cars are zipping around on the street. My thigh touches his and there's that electric energy between us—just like always—but the massaging energy from him begins to encircle me, moving through my lungs, my blood, cutting into my brain. I look up, studying his face, yearning for Tre to be back inside his skin. But I feel so content next to Damien. Maybe Damien is enough right now, in this moment.

"So, Oshun," he says, placing a hand on my shoulder, holding me firmly in place. His touch is hallucinogenic, making my muscles weak, yet I can still feel that fear creeping across the back of my neck like tiny spiders. "I like your music." The weight of his warm hand presses into me.

"Oh," I whisper. "Thank you." With one hand, I touch the crystal necklace and close my eyes, taking deep breaths. All I can do is pray he remembers me somehow, pray he doesn't do what I think he's going to do.

"You seem different tonight than you do on TV and onstage."

"You've never met me before." I glance away, swallowing. I regain some amount of restraint over his mind control and exert my own will, my own fire inside not to let this happen to me again—especially not from him. "Let's go sit over there on the sofa. I'm cold." I attempt to stand, but his hand firmly keeps me where I am. Teetering on the edge of the world.

He reaches a finger out to my chin, tilting my head up to meet his icy eyes. His touch, which once made me want to yield to him, practically makes me recoil. "Maybe that's why I find you interesting tonight. You don't seem like the girl we've talked about at our meetings."

"Meetings?"

"Gatherings for the Annunaki. You've attended them, right?"

I have. I did, though the memories are vague—and creepy. Flickering candles. Haunting chants. Dark ghosts. Sermons about controlling the world. The dead body of a large man on the floor.

He runs a finger down the side of my face, a gesture both sensual and chilling. "You were important to the cause. I would hate for anything to happen to you. Like that reporter who, how should we say, saw you beneath your skin."

I tremble, and a flood of emotions tumbles around inside me. The outside world grows quiet, indistinct, and my heart pounds. I take a deep breath and draw on Oshun's fearless-ness. "You know," I say, "you remind me of someone. His name is Tre. I met him in Trinity."

His hand squeezes my shoulder tighter. I tense, but then frustration builds. Screw it. This is my chance.

I break free from his spell, his dark, energetic power, ripping myself free cell by cell. "In fact, you *are* Tre. We fell in love. Or at least I did. And then I left. I got rebirthed. And... I miss him," I whisper.

I can only see portions of his face in the dim light. The party is a good seventy-five yards away, and the color of the noise moves in waves of turquoise and liquid copper. Tre's lips look fuller, softer, more like the perfect lips I loved so much in Trinity.

"I miss *you*," I add. Then, without giving it a second thought, I let go of the ledge, reach for the sides of his face, pull him in, and press my lips to his.

The kiss is warm and soft and just what I remembered. It's a reminder that his name is still written on my heart. I place my hands around his neck, pulling him closer. He responds, leaning into the kiss, bringing his fingers to my cheek, his mouth is in sync with mine. The breeze blows my hair. I slowly pull back, smiling, eager to see if our kiss lit something inside of him, awakened him like some boy version of Snow White.

"Now, Oshun, babe," he whispers. *Tre doesn't talk like that.* "I have to admit, I feel like I've been drawn to you since the moment I laid eyes on you. Like we were meant to be."

The last line grabs me. *Yes, we were meant to be. Yes.*

He stands up slowly, holding out a hand to help me up, too. My mind feels fuzzy again, and I'm pulled like a magnet, yearning to taste him again. I take his hand, and it sends a buzzing sensation from my fingertips to my core, wrapping around my head like a warm bath. He lifts me up, pulling me into his body—much like he did a few times back in Trinity. I put my head on his chest, feel his heartbeat, so happy he's still alive. I press my hips closer, wanting to fold myself into him.

"You've got everything you wanted in life, right?" He lifts my chin to see his face, dipped down, just a couple inches from mine. "You've got it all," he whispers on my lips.

Yes, I think, *I do.* His lips tease mine, tickling and moving in. Yes, I have it all—as Oshun.

He moves his mouth to my ear, tickling my jaw with his breath. "You and me... we'll have it all. Together."

Yes, I think. *Yes, we'll be together.* I yearn to be with him forever, to soak in his wicked world.

He puts his hands on my waist, backs me into the brick wall by the elevator, pushes his thighs between my legs, and kisses me hard, his mouth pressing against mine. A very bad piece of me loves this power, this passion and desire. His hands are in my hair, along my waist, and I'm tugging on him, missing him, wanting him. The ash-colored energy that hovers above his head smothers any coherent thought in my mind.

He whispers in my ear again. "I need the snapdragon vial from your purse."

My body stiffens and I stop kissing him. That's a chemical. I remember, as Oshun. It's a poison, something used by the Russians that can't be detected in an autopsy. He wants me to give him something to murder someone.

I push him away slowly. "No," I say forceful.

"But we'll be together," he says. "Rule the world."

I inhale, gazing into his eyes, absent the sky blue of Tre's. The color looks like dark, stormy clouds, and his voice is that blood red. Fear whips through me.

"No." I shake my head. "No, we won't."

I begin to pull away from him, when suddenly his hands clamp down on the back of my neck, tearing at my hair, taking me by surprise. Damien—not my Tre—pushes me back against the wall, the brick jamming into the back of my head.

"Who do you think you are?" His dark red voice hits me hard, like a medicine ball to the stomach, and his brow bends in anger.

Breathing hard and filled with terror, I wriggle. But that first kiss comes to mind. It felt like Tre. I did something to him. I know it. I pulled something inside him, shook a piece of him loose. I take another risk despite his rage.

"I love Tre. He's in there, I know it. *You* know it. Remember, goddamnit!" Desperation clings to my words. "You saw the Berlin Wall fall, you... you... love chocolate ice cream—in waffle cones. You told me you ran naked in a rainstorm senior year. You want to go to New York City and see the Brooklyn Bridge in the fog, and a whole bunch of other places." The words come out fast in a string of desperate gasps.

A momentary flicker of confusion crosses his face, but it's gone in a flash. Still, it's enough to give me hope.

"And you drive a motorcycle, your dad had a helicopter, your cousin taught you to swim in some marshy, nasty lake and threatened that you had to swim or be eaten by giant fish with sharp teeth. Remember? You told me that. And we—you and me—we swung on a rope together, spinning in the sunlight, and kissed. We played cards for hours. And you listened to me write music. You told me I had a voice that sounded like sandpaper dipped in honey." A smile breaks onto my face suddenly. "And I fell in love with you."

His hand lets go of me, but his scowl is fierce and his eyes bounce across the concrete rooftop. There's a flash of recognition in his blue eyes, and they soften as if he's close to tears, looking more like Tre. He runs his hand through his hair. That mannerism. That energy, moving in silver rays between us. It's different. More like *us*.

But it vanishes like steam from a hot cup of tea. Instead of pulling out Tre entirely, I've fully enraged Damien. He bares his teeth and his face flushes. In a swift movement, he wraps his hands tightly around my throat, and I can't breathe. "Traitor." His voice is red dots and mustard spikes in my vision.

Like a trapped animal, I desperately push against him and claw at his chest, pull on his fingers, but his weight is steel, his hands like clamps.

My legs grow weak as I cling to his arms and shoulders, until the world begins to shrink into darkness, into a circle the size of a pinhole. All I see are his eyes, barely visible, dark holes in his head.

"Tre," I gasp the word. "Please. I love you." The pain is awful, tearing, crushing the life out of me. I struggle to keep my eyes open, begging for Tre to see me.

A silky caramel-colored voice interrupts my death. A partygoer, passing by. "You *have* to see my plastic surgeon— he is a genius."

Tre's body recoils, and he lets go of me and backs away into the shadows.

Sobs burn inside my chest as I fall to my knees, biting for breath like a fish pulled from water. My throat feels scalded and my windpipe bent. I look up and see two women, clad in tight cocktail dresses and long hair, walking toward us from ten yards away. When they finally see me, they stop and gaze down at me, frowning.

They give me thin, false smiles, scan me up and down. I stand up, dust my hands off on my bare legs, and rub my neck. "You're bleeding," one of them says, pointing to my knee.

I look down at the blood dripping down my shin, a scrape from falling on the ground just now. "Thanks," I say.

They go back to their conversation and walk past me to the party. "He's the best. He did my nose and my chin."

I search for Tre in the dim light, peeking around the corner of the wall and searching the heads of the distant party. I have to reach him and quash the monster inside him —if he doesn't kill me first.

I weave in and out of the crowd before spotting him briefly in the elevator, before the black metal doors close on him. I run to it, punching the button to the first floor repeatedly, touching my throat, which burns and is most likely bruised.

A wave of sorrow crashes over. Tre's gentle hands did this to me.

No, I remind myself. *He* didn't do this. Rebirth did. I take deep breaths, pushing away the distorted reality at play.

The doors open, and I step inside, jamming the first-floor button. The lights for each floor flash slowly and ding. I stand there, touching the crystal necklace around my throat, as Oshun's identity rattles through my brain. If I wake up in rebirth, does that mean Oshun goes away? Her hate and her evil doings? Will Xintra come get me? Will I be able to find Tre and catch up to him? Convince him of who he really is?

The doors open and I run through the lobby of the building and out the glass doors to the street. I look in both directions and see only a balding doorman, standing at attention next to me.

"Did you see a tall guy with dark hair pass by?" I ask.

"Hey," he says smoothly. "Aren't you that pop star, Oshun?"

"Answer the damn question!" I snap. I guess Oshun has stayed with me, operating in the background when necessary.

"Uh, yeah, that way," the man says, pointing to the left. "Down that alley."

I take off running in these ridiculous high-heeled shoes and bound around the corner, racing into a dark alley that smells of trash and spoiled food. He's got to be here. I slow my pace and search the dark, looking for his familiar shape.

The sound of tires rolling across the ground shows up slate gray in my Crayon Brain, and it grows in size and volume as the vehicle approaches me from behind. I turn to see a dark car moving slowly next to me, and a tinted window rolls down. Inside the car is a man with a face that looks like mashed potatoes. He sneers and wags a finger at me.

"Game over, Oshun," he says.

Panic courses through my body and I propel my arms and legs forward, sprinting over flattened boxes and trash, stumbling over cracks. My heart thumps in my head and soon, my legs move fluidly over the ground despite the heels. I can't even feel my legs moving anymore. It's as if I'm floating over the ground.

I turn the corner at the end of the alley, not sure where I'll go, when I hear the motor rev. I glance behind me over my shoulder and a flash of the black car roars into view. Terrified, I scream.

Something hard slams into my back. The world slows, and I tumble into the air. My shoulder and neck hit something hard with a thump, and my head lands on the ground with a crack. I am a pile of skin and bones, anchored only by the sound of my heart beating. *Thump. Thump. Thump.*

I blink, and the Snickers wrapper on the ground blurs and wanes in my vision. Muffled footsteps fade, as if a dial on a radio has been turned down. Until there is nothing left.

42

MADDIE

The words are barely legible. *Trinity Forest: No Trespassing. Keep Out.*

I gaze into the forest, the tall, dark pine trees hovering, whistling in the wind. The sun sets behind us. There's a good reason why I've never come here.

"This is crazy," I say, grimacing at Jared and then touching the barbed-wire fence with a single finger.

"Yep, but we're desperate," he says.

He is desperate. And me? I told him that I was in, told him that I would go to Trinity Forest with him. So here I am. In deep.

Without hesitation, I crawl through the fence. "Let's go then," I say.

When I walk into the dense pine trees, it's as if someone dimmed the daylight with a light switch. The air feels impossibly still here, and as I walk, I question every step I take. A breeze cuts through my clothes like they're nothing, like I'm nothing, and I shiver. Am I really going into this creepy forest now, on a Sunday night, when I need desperately to get back to school and focus on real life? I glance back at Jared and his face crinkles with worry. I inhale. Yes, *this* is why I'm doing this. He needs this.

Besides, we can't give up on Ember—not now. She's out there somewhere, and Jared needs peace. I can help him find that, even if it means charging into this totally creepy forest without any kind of plan. No provisions. No really good evidence that she's connected to this place, but right now it's all we've got.

"Maybe there's some sort of crack house here," I say. *They roped Ember in*, I think, *and they're holding her hostage*. "Or maybe there's a Hollywood agent," I add with a laugh.

"If so, you might very well get signed as some sort of really bad comedian, Mads."

Jared has caught up to me now and our feet crunch the leaves, crack branches. Owls hoot from the distance, and the howling wind sounds like a distant highway. The path starts to fade and the trees become denser, closing in—just like in haunted cartoon forests.

The ground rumbles and quivers.

"What the hell was that?" Jared whispers.

"Maybe an earthquake?" Logic. I have to go with logic.

But the part of my brain that defies logic bucks. I can't shake the feeling that something really ominous is happening here. With Ember, with the virus, with the earthquake. Something big. This was a terrible idea.

My cell buzzes. I'm surprised I still have service. I look at the phone; it's a Google alert I set up on the way home to keep us apprised of any news relating to Oshun. The blood drains from my head when I see the headline.

I grab Jared's arm, stop him. "Wait."

Pop star Oshun found dead in bathtub.

43

DAX

My hands tremble as I splash cold water on my face and stare at my reflection in the mirror, studying my droopy, bloodshot eyes. Man, I look like crap. I run my fingers through my hair, and out falls a clump of black strands. A cough tickles my throat, and after a second, I'm hacking uncontrollably. Stress. I'm pushing myself too hard.

I put on my Raiders slippers and shuffle into my bedroom, which remains bare despite two years of living here. White concrete walls, a mattress with no box spring, and a bedside table on cinder blocks—the glamorous life of a reporter.

I collapse onto the unmade bed. My phone lights up on the bedside table and I glance at it and see another message from a TV news station wanting to interview me about Oshun. Another claim to fame: the last big interview before she died. Her last words to me still haunt me. *"I want to say good-bye, because I don't think I'll be around much longer."* I thought she was talking about her fame, her career. I never thought it meant she'd end up dead.

How had she predicted her own death? It was as if there

was an invisible hand dealing her fate, controlling her life. She changed so much during those few days after I met her, going from über bitch to something a little softer, more reflective.

I pull out my laptop to start the project I've been building toward—my memoir. This will be the thing that catapults my career onto a whole new level. I type my passcode to unlock my screen, and an enormous pain seizes my fingers. My hands ball into fists and the muscles in my calves pinch. My stomach and back cramp at once, and the pain spreads as if my limbs themselves are being cut in half. I scream in agony, rolling into the fetal position, and rub my bicep where I got the injection earlier with Damien. Could I be having some sort of reaction to it?

My head pounds so hard, I can't even see straight. I shut my eyes, but the pain doesn't fade and piercing white sparks flash like fireworks in my vision. Fear spins furiously in my brain as I tally up the symptoms; the list is similar to the indicators of the virus.

"You'll be okay," I say over and over to myself. But my skin feels even clammier, beads of sweat roll down my face, and I can't stop licking my cracked lips. Lick. Breathe. Lick. Breathe. I try to shut my eyes to sleep but see only sparks. Instead, I stare at the bare white wall and then the small glass block window, waiting for the pain to disappear. I cough again, hacking until my stomach cramps and I heave, vomiting up my lunch all over the floor. I wipe my mouth and roll over, away from the acrid, nauseating smell.

It feels like something is choking me, cutting off all air to my lungs, and I feel so dizzy.

This is big. This is serious. I reach for my phone to dial 9-1-1, but it slips through my fingers to the floor. I gasp for air.

The room fades to a bright white, and eventually, all the pain is gone.

44

MADDIE

"Ember can't be dead!" Jared's voice is frantic.

I cross my arms over my chest. There's something about hearing someone died just after you interacted with them. It makes death feel tangible, like something you can touch and smell. The girl we just had dinner with and whom we saw in concert the other day is dead.

But she wasn't Ember, I assert to myself. She couldn't have been—even if Dax did question the theory in his story.

"No," Jared whispers, staring at my phone. "No. No. No. No." He sinks into the dead leaves and branches onto his knees. I sit down next to him, and together, we read the entire story.

Pop star Oshun dies at age seventeen after being found dead in her $19 million Malibu home. Officials say her body was discovered in the bathtub, and they suspect the cause of death was a drug overdose.

Sarah Shiles, also known as Oshun, stormed on the scene last year when her debut album Seasons *shot up to no. 1 on the billboard charts. Her new single, "Petals and Thorns," shot up to no. 3 this week, despite mixed reviews. Meanwhile, her hit song "Candy" received acclaim from music critics, who deemed it the strongest track on the album.* Rolling Stone *called her voice and her presence a "dreamy sound landscape that weaves you into another world."*

The pop star was also a lightning rod for controversy. Recent news stories referring to Oshun's erratic behavior, including spontaneously canceling a recent concert midway through her second song, examine rumors that she was somehow connected to teen Ember Trouvé, who went missing three years ago in Colorado and bears a striking resemblance to the pop star.

"She was erratic because she was a drug user," says one unnamed source. "She was not in any way related to that missing girl. She was just messed up."

Jared's body trembles, and I put my arm around his shoulder, pull him close. Oshun's story is so freaking sad. Ember's too.

Jared covers his eyes with his fists and I lean into him, resting my chin on his shoulder. Then my own tears flow, too. Not because Oshun is dead or Oshun was Ember. I cry because this is the culmination of a long marathon spent looking for Ember, climbing up hills and running fast toward hope, only to find hope was just a mirage. And I cry because I miss her. I cry because I couldn't save her. I cry because I could never reach her. Before she disappeared, and now.

"I thought we were so close," he says.

"It wasn't Ember, Jared," I whisper. "It wasn't her."

His whole body tenses and he pulls away. "Then why the hell are you here? Why?"

"I'm just trying to support you," I say softly. The air between our bodies is cool, and I want to lean back into him, keep him whole.

"Not an inkling of a thought—not even for a second—did you believe this was Ember?"

I don't say anything.

"Even *Dax* believed it."

I bite my lip, bracing for what I know will come next. My heart pounds. Not only will I lose a boy I feel something big for, I'll lose my best friend. Again. First Ember, then Jared. Shit.

I shake my head and stare through cloudy tears at the dead leaves on the ground before noticing a low fog, creeping quickly across the forest floor. It glides, twirling at the edges like a snake. It makes the hair on the back of my neck stand on end. People always said the fog in Trinity Forest steals your breath. The trees eat your soul. Something makes you dissolve. I thought it was just stories.

My stomach clenches tight. We need to get the heck out of here, right now.

45

XINTRA

Jeff Culver looks pathetic, still so much like Chris, the sad, broken fool I drew to Trinity so long ago, but enough time has passed in the outside world that no one would suspect he and this CDC official are the same person.

He failed me. He's letting me down just like the fool I put in charge at the FDA. He was supposed to poison the food supply with faulty genetics. That blew up and went nowhere. The food industry had no backbone and shut it down. Not enough Annunaki members. The virus and the storms are the key to the genocide. I control the storms from the cumulative power of my vortexes. At least I have that under my control.

He stands before me in a trance. He won't remember our conversation in the future, but he will do my will.

"What do you mean there are people trying to *cure* the virus?" I repeat. I'm so close to my destiny, to ensuring the world is populated by the worthy.

"I discovered there are private research groups funded by billionaire George Stepos, and they claim the government's vaccine doesn't work," he says in a monotone voice.

"Of course it doesn't work. The vaccine *is* the poison," I snap. "Eliminate the detractors. Put a sab out to bomb them or get close enough to use the snapdragon poison."

He nods slowly. "Yes, your highness."

"Now move into your position for the sacrifice," I say.

He backs into the corner, gazing straight ahead, and the sound of shuffling footsteps echoes through the tunnel. Two dark figures emerge from the fog, carrying a body.

Ember. Black and green bruises cover her shoulder and neck, and dried blood is caked around her mouth and her ear.

"Good," I say, pointing to the stone table in the center of the room. "Put her on the table."

Asa and Caius drop her limp body on the plank. I tilt my head, studying her, lifting her thin arm and dropping it again. It swings and dangles off the stone table. She wears thick cat-eye makeup and her parted lips are smeared with red lipstick. I run my fingers over the clumps of her blonde hair, which is caked with dried blood.

She looks so much like her mum. A vague wave of tenderness tickles me before it rolls into hate. Too much like her mum; she defied me, too, tried to ruin all that was destiny, all that was good. I should never have assumed I'd have a second chance with Dezi through Ember.

The electrical pulse hums in the air, the voices of the dead, fueling Trinity's rich energy. The robed rebirthers move into the room as commanded, the only sound their shuffled footsteps. The air smells of lovely rich, damp earth.

Zoe moves to Ember with a lit torch and ignites a pile of branches beneath her. A flame whooshes to life, spreading to the wood below.

"Let her burn," I say.

46

EMBER

A yellow-sounding crackle lights up my vision, followed by the army-green color of liquid dripping. *Drip. Drip. Drip.*

My neck aches and a shooting pain runs through my shoulder, deep into my bones. Voices hum gray and low around me, but they have no bodies, no heads. I cannot move. I cannot speak. I cannot see. Well, not anything that's actually around me --just my Crayon Brain going at it again.

But I can hear.

"What a waste." A voice with a lilting British accent. The color of a raging, dark hurricane. *Xintra.* Fear rattles inside my chest, a fish flopping on the shore. "I should have just killed her at the beginning."

The sickening sound of her robe flutters around my head —tiny gray and burgundy dots. "Her dead mum had a similar streak. I should have just sacrificed her, too."

Sacrificed?

Low humming and chanting surrounds me, showing up as rust-brown and black sparks in my vision as the sound grows louder, faster. Xintra chants unintelligible words over the noise, and the black chant becomes hypnotic.

The hurricane of Xintra's voice emerges in treacherous black and blue waves, flooding my Color Crayon Brain. "This, here, should serve as an example of what happens when dormant souls rise up." Xintra's powerful voice makes me feel ill, helpless, panicked. My heart pounds and my skin crawls, but I can't move. "All of the rebirthed shall adhere to my will and force any kind of rogue spirits into submission. And so, this Oshun, this Ember, she will be sacrificed."

No! I feel so hot, as if I'm sitting by a fireplace in the heat of the summer. I smell smoke. Wood. Like a campfire. The smell of burning hair.

The sound of the chanting grows quieter as the voices move away. I imagine hooded people vanishing like ghosts. Where do they go?

Zoe's silky voice moves closer, whispers near me, "That's a shame. She had so much potential."

Potential. Mom's painting flashes in my mind—sage greens and blood reds and midnight blues. Circles. Wispy lines. Splatters. Looping. Whimsical and flowing. The ankh cross. Life. Mom's almond eyes shine, the same brown as freshly polished rosewood. They're gentle. Forgiving. Her voice again echoes in my head: "Our Ember. So beautiful. So much potential."

A chain of flickering images appears in my mind. Tre's face in the rain. His crinkled smile and ridiculous hair. His kiss. Oh my God, his kiss. My parents cheering at a choir performance. My brother's high five. Maddie yelling at me from down the school hallway. The memories come together like a jigsaw puzzle. Kissing Tre on the rooftop at that weird party. A guy talking to me in a tattoo shop. Begging Jared on the phone to save me before darkness doused my consciousness. Running from the car, the man with the mashed potato face behind the wheel, in an alleyway. Me, tumbling through the air.

I lost myself and found myself once before. My parents used to call me the determined one in the Trouvé family, and I am not ready to die. I am young. I have so much to do.

My frustration folds into anger. No one is taking my life from me again. I screwed up once, and I'm not giving in again. I scream inside, and light washes away the black. My eyelids flutter open. Feeling as if I'm swimming in sticky, thick glue, I sit up from a lying position on what looks to be a long stone table. In a dark room where water drips from the ceiling, candles flicker in sconces; the wet earth plugs my nose.

I'm in Trinity, and Zoe stands at the foot of the table.

I sit up straighter, and suddenly, it all makes sense. Something is burning. Me. *I* am burning. Flames lick at me from a small fire lit beneath the stone table. I'm being cooked alive. Set on fire. Like a pig on a platter. The orange and yellow flames crackle as if they're teasing me, touching and releasing with each breath. Instinctively, I scream and jump off the table. The flames burn my ankles, delivering scorching pain to my skin. I reach down and cover them with my hand, crying out.

"You... you're awake!" Zoe's face mirrors my own shock. She looks more human than I've ever before seen her. Scanning the dark room, I see we're alone.

"I'm not ready to die."

Dizzy, I stumble, backing up slowly away from her. I can still feel the heat of the fire. My heart pounds so loud in my chest, perhaps it will snap through my ribs and my skin. Perhaps Zoe will push me back into the fire, tackle me, strike me with some psychic power.

Breathing heavily, I pause, waiting, considering my next move. My heart thumps even louder, a kettle drum in my ears. Zoe could attack me anytime. Or maybe Xintra. But her expression doesn't change. It's curiosity. She remains still and only watches me.

My fingers graze the crystal necklace still around my throat, and I remember how I lost the crystals last time I was in Trinity. Hope and euphoria ignite inside me, and I know where I need to go, what I need to do. I race through the dim room, past the flames and smoke and the table where I was to be cooked alive, away from Zoe.

She stands completely still. A statue. Of course, she is no dummy. She knows my odds are slim. Yet still, I sprint through the maze of dark hallways, ready for anything to grab me from behind. When I come to the familiar Y in the hallway, my breath catches in my lungs. Thoughts shuffle in my mind as I reach for the memory of which direction to go in. It was so long ago when I was in Trinity. A lifetime ago. Left. I think it was left. No, I *know* it was left.

I glance over my shoulder and see no one pursuing me, hear no shouts, only the creepy humming sound dancing and twirling through the shadows behind me. I get to the stairwell, and I climb on gummy worm legs in these high-heeled shoes. I stretch to land two steps at a time in the short miniskirt. Outward, my body is still thick and awkward, and pain jabs my shoulder, my head, my hip, and my neck from being struck by the car. But on the inside, I'm frantic and euphoric. *I'm back and maybe, just maybe, I'll get out alive.*

Outside the house, thunder rolls and heavy clouds flood the night sky, each one more ominous than the next. I maneuver through trees and bushes, over rocks and around stumps, while thunder snarls and chases me, hurtling cracking bursts of lightning from the sky. I duck my head, as if that position is somehow going to keep me from being struck by, like, a billion volts of electricity.

I must get to the canyon wall. I stop and yank off my ridiculous heels, and the jerking movement delivers biting pain to my bruised left side. I chuck the shoes into the bushes, worried for a second that was an impulsive, stupid move. But I think I can run way faster in bare feet than heels. Grimacing from the sharp pain of the rocks and sticks, I run on the balls of my feet and try to remember Mom's notebook. My brain still feels so fuzzy after all those months of being lost, underwater in Oshun's consciousness.

My mind flips through the pages of my memory. The Egyptian symbols, the list of crystals.

I dart across the open meadow and run past the lake. Memories of Tre and Lilly and Pete flash through my head. They're gone. They're all gone.

The cliffs loom in the distance and I think how it all would have been different if I'd caught up to Tre in Los Angeles and shut Damien down. But now I'm trapped in Trinity again, and more people will die at his hands. A sob rises up from my throat, but instinctively, I push it down, determined to focus on actually making it out of here alive.

Stay focused, Ember.

I make my way through bushes, ducking under trees to get down to the meadow. I hear a familiar sound. The *aak-aak* pounding in bright, reflective-orange starbursts. *The Alarm Clock Bird.*

The sound slices into my optimism and I want to find the bird and kick and beat it to death. I turn around, searching for the sound through rain that comes down in sheets like gray cellophane. Then I see her, standing at the top of the hill in clear view: Xintra. That awful little shrike bird sits on her shoulder, glaring at me with dark, beady eyes. Xintra wears a cool smile on her face. She found me. Fear zaps me and sucks my breath. Crap.

47

MADDIE

Jared moves too slow, and the fog makes it hard to tell which direction to go. Even the forest feels denser, like the trees multiplied since we came in here half an hour ago. We didn't get too far beyond the barbed-wire fence, so we should be able to just dart right out of it. I don't know if it's real or if it's my imagination, but I think I can hear something like a breathing sound. No wonder people say never to come to Trinity Forest.

Suddenly, I'm running, scared and pissed at Jared for bringing me here, for taking me on his crazy train to a creepy forest for no legit reason. Goosebumps cover my arms and neck as Jared and I race through the forest, ducking under trees, crunching branches.

"Mads, I think the exit is this way," he says, panting and pointing to the right. "The fog opens up over there."

But it feels all wrong to me. In fact, something in my bones tells me that is absolutely *not* the way home. "No," I say nodding in the opposite direction. "It's this way." I turn and duck underneath a tree branch.

"Maddie, I feel it. We really need to go the other way,"

Jared says. He hasn't moved. "The fog forms a tunnel, opening up."

I turn around to face him, panting, and put my hands on my hips. "Listen, I have gone on your wild-goose chase for several days now. I blew my grocery money on it. I ditched classes for it. I went along. So far, *your* gut has gotten us nowhere good. I say we go *this* way. It's time to listen to *my* gut."

With that, I turn and run, praying he follows.

Without another word, he does. And thank God, because within a few minutes, we get to the barbed-wire fence, and I'm panting, a side stitch eating at my left rib. Suddenly, I feel ridiculous that we ran out of there like two scared little kids, but relief comes just the same. I know it's illogical—it's just a forest—but the ominous feeling in that place was real. Going there was a crazy whim, and in fact, this whole trip has been that way. Just one giant splash of crazy.

Breathless, we walk to the car, neither of us talking about how disturbing that was, how wicked that felt, or how panicked we both became. And we don't talk about how I probably screwed everything up by finally verbally shaking Jared for believing Oshun was really Ember.

Inside the car, the radio plays Oshun's annoying pop song, "Follow Me." My hand flies to the dial, and I change it immediately to a reggae song, a tune that makes me feel like I should be on vacation with a fruity drink in my hand. The air is hot and stuffy, and the mint air freshener dangling from the rearview mirror only makes it worse. I roll down the window and the fresh mountain breeze blows in my face as we rattle down the dirt road.

In the silence, a gulf opens up between us. Jared gazes out the passenger window for a long time.

"I'm quitting my job at Safeway," he says suddenly.

"Really? Are you going back to school?" I can't help but

feel a feather of hope—maybe now he'll move on, get his life back. "I have friends you can live with if you end up in Fort Collins."

"I'm going to Hawaii."

"Okay..." I say.

"Oshun gave me a voucher for a free flight to Hawaii that night at dinner."

"Really? Was she, like, hitting on you?"

"No," he says, disgusted. "She's my *sister*."

The word makes me clench my jaw. He *still* thinks Oshun was his sister! "Why did she give you a ticket?"

"She said it was for special fans."

"You weren't a fan." I turn left onto Tennessee Pass and glance at him with a quick smile.

He smiles and gazes out the window.

"So, she just gave you one plane voucher?"

"Yeah, maybe you would have gotten the prize, too, if you'd stuck around at dinner." He quashes a small smile but doesn't look at me.

"She pissed me off."

He pulls a coin out of the pocket of his shorts and twirls it between his fingers. "I also found this coin just a minute after she handed me the ticket. It says the name of a Hawaiian volcano on it."

I glance over at it while I drive down the twisting highway. For unknown reasons, I want to take that coin and throw it out the window.

"Weird."

"I think it's a sign. You know, telling me that I'm supposed to go," he says. "Especially since she died and all."

"You sound like your mom," I say, and immediately regret it. His mom always saw signs in everything, and everyone told her she was crazy because of it. I liked her, but still, she was weird.

He opens his mouth but doesn't say anything. He stares straight ahead as we wind up the twisting mountain pass.

A little later, we pull up in front of his grandma's house, which sits high on a little hill and has a tiny lawn wrapped by a chain-link fence. The car engine hums, and Jared twirls the silver coin between his fingers.

"Want some company? I could use some Hawaii." I nudge him with my elbow.

"Naw," he says. There's a hollow sound to his voice.

I put the car in park, reach out and touch his hand, lean in closer across the console. "Hey," I whisper.

He looks into my eyes, and the electrical current between us is still there. I lean in, tilting my head and brushing my nose across his stubbled cheek. He smells like cedar and menthol, and with one hand, I touch the mess of hair at the nape of his neck.

I kiss him softly. The feel of his lips stirs me again, but Jared isn't really there with me. He's sad; I can feel it in the way his body stiffens and his lips are slow to respond. After a few seconds, I pull back and gaze into his hazel eyes and point my finger at him. "You can't shut me out," I say.

But he will. I know this. Classic Trouvé style.

There's a long, awkward pause and we both take in a long inhale to say good-bye. I don't want him to get out of the car.

"Text me when you get home, Mads. And yeah, thanks for going with me on this whole road trip."

"Anytime." He doesn't make eye contact. Instead, he climbs out of the car, slams the door shut.

It's in that sound alone, the heavy thud of the door shutting, that I know he's going to slip away like sand through my fingers.

I pull away, and the tears roll silently down my cheeks.

48

EMBER

An explosion shakes the ground, and the sky lights up for half a second. I fold my body inward and throw my hands over my head before peeking through my wet hair.

Flames roar from a pine tree less than fifty yards away. I turn and run up the hill, away from Xintra, pulling on branches to hold myself steady, zigzagging, ignoring the pain in my bare feet. I'm breathless as I make my way through the uneven terrain, the rain coming down in sheets now and the thunder booming in all corners of the canyon. I glance over my shoulder, but Xintra doesn't chase me from her perch.

Another boom, and then a sizzling crack. Lightning strikes another tree just in front of my path, igniting an orange blaze of fire. That has got to be Xintra. She has some strange, witchlike power. I remember from Mom's notebook: sorcerers controlled the weather and storms.

Shoving down the fear, I move ahead, tromping through the thick, wet brush and pine trees until eventually, I reach the familiar sight of the limestone cliff. I pant, grimacing from the stabbing pain eating into my feet, and rest my hands on the yellow-brown rock wall.

The cliff looms above like I remembered, and when I crane my head up to see it, I have to blink away the large raindrops that patter against my face. The storm has produced deep puddles and muddy streams that flood down an incline along the base of the wall.

I touch my necklace and recall the pages of Mom's notebook. I was supposed to find the ankh cross; that was circled, I know that. I scan the wall, looking for the cross with the looping top.

My heart pounds in my head as I stomp through the mud, squinting in the rain, searching for the ankh cross, for *anything* that might help me escape. Icy water rushes over my feet, unleashing biting pain, which after a minute, diminishes into numbness. I slide down the muddy slope along the base of the cliff, and notice the rainwater appears to be draining behind a salmon-colored boulder the size of a duffel bag.

A deep rumbling roars above the rainstorm, showing up as dark moss-brown spots in my vision, and the color and sound grows with intensity—but it's not thunder. Above, three large boulders break off the cragged cliff wall and barrel down toward me. A pang of fear moves through my spine to my fingertips.

I freeze for an instant before crying out and diving into the tall, wet grass. I whimper, throw my hands over my head, and bury my face into the ground. The rocks crack when they land, like bones snapped in half, missing me by just a few yards.

Terror seizes me, making my fingers tremble and my throat clamp shut. From the grass, I gaze back up the wall to the duffel bag boulder and notice something just above it. It's faint, but it looks like another small engraving in the rock.

"Yes!" I whisper, before scrambling up the muddy slope. There's another crash of thunder and lightning. A lodgepole pine tree just a hundred yards or so away roars with flames.

Blocking out the chaos, I squint in the rain until I can just make out a carving of a face. It's a pharaoh's head atop the body of a lion, carved into the rock. A sphinx. I squat down and run my fingers over the picture. I remember Mom's notebook. "The sphinx guarded secrets," I whisper to myself.

But what? What is it guarding? I slap my hand on the rock wall, frustration and panic wracking my body. "I don't get it!"

An invisible clock ticks loudly in my head, a reminder that my death is imminent unless I figure this out. I let intuition take control. Something tells me I need to move this rock. Adrenaline surges and I squat down, place my hands on the rock, and grunt, pushing and heaving it forward. Once. Twice. Three times. The boulder slowly moves, rolling, shifting, scraping along the cliff wall.

My heart practically leaps out of my chest. Hiding behind the boulder is another carving. There, in perfect indentations, is the ankh cross!

"Life!" I squeal.

Above the folds of the cross, about the size of my hand, is a tiny hole or indent in the wall. It's just the right size for a crystal. Mom's notebook had a page with several symbols. Above each one, there was a different colored dot. Was this one a red-brown color? Clear? I quickly take off the necklace and thumb through the stones, checking for the size that might fit.

I remember—the colored circle above the cross was light red. Mom scribbled the word *agate* next to it. My fingers stop on a milky amber stone. "Agate," I whisper. "Known for good luck."

Without hesitation, I place the stone into the hole above the carving of the ankh. It fits perfectly. The rain is blowing sideways now, the wind howling, and I grin and step back, waiting for *something* to happen.

The ground violently shakes, and something cracks and

moans. My Crayon Brain sees lime-green blobs, followed by the bright white and yellow lights of a deafening crash. My heart drops into my stomach.

Thirty yards away, two trees break in half and tumble to the dirt. I touch the cliff wall, and it vibrates like a washing machine. The ground buckles and rolls, and I'm thrown to the ground. Rocks dig into my bruises.

I look up, and another boulder now rumbles and flies off the top of the cliff. Before I can even process what's happening, I throw myself down the hill again. Pain shoots through my head and neck—and my back where my skin is still tender from the tattoo. The rock comes crashing down, rolling past me, a steam engine barreling just feet away. My heart pounds loud in my head and my fingers tingle. The rock nearly bashed me. I pant. Holy crap.

With fingers buzzing from the adrenaline, I scramble up from the ground again and move back to the location of the ankh cross carving. A crack now runs from it and down the limestone rock, creating a yawning hole at the base by the ground. It looks like the opening to a cave, but it's no bigger than a doggy door. The agate crystal must have triggered the cliff wall to crack open.

Rain pounds the ground, and water gushes past me, rushing into the opening of the cave. I stick my head inside, trying to see where the water is headed. Maybe it's flowing to a river or a lake outside this place. Maybe it's filling up one big hole at the bottom of the cave.

I bump a few rocks loose with my hand, and they thump, splash, and echo far below. Xintra's bitter voice rises in the distance, her words indistinguishable, and I swivel my head to follow the sound. She is not going to relent.

I stare at the hole, knowing that my life rests upon this decision: whether I stay here and confront Xintra, or hide inside this cave. I don't know where it goes; it could be an animal's den or a hole to nowhere. But the storm is raging out of control, the lightning is scaring the crap out of me, and Xintra will torture or kill me when she catches up to me. Just the memory of seeing her smiling on the top of the hill makes my stomach lurch.

I've got to take a chance.

I climb inside the hole.

On campus, life seems relatively normal. People with back-packs zip past me on bikes. A couple of girls lie on their backs on the grass, eyes closed, shorts rolled up to their hips, shirts exposing their stomachs, soaking in the sunshine. A guy dangles from a dorm window, yelling to a friend over the beat of rap music. "Hey, get some limes, too!"

Inside, the dorm reeks of incense, and a cluster of girls crowd the hallway. I squeeze around two of them in the midst of a heated argument near the bathroom door. "I don't care what she says. She's lying," one says.

I move quickly past their bickering, step over someone's dirty sock lying in the middle of the hall, and move past a door with a whiteboard covered in scrawled cusswords and a fat, hand-drawn heart. These are the days when I wish I hadn't signed up to be an RA. I need a quiet apartment—a place where real upper classmen go.

When I get to the door to my room, I breathe a sigh of relief. Normalcy. I unlock it, swing the door open, and instantly, I'm confused.

It's empty. Or at least the half where Emily lives is. It's

totally cleaned out. The only thing left is the built-in desk and bookshelf—also empty—and the bed. No sheets. No fluffy, furry neon-green pillows. No posters. No peach body spray smell. Nothing.

I dash out to the hallway and call to a lanky guy with a baseball cap passing by. "Hey, do you know what happened to Emily?"

"Emily?" he asks, turning around and continuing to walk backwards, away from me. "She that chick with the hair down to her butt? The one that—"

I nod. "Yeah, my roommate. Where'd she go?"

"Ah, man," he says, slowing down and shaking his head. "You didn't hear? She's dead."

My heart lurches to my throat. "Seriously. Did she drop out of school?"

He touches his palms together and then touches his fingers to his large hook nose before pointing them at me. "Sorry."

"But... how?" I feel dizzy.

"Virus. They have a free vaccination in the lobby at two o'clock. Hey, I'm late. I've got to go." He turns around and practically runs down the hall.

Dead? The virus? I didn't even know it was raging here. Emily? My snoring, rude, slovenly Emily—dead. I back up into my room, sit down on my bed, and put my face in my hands. And bit by bit, I fall apart.

My stomach twists at the idea that Emily is no longer breathing. I recall the way she'd pucker her lips after putting on lip gloss, applying and reapplying it for what seemed like hours on Friday nights. The way she seemed to just breeze through classes as if they were her lowest priority. I never saw her study, but she always aced her exams. Her focus here at school was boys. Different boy every week, it seemed. Someone who slept next to me for several months is no longer breathing. She no longer has a life, is no longer moving through the world.

I feel light-headed. Every emotion and turn of events is piling onto me now, tumbling in my mind. First, losing Ember. I remember her glowering look in the hospital before she disappeared. Then giving mouth-to-mouth to the guy in the LA hotel lobby. Kissing Jared, feeling that crazy connection. Feeling that strange sadness when we read that Oshun died. Jared wanting to run off with some coin in his pocket and being so distant when I dropped him off. Now Emily? Everything I touch crumbles beneath my fingers.

A few minutes later, a knock on the door makes me snap my eyes open. I wipe my face with the back of my hand, sniff away the snot dripping off my nose, and open the door.

Mom? I don't know why she's here, but without a word, I crumple into her arms and she holds me up by the elbows. I tremble and sob, and let everything pour out of me. "Everyone is dying, everyone is dying," I say over and over, my voice gurgling.

She whispers shushing noises into my hair, and brushes it down with her hand. She's always been a hoverer, but right now, that's exactly what I need. I've never felt so absolutely alone and now, here she is. Like magic.

I sink into the softness of her silky blouse, the fullness of her body. She always hated her body's shape, but I loved it, especially as a little kid. She was always a big, comforting pillow.

"Baby girl," she says.

I look up at her, blinking away the tears that now slow to a drip. "Why are you here, Ma?"

"The school called me, looking for you to talk about Emily. I called you but couldn't reach you. So I called Ember's grandma, and she said you were on your way back here. I got worried."

I feel suddenly guilty for avoiding her calls.

"Sorry." I go back and sit cross-legged on my bed. I turn away from Emily's blank wall, the empty bed, the reminder of death. Of people who disappear. "You drove all the way up here?"

"I worry," she says with a shrug and a grimace. "It's what I do."

"Where's Dad?"

"He had to work. But he sends his love." She pauses. "So where have you been, sweetie?" I feel her gaze on me. Here it is: the Mom Inquisition.

"With Jared. We were trying to find Ember."

She nods, saying without words, *Of course you were. Like always.* "Did you find her?"

She knows the answer. "No." I consider telling Jared's wild Oshun theory. But I feel like Emily's death has sucked all the energy from my body and I can't talk about anything else that makes my chest tight. "I feel like I lost Jared, though. He's just really shutting me out."

She frowns with one side of her mouth.

"I think I love him," I say, tracing my fingertips.

"Of course you do." Mom says tilting her head.

I wince. "You *know* that?"

"Of course. You've probably always loved him, Maddie. Both those Trouvé kids. Don't worry about Jared. He'll bounce back. That boy is made of rubber." She pauses and squeezes my shoulder. "There's a sign for free vaccines downstairs. Your dad and I got one at the clinic at home. Are you going to get one?"

I look at my closet door. I think that's where I put the medical mask she sent me. I should wear it. Or did I throw it out? I can't remember. I should have given it to Emily.

I shrug. This whole room is probably one giant petri dish for germs. Death germs. But the vaccines just *feels* wrong. I feel like I'd rather just hide out in some cabin if a pandemic took hold than stick a needle filled with who-knows-what in my arm.

"Well, you know what I think..." she says.

I roll my eyes and sigh. "Yeah, Ma, whatever." She's going to lecture me.

"I think we need some ice cream."

Surprised, I laugh through my snot and tears. Ice cream is Mom's tradition. Whenever some guy broke up with me, the answer was ice cream. When I broke my arm jumping off the couch in fourth grade, the answer was a cast and chocolate ice cream. That's probably why Mom's built like a pillow—trying to solve all my drama with ice cream.

"Sure," I say, wiping my tears and standing up. "Yeah, that sounds good."

We walk down the hallway side by side. I informed her in eighth grade that putting her arm around me in public would permanently scar me socially. She still adheres to that advice, walking without touching me, our footsteps in sync, stepping over pizza boxes and the extended legs of two guys listening to iPhones on the floor. This time, I put my arm around *her*.

50

EMBER

I squeeze through the cave's tiny opening, and the cool, musty air tickles my skin. It's so confined in here, I feel like I'm crawling through a dark water culvert. In the distance, branches break. Red triangles in my Crayon Brain—that must be the sound of Xintra coming after me. She isn't going to let me out alive, a reality that pokes my nerves like a hot iron.

Quickly, I crawl deeper into the hole, whispering to myself under my breath. "This has to be the way out. It has to be."

Lodima, that strange woman I met outside the forest, tucked that ankh cross necklace into my backpack before I first came into Trinity Forest. That symbol again showed up in Mom's notebook. The carving of the cross and the agate opened this hole. This has to be an exit. I have to trust this.

I have no idea where I'm headed. All I know is I'm moving away from Xintra. I move faster, on hands and knees over the wet rock floor, which is covered in moss so slick it feels like oil. My breath is loud despite the thunderous beat of the rain outside that floods into the cave in a steady stream over my hands and feet. This tunnel slants downward, like a water slide, and I clench the rock floor with my fingernails to keep from losing control.

My breath becomes ragged, and I try not to whimper. Thunder crashes again outside the cave, followed by the sound of deep, cracking thuds at the entrance. The sound shows up in my vision as dark mud colors twisting and turning. I look over my shoulder and watch an avalanche of rocks tumbling to the ground one by one, piling up and around my hole, my only exit. Only small patches of moonlight seep through the top edges of the cave entrance. The immediate and sudden darkness takes my breath away. It's like the world is closing in on me.

For a few seconds, I just stare at the blockade, panicked; my options are getting more limited by the second. I slide some of my wet hair out of my eyes with a shaky hand and begin to hyperventilate. No. I won't do this. I won't fall apart. I take a deep breath, filling up my lungs with air and my mind with confidence, expanding my rib cage, slowing my heart rate. I will get through this. It will be fine.

It seems to calm me, and I move forward again, deeper into the dark tunnel. But my hand slips, and I slide unsteadily forward onto my stomach. I let out a sharp scream. The tunnel is too steep and slippery and my weight pitches forward. I'm nothing but a lost stone, careening alone, tumbling down the inky tunnel. I scream again, knowing that this time, I may actually die.

I spin side to back for a long while, until suddenly I'm launching into the air. I land with a splash into a pool of water that is so cold it sucks the breath from my lungs. The shock seizes my muscles, and water shoots up my nose.

Coughing, I splash in the water and gasp for a breath of air, completely disoriented. When my eyes adjust to the darkness, panic again chokes me: I'm floating in a pool of water inside a cave that's about the size of a two-car garage. There is no ledge to the pool, nowhere farther to go in the room. It's just rock walls, water, and the steep tunnel from which I fell. It looks like a laundry chute.

I shriek and bang my fist on the water. "Shit! Shit! Shit!" The ankh cross should have been the clue to get out. But this is not out. The tunnel leading back up is impossible to climb. I feel so betrayed—by Lodima, by Mom, by everything.

The water slaps my collarbone, and the top of my head touches the roof of the cave. The only sound is my panicked breathing and the steady splashing of rainwater coming down the tunnel and into the pool.

I let out a deep exhale again. "No, you can't panic, Ember," I say. "I will not be afraid. I've come too far." I've made some mistakes—big ones—but I'm not going to let fear and this stupid cave get the best of me. There has to be another clue. Another way out. Xintra got in and out of here. I can, too. "Screw this cave," I say aloud. "I'm going home."

I shiver and my hands grow numb from the cold. I claw at the edges of the slick, jagged limestone wall. Even if I can climb back up, the exit is blocked by boulders. A dead end. And if I were able to get those rocks out of the way, Xintra would be waiting for me. But if I stay here I will drown.

I slide my hips up onto the ledge and begin slithering up into the gushing flow of water. It's too much, the slope too steep and slippery. I lose my grip eventually and skitter back down, splashing into the pool. I wipe the water from my eyes and growl. This is just like when I tried to climb the cliff wall here so long ago. It's total déjà vu.

This time, the water will rise, eating up the oxygen in the cave, drowning me. The thought makes me pant and a surge of adrenaline pumps through my veins.

I try again, pulling up my hips, clawing the slippery rock with my fingertips. I get up a little farther, but the tunnel is so steep that I can't even get into a crouch or a crawling position. My feet search for traction, but it's as if I'm on a treadmill—a treadmill that's wet, covered in oil, and tilted upside down. The water gushes over my hands, and they're so cold, I can't even feel them.

The next instant, my fingers slip, tearing my thumbnail, and my stomach slams against the rock. I slide back into the water.

I continue this for a long time, trying over and over. Determination and fear driving me. But then, I grow silent. It's too steep. It's not going to work. Tears pool in my eyes. My teeth chatter.

The water is lapping my chin now. I had my chance earlier with Tre, but now, I will die alone. In this cold pool of water. In this twisted vortex. I. Will. Die.

I dully gaze ahead, waiting. My teeth stop chattering—a bad sign for hypothermia. I adjust my grip on the ledge... and wait, what was that? I walk my fingers backwards, and they dip into some indents.

I pivot around and squint at the wall. Maybe it's just wishful thinking, but it looks like another small stone carving the size of my hand. Another carving. I lean in close. It *is* a carving.

I suck in an excited breath. "Yes! Yes!"

This one depicts a star, and it almost looks like a stick drawing of a person without the head. I trace my fingers along its shape. A seba, an Egyptian star that's related to gates and doorways. I remember it exactly from Mom's notebook, reading it so close to Tre's body beneath the overhang in the pouring rain. *Tre.* Blood pulses again in my body as the motor of my brain turns on. I have to get out for Tre.

I ran away from him, gave him up, and actually opened my eyes from this nightmare. But that can't be how this ends. I *will* get out for Tre, now some guy named Damien, doing

Xintra's will. I have to find him, wake him up from his own nightmare, too.

I gaze at the seba. If I remember correctly, when it has a circle around it, it becomes the duat, a symbol of the place of the dead. A chill runs down my spine.

"No, Ember," I whisper to myself. This one has no circle. It's a doorway. And there's a hole above it. A hole for another crystal. I need to try another crystal!

Quickly, I take the necklace from where I tucked it into my bikini top next to my breast, careful not to drop it in the water, and I squint in the dark to find one that might fit in the hole. I pull a clear one off the thin wire, put it up to the hole, but it's too big, just by a mere millimeter. I want to shove it in, force it. But I resist the urge.

I try two others, and they're all either slightly too big or the wrong shape entirely. "Come on!" I whisper, frustration whipping through me.

I pull on a light purple one, the size of a dime. Amethyst. Mom's book said it inspires bravery, preserves soldiers from battle wounds, aids the warrior to victory. "Sounds fitting," I whisper, grateful that I can so clearly recall pages I've seen. Mom used to tell me I had a photographic memory, though scientists say there's no such thing.

I slide the crystal off the necklace's thin wire and awkwardly place it into the hole above the star. I exhale a huge breath as it slips into place, lock and key. I grin, relief flowing through me, as I wait for something to happen.

A loud scraping of rock reverberates through the cave, and a rush of satisfaction fills me. But it lasts only for a fraction of a second, because the water begins swirling fast, clockwise around the pool.

The water threatens to sweep me into some sort of spinning vortex. The current is strong, like a riptide, and I screech, pant, grunt, and cling to the rock wall tightly, my fingers digging into any crevasse and ledge on the slippery rock. Water splashes in my face and rushes up my nose, and I prop my feet up high on the cave wall, clinging to it like a bug onto the windshield of a moving car.

I will not die this way. Not now. I won't. I will not be pulled under again. I am stronger than this torrent of water. I scream, releasing my fury and frustration, though the sound of my voice is barely audible over the roar of the water's current. A rush of power courses through me, strength I didn't even know I had inside. I won't be taken under.

After a couple more rotations, the spinning water slows, the tug of the current diminishes. I exhale when it's clear the water is lowering, draining like a bathtub. My head no longer touches the ceiling. Instead, it's a good five feet below it.

I breathe heavily, clinging to the wall until the water drains enough that I can actually stand on the floor of the cave. I look up. The ceiling must extend at least twelve feet high. Meanwhile the water circles at my knees, still tugging hard. I brace myself on the wall. "Yes!" I whisper, giddy joy unfurling from my chest.

When the water gets to my ankles, I let go of the wall and laugh. I jump up and down and scream, but then slap my hand over my mouth to mute my excitement. My predator waits for me at the top of the tunnel.

"Oh my God," I whisper. "What the hell?"

The water is draining into a small hole once again, with an opening the size of an air vent. It sits just below where I was floating, directly beneath the seba carving I found.

The idea of another dark hole is alternately demoralizing and hopeful. The crystals are doing *something*, but I don't know how many layers of holes and water and near-death experiences I can take. Part of me worries that this is going to be another twisted reality, like the days I climbed those cliffs in Trinity, hiked forever, only to be put back in the same starting place. What if I am truly locked in some sort of weird time dimension that only Xintra controls?

"It's got to be a way out," I whisper. If I say it, it will be true. My teeth chatter uncontrollably. I cross my hands across my wet, freezing skin, exposed from the miniskirt and skimpy bra top I'm wearing.

The water drains to the edges of my feet, and hesitantly, I bring my right foot down into the hole's opening. Pushing my toe a little farther inside, I can tell there's a sharp drop-off, a ledge, and the water trickles over it like a waterfall. I listen carefully, wondering if I'll be able to hear how far down the hole goes, or where it ends. But I can't tell, and I see nothing but darkness.

Just then, the sound of rocks scraping echoes above me, and I freeze, listening, glancing around the empty cave. Crap. I crane my neck to peer up the tunnel some twelve feet above my head. Then another scraping sound booms a faded black color, and a sliver of moonlight pierces through the darkness. Water still trickles into my cave—a deep turquoise—and splashes at my feet. More scraping, followed by more moonlight.

Xintra is moving the rocks. She's coming in here. As I bite my lip, my thoughts swirl as if they're in a blender on high. The hole is dark and ominous. I almost killed myself crawling through that tunnel up there, and then nearly drowned. I don't know if this is a hole in which I will die slowly from broken bones and starvation. Stuck. If it will throw me into an entirely different world—one much worse than this one—or if it will be yet another continuous loop you see only in Trinity.

But maybe I can get home.

I have to at least try.

I take a deep breath and climb into the hole, sliding slowly off the ledge. My feet slip on the wet rocks, my hands lose their grip on the wall. I hold my breath and disappear into darkness.

The world is gone and I'm falling. My heart lurches to my stomach. I'm on a blacked-out roller coaster ride, tumbling through miles of nothingness, another galaxy, another world. The water echoes, trickling like a crisp mountain stream, giving way to ribbons of iridescent color in my mind's eye. The spray of cool water hits me now and then, and it bounces around me as my body flies weightlessly through space.

51

MADDIE

The ice cream shop smells like a waffle cone factory and looks like I stepped into a kid's pastel coloring book. Large smiling teddy bears with big crazy eyes loom over us as we fill our cups with every kind of topping imaginable. Fruity Pebbles. Sprinkles. Maple syrup and marshmallows. Snickers bars.

"So how well did you know Emily?" Mom asks, stirring her ice cream just like me.

I take a bigger than normal bite of my concoction, the flavors of marshmallow and chocolate and fruit crunch swirling in my mouth. The ice cream isn't slowing the freak-out that's racing beneath my skin.

My roommate is dead. The person who slept next to me, who shared a bathroom with me—she was alive one day, and then dead the next. It's hard for the brain to comprehend. My forehead feels tight and I feel like I want to cry again.

I shrug. She moved in second semester, even though I was promised that as a junior resident assistant supervising all the freshmen, I'd have a room to myself. But they screwed up at residential housing, and she was homeless, and I was a sucker. Her bed went where my futon couch used to be.

"She left dirty tissues on the floor," I admit. "She talked in her sleep about ham and cupcakes. She talked *really* loud on the phone to her best friend." I don't mention that she would hook up with random boys in her bed while I slept right next to her. As the so-called boss of the dorm, I should have clamped down. And finally, one night, I did kick the last guy out.

"So you never even got to know her?" Mom frowns. "Where was she from? What was she majoring in?"

"Math. Tulsa, Oklahoma," I say. "I can't believe she's dead. It makes me so sad. I should have gotten to know her, been friendlier."

Not to mention, selfishly, that could have been *me*. I could have gotten the virus. If I had stayed here instead of darting off to Los Angeles, maybe I would have. Maybe I'd be dead. My head feels numb, and my eyes zone out, gazing at the crisscross pattern on the painted cartoon ice cream cone on the wall above Mom's shoulder.

She turns around to follow my gaze and changes the subject. "Okay, so how about instead you tell me about your little trip? You didn't answer your phone."

"Sorry," I say, putting a big mouthful of ice cream in my mouth. It's so cold that I have to bounce it around on my tongue. I don't want to talk about my trip. Not about the death of the dude at the hotel. Not about Oshun. Not about the kiss with Jared, or the fact that he's back to shutting me out. "It was okay."

"Just okay?"

"Yeah. We went to a concert?"

I shrug and look at my bowl of ice cream.

"Tell me more about Jared. Did something happen?"

"He's fine."

"Okay." She sighs, sitting back in the booth. She places her spoon on the table. "Do you want to pack up your stuff and move to a new dorm?"

"What?" I hadn't even considered what I would do now that my roommate dropped dead. But now that she mentions it, I suppose sleeping there tonight isn't so appealing.

"Or... your dad and I were thinking maybe you should come home. Take a semester off." She looks at the table while she tells me. This is why she came. She's afraid.

"No," I say automatically. I turn away and study the hand-painted bear on the wall, the ways its eyes are shaped more like footballs than golf balls. That's why it feels like he's glaring at you, watching you stuff yourself full of brown and blue fat.

"You know that thirty-five percent of Leadville is dead. The virus is hitting New York and Chicago. Half of Florida's schools are shut down. This is serious, honey. And now it's at your school?"

"I'm going to Hawaii," I say inexplicably.

"What?"

"Yeah, Jared has a free ticket and I'm going with him."

"You think viruses can't get to the islands?"

"At least it's warm there. Pretty."

"That's foolish." She frowns and stares at me; it's a piercing look that, years ago, would have made me bend to her will and confess all my sins. The Mom Vulcan Death Grip. Not anymore.

I am not going back to the dorm after this. I'll go to Lia's place. I won't be afraid.

I look at the bear painted on the wall. "Why do you think they made his eyes look like footballs?"

Later, Mom stops her car in front of my dorm, and I unbuckle my seat belt. A line of people snake around the building. Most of them have their heads down, looking at their phones, while a few sit on the ground, leaning against the brick building, soaking in the sun.

"Hey, looks like the vaccinations are still available, sweetie." Mom ducks her head to point out my window.

"Yeah," I say, grabbing my purse from the floor. "Do you have my bedroom at home all wrapped in bubble wrap and ready for me?"

Mom sighs. "I know you want to pretend things aren't serious. But they are."

I shake my head and climb out of the car. Through the open door, I lean in. "Ma, I love you. Thanks for the ice cream."

"Did it help?"

"Yeah," I say, nodding. I walk toward the three-story building that I call home, and as soon as I'm sure she has driven off, I dart over to my car, get in the driver's seat, and call Jared.

"Hey," he answers. He sounds like he has a runny nose. "What's up?"

"My roommate died of that virus."

"Are you serious? Mads... I just... you're never going to believe this. Dax is dead, too."

"What? Are you sure?" *Too much death* is the first thing I can think in response. It's all just too much. Too awful. Too sad. *It's just too freaking sad.* The edges of my vision blur in my periphery.

"I just read a big story about it. The virus. He got the virus." He pauses, and I can tell he's pushing down emotion. I think of Dax, how healthy he seemed when we ate dinner with him. He was at the top of his game.

"How can that be?" I whisper. A gasp follows the last word, and I hold my breath to chase it away.

Jared is silent. Again.

"Are you still going to Hawaii?" I ask, changing the subject.

"Looking at flights now."

"Seriously?" My tone makes me sound like a barking seal. I can't put my finger on why, but the fact that he's planning this trip makes me feel irrationally panicky. I feel like, somehow, if he gets on a plane, I'm never going to see him again. He's going to disappear, just like everyone else. I *feel* it.

"Yeah," he says. "I quit my job."

"That was fast."

Silence. I hear him breathing on the other end.

"So what are we doing, Jared?" I finally ask, addressing the question that lingers big and fat in my mind. "Us?"

"What *are* we doing, Mads?"

"You can't answer a question with a question," I say, trying to insert a smile into my voice, but inside I feel tense.

"I just can't think about anything right now. The only thing I can think about is getting on a plane and going to that volcano. I don't know why, but it feels right. Maybe I can figure things out there, forget all this stuff, all this pain."

"Oh," I say. Disappointment floats on the edges of the word. This is him, shutting me out, backing away and falling into the grave. Crumbling beneath my fingers.

"Who knows, maybe I'll come back a totally different person."

"I don't want that. I just want you back, Jared. The guy I've known all my life."

"I found a flight for eight a.m. tomorrow."

I cover my mouth, suppressing emotion. "Please don't go," I say. My voice cracks. "Come up here instead."

"Here?"

"Fort Collins. I can find you a place to live. Just... please don't go. I have a bad feeling."

"I'm sorry, Mads, but I'm going. I feel this pull, like I need to go to Hawaii," he says.

My shoulders slump in defeat.

"Hey, um, I'll miss you, Mads."

As if that's supposed to make me feel better. The gulf between us widens, and through the phone, I reach out to squeeze his hand twice. "Yeah, same here."

52

EMBER

The sun is blinding and hot. Strands of wet hair stick to my face, and my soaked skirt and top hug my body. I wipe grit and dust from the corners of my mouth and sit up. A breeze whips up the potent scent of sage. My entire body aches.

I squint in the sunlight and think for an instant that maybe I'm dreaming. I'm sitting amidst an endless span of brown prairie flanked by a wall of blue sky—and I have no idea where I am. No cliffs, no hills, nothing but a vast plain. No explanation as to how I landed *here* of all places. All I know is that it's unbelievably hot and there's nothing but barren land around me. I'm still soaking wet, and I escaped Trinity alive.

Relief rushes through me. I stand up and stumble through the vacant land, and a sharp pain stabs my foot. I stop, pull a cactus thorn from the sole of my bare foot, and then tiptoe carefully, zigzagging around the chewed juniper branches, thorny bushes, and cactus plants that hide atop the sandy earth. I yell until my voice is raspy and I'm out of breath. "Help!"

A rushing sound ripples through the air, golden brown,

and I can make out a car moving on a highway some five hundred yards away. I trot to the hot pavement, waving my arms in the air above my head, but the car is long gone. The asphalt scorches my bare feet, and I swear out loud, hopping from one foot to the next. I jog on the shoulder of the road, looking for any car, any sign of life.

I walk along the highway, and judging from the sun, I'm headed north. I have no idea where I am. In the Middle East? Maybe Africa? California? My breath knots in my chest, as my reality and the sheer enormity of all that has happened to me dawns anew. It overwhelms me, like a reservoir dam bursting open, flooding me. My body trembles and hot tears drain from my eyes. Shaky, I sink to the ground next to the pavement of the highway, tucking my knees up to my forehead.

The highway is absent all cars and extends for miles on a flat plain in both directions. The sun's glare burns into my skin. I fold my head onto my knees, feeling so entirely exhausted and absolutely directionless. I've got to get to Los Angeles and find Tre. I've got to wake him up just like I woke up. I've got to find Jared and Maddie. I want to be *home*.

Through my legs, I gaze at the black henna lines weaving up my hands. The black nail polish. This is real. I'm in the middle of freaking nowhere after a crazy roller coaster ride, and it was all real. Xintra is going to ruin the world in a matter of months, and I'm out here like a freaking homeless person, wandering the desert.

I scan the terrain, trying to decipher where I might be. I don't know. Wind blows in small dirt circles in the distance. Mini tornadoes. *Vortexes.* I put my head down on my knees again, and a chill runs through my spine. I don't want to think of the Trinity vortex or anything else creepy. Instead, I gaze at the lined grooves in the black pavement and the pits that dot the surface. My eyes grow bleary.

"Hey, missy, you okay?" The voice startles me, and I jerk my head up.

A rusted car the color of old oranges hums next to me on the road. The voice belongs to the driver, who leans over the seat to an open passenger window. He looks to be about fifty and has a face with droopy jowls. "Listen, I don't know what's going on here, dearie," he says, "but I'm guessing you need a ride?"

I bound up. "Yes! Yes, I need a ride," I say, tugging on the door handle of his car before he can change his mind.

His car smells like leather and sweat, and I sink into the seat, tugging on my miniskirt, which creeps up my thighs.

"Where ya headed?"

"LA"

"Where?"

"California," I say, bouncing on the seat. I want this man to step on the gas and drive. I need to get to Tre.

He laughs and puts the car into drive. "Well, I'm not going that far. But I can take you to a phone so you can call someone who is."

"Yeah, maybe I can just use your cell?" I say, extending a hand. My body is sprung like a wire.

"I don't got a cell phone. But there's a store about two miles from here," he says, pointing down the highway. "I can give you a lift."

"Thanks." I sigh. If I had just walked a little farther, I would have found a phone long ago.

The car hums in jagged grey lines and an air freshener masquerading as a cardboard cutout of a pink pig swings from the rearview mirror. It moves back and forth like a grandfather clock.

"Where are we?" My voice is hoarse.

The man does a quick double take, and surprise washes over his face. He looks back to the road. "Well, we're coming up to Corona."

"And where's Corona?" The dark horizon is flat with no trees or houses. Just one long fence lining the highway.

"New Mexico, my dear."

"Oh." Freaking New Mexico? I squeeze my nails into the palms of my hands. I have no idea where Corona is in the state. But wherever it is, it's the middle of nowhere.

"I'm Jerry," he says.

"Ember." *My name.* I finally have control over my own mouth and words and identity again. The idea of it makes me smile.

"Well, Ember, I'm guessin' you might be lost. Want me to take you to the sheriff?"

"No, it's okay—just a phone," I say, looking out the window. We come to a few scattered adobe buildings and sunken clapboard houses that apparently mark the town of Corona. A mangy dog barks behind a barbed-wire fence, protecting a pile of miscellaneous junk and a rusted car.

The sight of civilization, as meager as it is, breathes some life back into me. Jerry swings his car into a dirt parking lot and stops before a faded red store with large dirty windows. He puts the car in park and turns to me. "My wife is expecting me home now, but Russ in there can let you use his phone. Is there someone you can call?"

I nod. "Yeah, thanks."

I push open the car door and walk up the concrete steps to the store. The sound of the car engine hums apple green and the headlights pull away, leaving me in the dusk light.

Inside, the scent of air-conditioning coolant fills my head, and a radio plays country music. It sounds like a bowl of red cherries. A large man stretches out on a metal folding chair behind the cash register, a straw cowboy hat covering his face.

"Uh, hello?" I ask.

The man bolts up in surprise, leaning forward onto his thick thighs. "Yello there, young lady, what can I do ya for?"

"Are you Russ?"

"That'd be me."

"A guy, uh, Jerry, gave me a ride and told me I could use your phone."

Russ stands and breathes heavily through his nose like a sleeping dog. He scans me, eyeing my ridiculous outfit, lingering on my bare feet.

"I'm lost."

He nods, irritation seeps through a smile, and he reaches under the table and slides an iPhone onto the counter. "Jerry likes to volunteer me for the lost and found."

I look at the phone. I need to call Jared. Or Maddie. But then, what do I even say? They'll want to put me in the mental ward somewhere. Load me up with drugs. I feel nauseous even thinking about having the conversation about where I've been.

"Can I use your restroom?"

He points to the back corner, and I escape his nosy gaze in a bathroom the size of a coat closet. I gaze at myself in the faded mirror. I look like a drowned rat with wet hair and black makeup smeared around my eyes. I have a perfect, thin nose. I touch my plump lips, gaze down at my enormous breasts. So weird. The skin on my back feels achy and sore, as does my shoulder, neck, and head.

I turn around to look at my body in the mirror. Deep purple bruises dot my shoulder and neck, visible with this neon-green bra top I'm wearing. There's a scab forming on my scalp. Even my ribs hurt—all this undoubtedly from when I got hit by the car.

I turn around further and gasp when I see the enormous tattoo, still new, on my back. It's red along the edges, and the ink is scabbing white. I sigh, groaning, remembering that lucid moment in the tattoo shop. That guy told me I did this to myself. He showed me the picture. But it looks so much bigger right now in the mirror. The pyramid sits perfectly centered on my spine and extends out to the bottom of both my shoulder blades. The curling lids of the eye cross over my vertebrae. Trinity's pyramid.

Disgust turns my stomach. Xintra totally had her way with my body. The tattoo is huge. And weird. Like never-wear-a-swimsuit weird.

Then I recall what I know about the eye. It helps ward off evil. Yeah, I think that's what I read somewhere. It's the Eye of Providence. It's going to be a good-luck charm for me, I decide. It has to be. It can't be a reminder of what a giant freaking mistake I made.

I splash water on my face, getting the grit and sand out of the corners of my mouth. I inhale and stare at myself in the mirror once more. I have to get the hell out of Corona and *find Tre*. I run wet fingers through my hair, scrunching it to bring back the natural curl, and then stand up straight, open the door, and stride back out into the store. The iPhone is still sitting on the counter, a spec of an object in comparison to the large man leaning over it.

"Where ya coming from?" He takes off his hat and scratches his sweaty dark hair.

I pick up his phone off the linoleum counter. "That's hard to explain. I don't really know how I got here, but I wasn't in New Mexico this morning. That I can say."

He nods. He must assume I'm caught up in some suspicious business, which in a way, I am. But the look of contemplation that appears next tells me that's not exactly it. He knows something more than I do. Something important.

"What?" I ask. The edge in my voice surprises me. Maybe there still is a little bit of Oshun inside of me, a girl who gets what she wants and demands a lot from everyone around her.

"You didn't happen to be out by them storm clouds, did ya?"

"Storm clouds?" I look at the phone and dial Jared's number.

"Every once in a while, we get them clouds that stretch for maybe a quarter mile out in the prairie. The clouds touch down to the dirt in just one spot, like it was raining just on that one part in the desert. Dragging something up from the ground or somethin'."

The blood falls from my head and I stop and look up at him. *That's* how I got out of Trinity. Some freaking vortex exit.

"Sometimes, people will go missing. Dogs. Whatever happens to be close. Phones go dead. Power goes out. In '89, a truck flipped over."

My mouth feels dry. "Wow."

Russ nods, takes his seat in the corner before adding, "You know, you kinda look like that singer star who done died the other week."

"Who?"

"Um, her name was Oshun something or other."

"Died?" I ask.

"Yeah, she died in the bathtub, or maybe it was a swimming pool."

Oshun is dead. I should be happy. I should dance. But the idea that Xintra controlled everything about my life, even when I supposedly died—reminds me that when I gave up free will, I became just a shadow trapped in a box. Disgust scuttles across my skin.

I give Russ a shrug, shake my head, and turn away with

the phone to my ear. I dial Jared, listen to the phone ring forever, then get his voicemail. Just like I always did.

I stare at the packs of spearmint gum on the shelf and decide to dial Maddie's number next. On the third ring, she picks up.

"Maddie," I say. "It's Ember. I'm in Corona, New Mexico. And I need help."

53

MADDIE

"Emby? Is that really you?" I bolt up from Lia's couch, where I've been melting under a pile of nachos and Cherry Coke since Mom left earlier. Blood rushes furiously into my heart and head. This has to be a joke. But it *sounds* like Ember. My words spill out on top of each other. "Now *where* did you say you are again? Are you okay? Where have you been? Tell me, oh my God—are you home? Wait—"

"I'm in New Mexico."

My brain breathes for a second. "Okay, okay." How do I handle this? Do I call the police? I have no idea what kind of crazy stuff she has gotten into. Where has she been?

Lia sits up and tilts her head in confusion. I open my mouth and eyes wide, shaking my hand in the air to silently tell her this is huge. So huge.

Ember's voice is urgent, a hushed whisper. "And I need you to get me. Can you get me?"

"Of course. Of course." I pause. "Should I come now? I'll come now. Have you called anyone? Does Jared know where you are? Where in New Mexico?" I stand up, pace, tug my hair with my free hand, reminding myself that I won't get any answers if I don't shut up.

"Long story. Can you come right away? I have no money, no car, no phone, no ID." She pauses and then laughs quietly. "No shoes even. And I'm at a store..." She pauses. "It's called Russ's Place."

"Yeah, yeah, of course." I put her on speakerphone and type the business name into Google. "Hang on. I'm looking it up on my phone now."

Lia leans into me, and whispers too loud, "What's going on?"

"Ember! She's on the phone!" I say.

"Ember?" Lia asks. "Like missing girl Ember? Who you talk about all the time?"

"Yeah!" I say.

Lia's face is a mixture of shock and delight, and she shakes her head before leaning in with minty gum breath and shouts into the phone, "Well, hi, missing girl Ember. I'm so glad you're okay."

"That's Lia," I say.

"Oh," Ember says.

I look at a map on my phone. "Looks like it should take me about seven hours." It doesn't matter that I just drove all the way from California and haven't been on campus for more than five hours. This is huge.

"You're the best." Ember sighs. "I owe you."

My pulse is racing. "Where have you been? Are you okay? Can I call, uh, the hospital? The police? The media?"

"I told you, it's a long story." Her voice sounds tired, like she's survived a war. My mind goes to dark places, imaging terrible things happening to Ember, being tied up, abused, or held hostage. My stomach cinches tight. "But I'm fine," she adds. "Just hurry?"

I smile and sigh deeply, tears pricking my eyes. I cover my

mouth and emotion bubbles up my throat. "Can you stay on the line while I drive? Just to be sure you're okay?"

"No, I can't."

"I'll call the police, though, okay?"

"No, please don't."

I frown. "Okay, well, yeah, sure. See you soon."

I click off my phone and frantically spin around to look for my purse.

"So where is she?" Lia asks.

Where's my purse? I need to find it. I duck down and scan the tiny apartment before spotting a leather strap beneath her Ikea desk. I snatch it up, throw it over my shoulder. "Gotta go."

"Now?" Lia flips her head to watch me run to the front door.

"Call you later," I say, swinging open the door and dashing down the metal staircase to the parking garage.

Lia calls to me through the open door, "But we were just starting the movie!"

As if I'm going to sit around and watch a movie when Ember is back from the depths of oblivion. Lia can be so clueless.

My body feels like it's been set on fire, and I scramble to unlock the car and dial Jared at the same time. This is really happening! She's alive. Oh my God, Jared is going to freak. He has to come with me. Unless he's already on his way to Hawaii.

I'm getting my friend back. My Ember. My Jared. My sanity, too.

The phone rings but Jared doesn't pick up, so I leave a message. "Hey, it's Maddie. Your sister is alive. Alive! Holy crap! I'm going to drive to New Mexico to get her. So yeah, just call me when you get this." I hang up, toss my phone in my purse, and gun the car out of the parking lot.

54

EMBER

I sink down onto the concrete step and lean against the front of the wooden building. The ambient sound of wind is pale yellow. My head throbs, and I gently touch my neck, my flesh tender from being hit by the car. I remember the driver's face, so clearly etched in my memory. The sneer on his uneven face. His skin like mashed potatoes. My stomach clenches.

Then I remember what happened just before, sitting on the edge of the world next to Tre—finally in the free world, yet not himself. That kiss told me I loved him, and the way he kissed me back told me he loved me, too.

I have to find Damien. He had a tech company. I have to find him. I look at the sky. It's black now, stars scattered across it like splattered paint. A chill moves through the air. I wrap my arms around my legs, and the neon *Open* sign of Russ's shop shuts off.

I rest my cheek on my bent knees and shut my eyes.

"Hey…" It's Maddie's tangerine voice.

I open my eyes, and the sight of her is like warm

sunshine. I jump up to stand, throwing my hands around her neck. "Mads!" I want to cling to her. She is all that is normal. She is all that is safe. She is real life. "Oh God!"

She hugs me back tightly, and I smell her scent, the hint of red cherry licorice and fruity shampoo.

I cry out and pull away when her fingers dig too tight into my tattoo and the bruise on my neck.

"Oh!" she says, freezing with her arms and big brown eyes wide. She touches my blonde hair with two fingers and crinkles her forehead. "You... you're... really Oshun?"

Without answering, I run to her Honda and climb inside. It feels warm and cozy like a cabin on a snowy night.

She climbs into the driver's seat and her eyes search me, confused. She opens her mouth and shuts it, opens it again. "That was really you? That day at the restaurant in LA?" Her features scrunch together in typical pensive Maddie fashion. "Why did you act like we were strangers? You were so *weird*."

I shake my head and shrug. "I... don't remember."

"Why?"

I sigh. "I was out of it."

"Your brother was totally convinced it was you, but it didn't make sense to me." She shakes her head. "I started to think maybe he'd lost his mind. I didn't believe..."

I shrug. "Yeah."

"Wait—I read a story that Oshun died of a drug overdose in the bathtub. That was, like, fake news? Did you fake your death?" She shakes her head quickly in disbelief.

I shrug, speechless. How can I explain?

"Why did you run away? How the hell did you become some crazy pop star?" She turns and gazes at her steering wheel and rakes her two hands through her hair, pulling at the scalp. "It doesn't make sense. *Why?*"

If I tell her I was rebirthed, that I was stuck in a dark vortex and that a psychic chick named Xintra was controlling a secret group of people, she'll call 9-1-1 and lock me up in a mental institution. They'll pump me full of medication that I don't need and I'll lose control of myself. Again.

"I can't explain it right now," I say, hesitating. "I'm just really tired and really hungry. Can we go someplace and eat?"

She looks ticked. "It's three in the morning. This town has, like, a hundred people in it. Nothing's open." She puts the car in reverse. "Listen, I'll just drive until we get to civilization, find a hotel, snacks, whatever. Okay? Talk if you want. I'm here. I'll get you home."

I nod, so grateful she's here. I can't believe she drove through the night to the middle of nowhere alone—just to come get me. I can't believe she's still actually here for me— the second time I disappeared. My senior year was a blur of stupidity and I totally shut her out.

But here she is.

She keeps turning her head to look at me and then back at the road. Then me again. I just grin, so pleased to be in the car with her. I want to pour my story out, but will she even believe me? It's crazy.

"I can't believe we finally found you." She takes a drink of her Diet Dr Pepper and wipes her mouth with her wrist. She holds out the drink to me with a straight arm. "You want some?"

I nod, and tilt the bottle to my lips. The carbonated drink sizzles and pops and I gulp and gulp until there's only a little bit left in the bottle. I stop and hold it up to see the last bit splashing around the bottom. "Sorry."

She waves her hand at me like she always did. "Whatever. We thought you were dead. It's been years! Holy crap, it's been *years!*"

Years. I knew this when I was in Trinity. But the reality that I've wasted so much time because of that one mistake, because I went off the rails senior year, it hits me like a line-backer, and my breath contorts in my abdomen.

"Yeah," I whisper. Maddie's face is rounder, but she looks healthy. Her hair is longer now, down past her shoulders. "You look good."

"Thanks," she says, glancing at me in the dark. "And you... look... like Oshun."

I grimace. "Weird. I know."

Without warning, she pulls the car over on the highway, puts it in park, and swivels to look at me. "I'm sorry. I can't drive. You *have* to tell me how this all evolved. What *happened* to you?" Her voice breaks with emotion and tears stream down her round cheeks. A hard sigh slides out of her throat and she shuts her eyes and shakes her head. Then she reaches out and squeezes my hands.

I cry, too, grimacing, my nose filling up and my eyes going blurry. Regret and relief and sadness and joy muddle together, weaving into one giant ball of blubbering mess. "I... I'm so sorry, Mads," I say, reaching to hug her again. "For everything. For leaving. For quitting. It was all so stupid."

"No," she whispers into my hair. "No, Emby. You were lost. You couldn't find your way."

My body convulses, and every emotion from the day my parents died, all the way to stepping into Trinity, to loving and losing Tre, to running from Xintra and jumping through a hole in a cave—all of it crashes together in a blue and black and gray torrent of moaning that emanates from my core. Eventually, it's all soothed by Mads, stroking my hair, rocking me.

After a few minutes, we pull apart, both of us giggling at our snotty crying fest. She leans over and reaches into her glove compartment for some paper napkins and hands me one and then blots her nose and tears with her own.

"I'm sorry I didn't believe it was you," she whispers. "Jared. He knew. He never gave up."

"Really?" My brother always seemed so checked out after Mom and Dad died.

"Yeah. He's been ruled by the belief you were alive, that you were Oshun." She opens her console between the seats and pulls out a bag of licorice, shoves it into my abdomen just like she always did. The sight of the red candy makes me light up.

"So hungry!" I say, reaching into the bag and pushing three pieces into my mouth at once. "Mwanks," I mumble with full cheeks.

"I always say it's the best medicine," she says. "Oh, and music." She turns on the radio and finds an indie band on her phone—the Stone Keepers. We listened to them all the time sophomore year. I smile, leaning my head back on the headrest, shut my eyes and watch the bright bubblegum-pink and mint-green stars move through my vision. *Home. I'm going home.*

But Tre. That invisible belt wraps around my chest and squeezes tight. I have to get to him. I'll ask Mads if she'll drive me to California. Or maybe I can get a credit card and buy a ticket there. I can't just pretend he's not living like a shadow in his body like I was, doing terrible things in the world. The mere idea makes me squeeze my hand tight, my nails digging into my palm. Blood thumps in my temples.

"I've got to get ahold of Jared," she says, dialing her phone. "I'm worried he went to Hawaii."

"What?"

"Yeah, he was going to take a trip to some volcano." She stops and points at me. "In fact, he says *you* gave him the voucher for a flight, and after seeing you he found a silver coin with a pyramid and the name of some volcano on it. What was that about?"

"No," I say swiftly, shaking my head. Panic seizes my body. "No. No. No. He can't go there. Call him. Call him now!"

She holds the phone limply and frowns. "I am, but why are you so upset?"

"I can't explain. But just get him."

She puts the phone on the car stereo and we listen to it ring over and over. We get his voicemail. Panic flaps inside my chest. "Call again."

Maddie dials again. The phone rings and rings, and I squeeze my fingernails deeper into my palms. I don't remember giving him a coin. I don't remember giving him a plane ticket. Why did I do that? I'm furious with myself, and my whole body is trembling.

But this time, he answers. "Hey."

"Jared! It's me, Ember! Don't go to Hawaii!" I shout.

"What? Who? Maddie? Is this you?"

Maddie speaks up. "I'm here with Ember in New Mexico! Jared, she's back! She's okay! And she says—"

"Don't go to Hawaii," I say. "I wasn't in my right mind when I gave you the ticket."

"Oshun? I'm so confused. What's going on? You really *are* Oshun? Wait, I thought you—she died." His voice is filled with white joy the color of bubbles and it inflates my whole body.

"I did die, and I didn't. I can't explain. But where are you?"

"I'm at home."

"Don't go on that plane. You can't," I say, leaning forward to the dash of the car, as if I could reach through the plastic and grab Jared by the shoulders and shake him.

"Wait—you really are Oshun! We *were* right, Mads!" Jared says.

"*You* were right," Mads says softly, looking at the steering wheel, her brow flickering.

"How?" Jared asks. "Are you Oshun? Or are you back as Ember? Regular Ember? I don't get it."

"Yes!" I yell, banging my hands on my thighs. "I'm back! Me. Ember!"

Maddie joins my enthusiasm, clapping her hands like a child. "She's back!" she yells, bouncing on her seat.

"Hang on. Holy crap. Just a sec," Jared says, and I hear footsteps and a muffled conversation. *Gram.* I hear Gram's voice, confused at first and then urgent.

"Ember?" Her voice comes on the line and it sounds shaky and unfamiliar, and for the first time her voice is purple, the lightest shade I've ever heard in it. Usually her voice is coffee colored and has an edge like shattered glass.

"Yeah, it's me," I say, high-pitched and gentle.

"Oh my Lord," she says. "So you're on your way home to Leadville now?"

Where is home, anyway? I look at Maddie and she's nodding. "Yeah, I guess that's where Maddie's taking me," I say. "But maybe we can go to LA first?"

Maddie's face is incredulous. She frowns and shakes her head.

"Okay, we'll go to Leadville for now." I will get home, make arrangements and then get back to LA. I'll find Damien, figure out how to yank out Tre.

"Where did you go? You just... vanished," Jared says. They must be on speaker. I imagine them huddling together in her dark bedroom, the mustard-brown curtains closed and the floral wallpaper peeling above her double bed.

"You left me when I went into the coffee shop that day, Ember," she says. Her voice may be light purple but it still sounds cutting. "Where did you go?"

I decide to be honest. "Trinity Forest."

Maddie's eyes get huge and she covers her mouth with her hand. "You're kidding."

I shake my head and stare at the glowing clock on the dash. It says four o'clock in the morning. "No. It's true," I say.

"We need to tell the police, Emb. We have to," Jared says.

"No," I whisper. I cover my eyes with my hand and squeeze. There's no way the police can stop Xintra. She's above the law. She's above the universe's law.

"Did someone kidnap you? Brainwash you? Drug you?" Jared asks. "You have to tell us. I mean, we went through so much trying to find you." His voice cracks, and I can hear emotion hovering at the edges of his voice.

"I went willingly at first, but then... I couldn't get out of it."

"Really? What did they do?" Maddie asks.

They? Xintra? The Trinity vortex? I don't even know how to begin to answer.

"See, Gram? I told you Ember was Oshun. She was. She was Oshun just like Maddie and I thought," Jared says.

Maddie looks like a dog caught digging in the trash. Guilty. Though I'm not sure exactly why.

"Trinity?" Gram asks. "Ember, I think you need to go to the attic and look through your mother's things as soon as you get home."

My pulse quickens. "Why?" I ask urgently. "What do I need to see?" *The crazy woman notebook?*

"I don't know. I just think things up there will be *helpful*. That's all I can say. It's all junk to me. You might think differently."

55

MADDIE

My head buzzes with the news that Emby was actually Oshun, that she is finally sitting here in the car with me, totally normal. Not at all the same person she was at the restaurant. I want to pummel her with questions. Demand them, really. She has no idea how much Jared and I went through, how much it took to go looking for her, searching, telling the world to bring her home. It's like two different feelings jostle for control of my brain. One is seriously ticked at her for divorcing her life and parading around onstage as a total skank and leaving the rest of us to mourn her disappearance. The other part of me treasures her and our history and yearns to keep reaching over and touching her arm, just to make sure she won't disappear again.

We've switched places so she's driving now—I'm desperate for some sleep—and I lean my head on the window, listening to her conversation with Jared play out on the car stereo. Her grandma seems to have gone quiet, and maybe she isn't even on the line anymore. I can't help but wonder what this whole thing means for me and Jared, whether we'll still be *more than friends* or if that was just a fleeting thing between the two of us. A stress fling.

"So, Jared, was there really a shooting at the restaurant where you worked?" Ember asks.

"Yeah, so freaking sad." He sighs. "But I wasn't working there anymore when it happened. I got fired because I was spending so much time looking for you. But I knew a guy who died." A hint of irritation scrapes the edge of his voice. He, like me, might feel confused and hurt by her disappearance and comeback.

"I caused that to happen," Ember whispers. I open my eyes and glance at her. She covers her mouth with a free hand. I still can't get used to her with that white-blonde hair and the nose. Don't even get me going on the boobs in that tiny top.

"Where are you working, where are you living?" she asks.

"With Gram. Just quit my job at Safeway."

I can't help it, I chime in with my badgering. I need to know. "How on earth did you end up as a pop star, Ember? It doesn't make any sense." I try to keep it light, hide the frustration and confusion broiling inside, but I'm not sure I pull it off.

She turns her head to look at me, probably surprised that I'm awake. "Uh. I don't know. I gave in to Trinity. Screwed up. It was the only way out."

"Who was it that hurt you in Trinity?" I demand. "Tell us."

"It's bigger than anything you can imagine."

I sit up straight and gaze at her, jutting my jaw. "Why are you so freaking secretive?"

"I'm not trying to be, Mads," she pleads. "I'll get to it. Sometime. I'm just so tired. Really. Please, I'm begging you. Tell me all about your life instead."

"My life?" Again, I'm part thrilled she's asking. That we're talking again. But I can't help but be frustrated.

"Jared, you should go back to sleep," Ember says.

"I don't want to hang up. I'm afraid I'll lose you again."

"You won't, promise," she says. "Let's talk in the morning."

"Okay," he says, but I can hear the reluctance in his voice. "I love you."

"Same." She hangs up the phone and looks at me. "We have so much catching up to do. If you're not tired, I want to know. Please tell me. I've missed out on so much."

"My roommate died this week from the virus." The words just dump out of my mouth. That's what's happened. That's what I've been dealing with. "Oh, and I gave mouth-to-mouth to a guy in a dingy LA hotel who died from the virus, too."

She's stone still, staring wide eyed at the road. I know she's freaking out because her nostrils flare.

"Sorry. You're probably scared to be alone in this car with me now that I might be infected," I say. "Did you get the vaccine?"

"Don't get the vaccine!" she says firmly. She exhales and gazes at me with compassionate Emby eyes. "I'm so sorry. This must have been terrible for you." She shakes her head and purses her lips. "I... I'm just so sorry."

A moment passes between us. Something not like understanding and acceptance, but maybe a temporary truce. She's not ready to talk, not yet. Okay. I mean, not okay. But what can I do, other than press on? Keep her talking almost just to convince myself that she's real. That she's back.

"On to happier things," I say finally, dabbing tears from the corners of my eyes. I do not want to be like Mom and dwell on all the bad stuff going on in the world.

We talk for hours, catching up about school and what everyone from high school is doing now. It's light and we laugh and it sort of feels like old times. But the story of what really happened to her stays locked away, forming a thick barrier between us.

Ember shakes me awake when we arrive in Leadville later in the morning, and I watch through the car window as Jared greets her outside the driver's-side door with their grandma by his side. Their reunion is emotional, and Emby is sobbing, her entire body collapsing into the shared three-person hug. I can't understand what Emby is saying, just repeating something like "I'm sorry" over and over. Her voice gurgles and Jared's cracks. Her grandma backs up after a moment, removing herself from the hug. She watches Jared and Ember with crossed arms. But I can see emotion there, because her eyes scrunch up and her lips quiver.

I follow them up the steps and inside the tiny turquoise house. "I'm just so tired," Ember mumbles. Jared wraps his arm around her shoulder and walks her upstairs to her bedroom, full of all those musty boxes.

I lie down on the couch, and Gram walks by wordlessly, pulling a plaid throw blanket over my shoulders and legs. It smells like mothballs.

I smile and shut my eyes, sinking into the familiar sofa, when a hand strokes my hair. I open my eyes and see Jared's face near mine. He squats in front of me with those crinkled eyes and that crooked smile. "Thanks for getting her, Mads."

"I didn't believe you," I whisper, remorse turning my stomach.

"Well, it was pretty unbelievable," he admits.

"Are you still going to Hawaii?"

"I never even packed," he says, laughing through his nose and smiling. "I guess I decided that I can't run away from life. That maybe I—"

"You're made of rubber and you always bounce back?" I interject.

He smiles. "Yeah, maybe." He brushes my hair away from

my eyes with his hand and leans in gently to kiss me. I kiss him back, our lips pressing together gentle and sweet like butterfly wings. I kiss him with my eyes closed and inhale his cedar scent, grazing his cheek with my fingertips. I smile, my eyes droopy.

I didn't lose her. I didn't lose him.

56

EMBER

The attic feels like a sauna, but the sweet, savory pizza tastes better than anything I've eaten in a long time. I take a third slice of ham and pineapple and dangle it above my mouth with one hand while peeking inside a cardboard box with Mom's name on it.

Maybe she left another Crazy Woman Notebook up here with some secrets about how to expel Damien from Tre. I've got to understand Trinity first, make a plan and then get to California. He needs me, and sitting here feels like a betrayal to him. Every muscle in my body feels wound tight, like I'm working against a ticking time bomb. I have to get him out from under Xintra's spell as soon as possible. But I have no idea how to do it and still don't really understand how I even woke up from my life as Oshun.

Across the room, my brother's messy hair falls into his eyes and his T-shirt is pretty rumpled. He still doesn't fold clothes, but he looks so much older now. I think again about how much time I lost with him. Lines extend from the corners of his eyes like sunrays in a child's drawings—just like Dad's. It really does feels so good to be around him again.

He and Maddie sit incredibly close, their legs touching, shoving each other and giggling. Maddie rips through a box like it's Christmas, and Jared gazes at her for a long time. Hmmmm.

"So why didn't Gram give us more instructions about what to look for? Or come up here with us?" I ask.

"She has a bad back and can't climb the ladder very easily. I didn't want to risk her falling on the way down," Jared says. Man, he is a softy about her. Another weird thing that's changed since I left.

"She just said to *look*," he adds. "She didn't know exactly what we should hunt for. But she had a hunch there were important things up here."

My head still feels thick and heavy as I peer into a box containing a spatula, some of Dad's Tom Clancy books, and a pink lace pillow.

"Oh, I forgot," Maddie says, moving over to me and patting my shoulder with urgent, wide eyes. She reaches into her hippy leather purse and dramatically presents a balled-up napkin to me—her two hands outstretched. "For you."

"I don't want your trash." I giggle and push her hand away before pulling a couple of art history books out of a cardboard box and then grabbing a bejeweled bronze African elephant the size of a toaster. Mom always loved how some African cultures saw elephants as a symbol of strength and wisdom.

"No, it's not trash. It's a gift," she says, grinning beneath that signature tuft of dark bangs. "For you."

"So, your used napkin is a gift?" I smirk and study the bronze elephant, wondering if I should display it on my dresser. That is, wherever I end up living. *After* I retrieve Tre and we live happily ever after.

She shrugs and smiles. "It's my super fancy wrapping paper. But it *is* a gift. Open it." I take the napkin and feel something wrapped inside. "I'm so sorry I wasn't there for you. I didn't believe it was you at the restaurant... I mean, you were so full of yourself, so hoity-toity—not to mention so freaking weird."

I snort and frown. "Well, I'm sorry, too. I shut you out—before graduation." I unwind the paper and pull out a bracelet—with a delicate, looping ankh cross dangling from it. Stunned for a second, I'm completely taken over by emotion.

Maddie's dark eyes dance as she watches my reaction. "It's cool, huh?" she asks breathlessly. "It's not new—I know, tacky. But Jared and I met this woman in a coffee shop in LA, and she said she knew you were Oshun. She said I would know what to do with it. I think it's a good-luck totem. She said no matter where your life may take you—"

"Your true path will be shown to you." I finish the sentence for her. I hug her tight, inhaling the familiar scent of shampoo and pizza sauce. "Thanks so much," I breathe.

"You've heard of that saying?" she asks.

I nod. "This woman, did she have long gray hair? Braids?"

"Yes!" Maddie sits up on her knees.

"What was her name?"

"I looked it up later, and it meant *guide*. Right, Jared?" She looks at my brother. "It was something like, Lo..." Maddie frowns, trying to remember.

"Lodima," I say.

"Yeah, that was it!"

I gaze at Maddie with wide eyes and then look down at the bracelet. I found my path. I weave my fingers through the chain. My entire body is elated, like this is a gift not only from Maddie but also from Lodima, from Mom. The ankh cross —*life*—guided me out of Trinity.

A stabbing pain strikes my chest. It guided *me* out of Trinity as myself. But it didn't do jack for Tre. It didn't help him. He's on the outside, but not as himself. Without any warning, the thought makes me cry, and my shoulders shake and a series of sobs climb up my throat.

"Hey, don't cry," Mads says, touching my shoulder.

I push away my tears and emotion, knowing the more I cry, the more questions they'll ask that I can't answer and the more they'll push to get me psychiatric help. Before we came up here today, Gram tried to tell me we needed to call a doctor and the police. "We have to have you evaluated. We have to tell everyone you're back," she told me, leaning against the doorframe of the musty room upstairs. Back to her icy disposition.

"Later," I told her. She just shook her head and left the room.

I put the bracelet on my wrist. The silver cross reflects the sunlight. I wipe my eyes, shove the emotion back down and manage a smile.

"You know Lodima?" Jared asks. "She acted like she knew you."

"Kind of," I say. "She gave me cryptic warnings not to go to Trinity."

"Really?" Maddie says. "Why didn't you listen?"

Why do we do all the dumb stuff we do?

"Check it out," Jared says, holding up a framed oil painting of Elvis, dressed in his standard white rhinestone jumpsuit.

Maddie's face lights up with sarcastic delight. "Oh. My. God. Classic."

It's got to be Dad's. "We *must* keep that painting," I say.

"Yeah," he says, setting it aside. "For sure."

Maddie rips into a large cardboard box labeled *Dezi*, Mom's name, before reaching in and pulling out a long bright turquoise and orange necklace and matching earrings from a little wooden box. She tosses a white stuffed bunny out of the box and onto the floor.

I like seeing Mom's belongings again. I don't feel that awful black guilt anymore. I smile when I see her things: blankets, old magazines, a handmade pillow I sewed for her in third grade.

Finally, I reach a hand into a black trash bag and pull out a metal box about the size of a footstool. A painted symbol decorates the top of it: the looping ankh cross. The same as Lodima's necklace and, now, my bracelet. I inhale sharply and look at Maddie.

"What?" she asks, leaning over to look at the box. Her eyes widen with excitement. "Dude," she says. "Weird. That's the same symbol as the bracelet! What are the chances?"

I lift the lid to the box, revealing a stack of envelopes, letters, charcoal sketches, and a small pink journal. I pick up one of the envelopes in the box. The return address is for Lodima Alden in Crestone, Colorado.

Holy crap. Mom really did know her. Mom knew Lodima.

"Lodima!" Mads says. "Double weird."

I open the journal to a random page and catch a few sentences in Mom's scrawled handwriting. The words give me goosebumps. *I was not a religious girl. Mama stopped taking me to church after my brother and Papa died. But this felt creepy, dangerous and bad.*

Maddie's bright tangerine voice pulls me out of the pages. "Wow! This painting is *really cool!*"

I look up, and Jared is flipping through several of Mom's painted canvases leaning against the wall. Colorful, swirling flowers and mountains. There's one painting of a brown-haired girl swinging off a rope into a crystal-clear lake. A dark-haired boy, blue eyes, tattoos on his arm, smiling from the water. "Wait!" I say.

Jared pulls out the painting to reveal the whole picture.

The large cottonwood tree. Lilly. Tre. Pete. Me. Chris on a log in the distance, a cigarette in his hand. "That's me. And Tre. In Trinity. Mom painted *me*."

"What?" Jared asks.

I crawl over to it on my hands and knees and study the girl on the rope swing, and sure enough, the likeness is eerie. Curly hair. The large brown eyes.

"Wow, that's crazy," Maddie says, squinting over my shoulder. "It *does* look like you. And who is Tre?"

"Him," I say pointing to the shirtless figure with the tattoo on his arm. "I love him." My chest constricts, followed by a painful heaviness. The date on the painting is 1988, before I was even born. I gaze at the picture, both amazed by Mom's gift and longing for those moments with Tre again.

"Who is *this* wicked girl?" Maddie asks with delight.

I look up to see Maddie holding up a portrait of a teenaged girl with snow-white skin, sea-green eyes, red hair spinning wildly around her head as if she's possessed. My heart somersaults in my chest.

Xintra.

I forget to take a breath, and irrational fear sweeps through me—as if she's really here in the room with me.

"It's like she jumps off the canvas," Jared says.

"Her eyes follow you," Maddie says. "Don't you think, Emb?" She looks at me and then frowns. "Are you okay?" She touches my shoulder. "Tell us, what is it?"

A tiny breath attempts to eke in and out of my chest. This was all real. Mom knew Lodima and Xintra, somehow. Maybe this stuff of Mom's will tell me more, maybe it really will be helpful, like Gram said. Maybe it will lead me to understand how Xintra is using Trinity and how to pull Tre out of that spell. I need to find him. Bring him back alive. Stop the war she's waging on humanity. Every single task feels more impossible than the last.

I spent all those years shutting Mom out without really trying to understand her. I didn't want to be her. But now that she's gone and I can't talk to her directly, I'm realizing I'm more like her than anyone. I need to know her story. I need to tell mine.

Will Jared and Maddie believe me this time, or will they just assume I'm certifiably crazy?

"Nothing." I shake my head.

Maddie places both hands on the sides of my shoulders and turns me to face her. She looks me in the eye, and the sun casts a hazy glare into the room through the dirty attic window. "Listen, I know you've been through a lot, but you can still talk to me."

"Me too," Jared says, walking over to me.

"Yeah. *Us*," Maddie adds. "You have to tell us what's going on with you." I look away.

"Emb, come on." Maddie exhales a frustrated sigh.

"We need to know," Jared says. "We *deserve* to know."

His words hit me in the center of my chest. He's right. But when I tried to tell them about Trinity before, no one believed me and I wound up with a one-way ticket to the mental ward. Why would this time be different? Because I've been a pop star for the past year? Because the evidence is right here in this attic? *Something,* I think. *Give me something to cling to. I don't want to be alone in this anymore.*

Before Trinity, I kept everything inside, shut everyone out. And that didn't work out so well for me. But I've been so many people since then. And my brother, my best friend— maybe they've been different people, too. I don't know much. I don't know how to wake Tre and rip him out of Damien. I don't know how to stop the virus, or the vaccine, or Xintra. But what I do know is, I can't do it alone.

I bite my lip. "Well." I sigh. "You guys are never going to believe this."

57

DAMIEN

"And that, my friends, is how we will make the smartphone obsolete," I say, clicking off my PowerPoint presentation. I toss the implantable chip on the glossy cherry conference table and it slides a few feet into the middle.

Grinning, I lean forward, placing my knuckles atop the smooth table, and gaze confidently at my board of directors. Most of them aren't any older than thirty and a couple of them wear T-shirts and sneakers rather than suits and ties. They nod thoughtfully, and I can tell by their raised eyebrows that they are truly impressed. As they should be.

"Brilliant, Damien," says Fin, twirling his pen.

Of course it's brilliant. They love the idea, and they love even more that it comes from a guy who's just eighteen. I'm the story they can shout to investors about and use to spin a yarn to the press. The golden child who's taking the world into the next generation: device-free living.

Mitch, another board member, leans back in his chair, places his hands behind his head. "We put eight hundred million bucks behind this thing and plenty of time to ensure it's ready to be sold. Why are you pushing to get it to market so fast? Shouldn't we test it more?"

I walk around the room, stopping to gaze at the rainbow of exotic fish gliding through fake seaweed and coral in the floor-to-ceiling glass tank. If only the fish knew they were captives, inhabitants of a false world. Everything they see, feel, and experience is orchestrated. With the pull of a plug, their lives are over.

I put my hands on Mitch's shoulders, standing behind his chair, looming over him. I feel his shoulders sink. "Some call it crazy, Mitch. I call it ambition. Let's get this one done *now*. First mover advantage." I step away and his skeptical expression has faded to endearment. He knows innovation when he sees it. He also knows power. *My* power.

"To get people started, we're giving away the free injectables. Who doesn't want to be a living Wi-Fi beacon, able to capture anything, anytime?" I say.

They nod, shuffling papers. Mitch pushes a newspaper out of the way, folded to the entertainment section. I catch the headline, *Oshun's Death a Mystery*, and a photo of her sulky face, brown eyes. My heart dislodges and climbs up my throat, and I feel nauseous and a tad disoriented. And, oddly, *sad*.

I grit my teeth as—*flash*—a vision emerges. It's Oshun... but she's no longer Oshun. She's a girl named Ember, eating pizza on her knees in a dimly lit attic with a boy and a girl, and somehow, I know she's in Leadville, Colorado. I *feel* it just like Xintra told me I would. In her lap, Ember has documents that could undo everything Xintra has created. And I know I must find this girl, Ember. Destroy her.

I *will* destroy her.

"Donuts?" asks Steve, the only member of this board who still has doubts, who could be the snag in our plans.

I straighten up and gaze into the balding man's pale blue

eyes. In the fog above him, I see his weaknesses. His hidden shame over a failed business and his ex-wife's taunts about his premature hair loss.

I decline the donut. "Let's move through the objectives for the next two months."

As we plan for production cycles in Chinese factories, I think of how they're all just followers. They do what I tell them, when I tell them. And our foreign counterparts? They'll secretly add the carbylamine-choline-chloride serum, or what we call snapdragon, in production so we can release it to punish those who disobey us.

"We need to staff up," I say, "hire technicians to implant free devices at health center kiosks at hospitals, malls, and schools nationwide." Before we adjourn the meeting, I stand up and clap my hands together. "Before you go, I'd like to give big thanks to a special person who helped this whole thing get started." I raise a hand and gaze dramatically at the floor. "She gave me a new take on life and she's been there all along with me. Here's to family. To Xintra. The one girl in my life I've loved since day one."

I wave to my sister, sitting at the head of the long table. Her hair shines like a silky red ribbon, a beautiful contrast to her pale white skin and emerald-green sweater. Gorgeous as a blooming rose, rising from a bed of thorns. She smiles and her eyes dazzle me, so pure, so green in the sunlight shining in from the window.

"To a new world," she says, raising her coffee cup into the air.

We all follow suit and repeat her words. "To a new world."

ACKNOWLEDGMENTS

Two decades of working as a journalist has taught me one important lesson: every writer needs good editors. This most definitely was the case for me when writing *Oshun Rising*. My editors Kate Angelella and Corey Ann Haydu have been critical to the trajectory of the Trinity Forest Series. Thank you both for continuing to coach me and offering such keen insights into how to unravel Ember's story. This tale would not have come come together without your brains and talent.

I'm also so grateful to copyeditor Jessica Gardner and designer Caroline Johnson, who has worked tirelessly with ßme on the covers and more. Thanks also go out to my generous beta readers who took the time to chime in on the story along the way— from crummy first draft to final polish: Jaimee Rindy, Ingrid McGinley, Amanda McCue, John Shors, Mel Finefrock and Kelly Dwyer. I couldn't have done it without you and your attention to detail.

I am especially thankful to you, my readers, the rest of my friends and family who have cheered me on, spread the word about my work, and given me the encouragement and momentum to keep writing.

THE STORY CONTINUES....

Get Venus Shining: Trinity Forest Book 3 on Amazon
    http://amzn.to/2z6ErUc

PLUS: Curious to hear the song from the tattoo shop? Check out this audio clip of Oshun singing plus get more behind-the-scenes goodies about Trinity Forest. Videos quizzes, character pages and more.
    Tell me where to send your free stuff:
    www.trinityforestseries.com/sign-up-now-venus

Made in the USA
Middletown, DE
14 February 2018